More about the characters you loved in
Golden Illusion!

"You know Joanna," Matt explained.

"Once she's got the bit in her teeth, there's no stopping her."

"Yes, I know," Claire murmured, nibbling worriedly on her lower lip. "Oh, Matt, maybe we should intervene. Joanna can be so headstrong. She has a tendency to just rush into things without thinking. If she angers Sean—"

"I know, I know. But, darling, you can't have it both ways. You've been wanting her to show some of her old spunk and enthusiasm. Well, now she has." A speculative gleam entered Matt's eyes as he stared at the doorway through which Joanna had just sailed, and slowly an amused smile curved his mouth. "It should be interesting, though. I've always wondered what happens when an irresistible force meets an immovable object."

Dear Reader:

Romance offers us all so much. It makes us "walk on sunshine." It gives us hope. It takes us out of our own lives, encouraging us to reach out to others. Janet Dailey is fond of saying that romance is a state of mind, that it could happen anywhere. Yet nowhere does romance seem to be as good as when it happens *here*.

Starting in February 1986, Silhouette Special Edition is featuring the AMERICAN TRIBUTE—a tribute to America, where romance has never been so wonderful. For six consecutive months, one out of every six Special Editions will be an episode in the AMERICAN TRIBUTE, a portrait of the lives of six women, all from Oklahoma. Look for the first book, *Love's Haunting Refrain* by Ada Steward, as well as stories by other favorites—Jeanne Stephens, Gena Dalton, Elaine Camp and Renee Roszel. You'll know the AMERICAN TRIBUTE by its patriotic stripe under the Silhouette Special Edition border.

AMERICAN TRIBUTE—six women, six stories, starting in February.

AMERICAN TRIBUTE—one of the reasons Silhouette Special Edition is just that—Special.

The Editors at Silhouette Books

GINNA GRAY
Sweet Promise

Silhouette Special Edition

Published by Silhouette Books New York

America's Publisher of Contemporary Romance

To Carol Brelish
No matter where she finally puts down roots,
she will always be my dear friend.

SILHOUETTE BOOKS
300 East 42nd St., New York, N.Y. 10017

Copyright © 1986 by Virginia Gray

ISBN: 0-373-09320-9

First Silhouette Books printing July 1986

America's Publisher of Contemporary Romance

Printed in the U.S.A.

GINNA GRAY

admits that for most of her life she has been both an avid reader and a dreamer. For a long time the desire to write and put her fantasies down on paper had been growing, until finally she told herself to *do* it. Now she can't imagine not writing.

ATLANTIC OCEAN

DOMINICAN REPUBLIC

VIRGIN ISLANDS

St. Thomas

ANITGUA

BARBADOS

St. Croix

PUERTO RICO

HAITI

CUBA

JAMAICA

THE CARIBBEAN ISLANDS

Chapter One

Wealth. Comfort. Warmth. The room exuded all three. Fine paintings, an exquisite cut crystal vase and a signed Paul Revere bowl shared pride of place with a bottle collection, a battered old hand forged copper scuttle and other items of whimsy. The furniture was of the highest quality and in excellent taste, but each piece proudly bore the marks of daily living, and each invited you to relax, to kick off your shoes and forget your cares. A cheery fire crackled in the stone fireplace and plush easy chairs cozied up to the hearth on either side. A pillow-strewn sofa, long enough for a tall man to stretch out on, stood foursquare before it. On the floor beside the sofa sat a basket of yarn, and draped across one arm was a half-finished afghan with a crochet hook sticking out of it. Underfoot, a thick oriental rug spread its faded beauty over the oak planked floor that had known over two hundred years of footsteps. This was a haven, a home, a refuge for the soul—not a showplace.

Two men occupied the fireside chairs. At first glance they appeared much alike. Both were big men: tall, broad shouldered, muscular. And both were dark and utterly masculine, with a commanding presence that immediately drew the eye. Yet there were differences. Matt Drummond's ebony hair was frosted silver at the temples; Sean Fleming's had the blue-black sheen of a raven's wing. Matt's face was rugged, with a weathered, lived-in look that was harshly appealing; Sean's was classically handsome. Matt's eyes were vivid blue; Sean's the deepest black.

The younger man sat slouched down on his spine, his long legs stretched out in front of him and crossed at the ankles. His head rested against the chair back, his hands across his abdomen, fingers laced loosely together. He looked almost boneless, nerveless. Only those who knew Sean well could detect the keen glitter in those seemingly drowsy black eyes, or see that behind that laid-back, easygoing façade was a taut restlessness, held rigidly in check.

And Matt Drummond knew him well.

Through half-closed eyes, Sean watched his friend leave his chair and walk to the old armoire that had been converted into a bar. He poured a generous amount of the finest Kentucky bourbon into two squat glasses, studied them, shrugged and added another splash to each for good measure. As he turned and started back across the room, Sean idly wondered what it was about these people, this place, that drew him.

Matt and Claire. Whenever he felt restless, troubled, unsure, he sought them out, preferably here in this huge old barn of a farmhouse that they called home. Somehow, just being around them calmed and soothed him, let him put things into perspective. It was strange, he thought with a wry smile. Strange...but damned comforting.

"Here you go." Matt handed him a drink. When he had settled into the chair on the other side of the hearth he gave Sean a long, steady look. "You know, ole buddy," he said finally. "Even though it's a cliché, there's a lot of truth in that old saw about opportunity only knocking once. You've always said you wanted to run for office some day. Well, if you're ever going to do it, now's the time, while you have strong backing. Turn Newcomb and his group down and they probably won't ask you to run again. And what with the incumbent retiring, the race for that Virginia Senate seat is going to be wide open."

"I know."

"When do they want an answer?"

"I told them I'd let them know in three weeks." Sean raised his drink and took a sip, exhaling a slow, raspy breath as the mellow bourbon slid down his throat. Holding the glass loosely between his hands, he rested it on his board-flat abdomen and stared at the dancing flames in the fireplace.

The fire hissed and popped. In the hall, the ancient grandfather clock ticked ponderously. The big room was lit by only two dim lamps and the fire, whose wavering glow was reflected in the polished oak floor and wainscoting. For a few minutes the two men sat in companionable silence.

Then Sean levered himself out of the chair and ambled over to the window. He twitched aside the green velvet curtain and looked out at the gathering darkness.

A light snow was falling, their first of the season—fat flakes that looked like feathers floating in the air.

What the devil is the matter with me? he wondered impatiently. *For months I've been feeling this . . . this vague . . . What? Discontent? Depression? Hell, you jerk. You don't even know what it is you feel. Or why. You ought to be turning cartwheels. Everything you've ever wanted, everything you've worked for, is within reach.*

So why wasn't he happy?

With a sigh, Sean walked back to the hearth and stared broodingly at the licking tongues of fire once again. "Before Newcomb approached me about running for the Senate, I'd been giving some thought to opening my own public relations firm, but I'm not sure I want to do that either." Grimacing, he sighed and raked an agitated hand through his blue-black hair. "Hell. The trouble is . . . I'm not sure what I want anymore. I feel at loose ends. Restless. Antsy." Sean gave a disgusted snort and shook his head. "I don't know. Maybe I'm going through a mid-life crisis or something?"

"At thirty-six?"

The dry amusement in Matt's tone pulled Sean's gaze away from the fire and his mouth twitched up in a self-conscious, half smile. "Well, something. I'm just not content with my life or my future anymore."

"So what are you going to do?"

"I'm—"

The peal of the doorbell halted Sean's words. He looked at Matt, a question in his eyes, but the older man merely shrugged.

Excusing himself, Matt went to answer the summons. A few seconds later Sean heard the murmur of voices and a soft ripple of feminine laughter and frowned. Sean liked women. Sean *loved* women. But tonight he wasn't in the mood for that kind of distraction.

Matt returned, bringing a young woman with him, and Sean's black eyes ran over her in automatic assessment. Nice looking, he thought idly. Great legs, too. A bit classy for my blood, but nice. Definitely nice.

"You remember Sean don't you, Joanna?" Matt said as he steered her toward the fireplace, and Sean felt a little dart of surprise.

This is Joanna? Claire's daughter? He eyed the softly feminine, poised young woman and expelled his breath in a long silent whistle. The Joanna he remembered had been a haughtily aggressive, rather obnoxious eighteen-year-old. There have definitely been some changes here, Sean thought as he noted the friendly sparkle in her hazel eyes.

The dark mole just above the left corner of her mouth drew his eye. It was a tiny imperfection that added fascination to her face, drawing attention to the otherwise flawless skin, the lovely curve of her cheek. The beauty mark was one of the few things about her that had remained the same. That, and the elegant bone structure of her face. It was that, Sean decided, which gave her that look of patrician aloofness he remembered so well. But it was softened by a mouth that was a tad too wide and curved now in a friendly smile. Her brown hair, which she used to wear in that god-awful frizzy style, now swung loosely around her shoulders in a shining cloud. It was, Sean thought a bit uneasily, the kind of hair a man wanted to thread his fingers through, bury his face in.

"Yes, of course," Joanna said. "You were Mother's press secretary when she ran for the Senate."

Smiling, she extended her hand and Sean took it between both of his. It was small and soft, and to his surprise, trembled ever so slightly. Even her voice has changed, he noted. It was gentler, softer, without that hard edge that had made everything she said sound like a command or a challenge.

"That's right. Hello, Joanna. It's good to see you again. It's been a while."

"Almost four years. I haven't seen you since Mother and Matt's wedding." Joanna cast a curious glance at her stepfather. "Speaking of Mother, where is she?"

"She's in the kitchen getting dinner. She'll be out in a minute."

Withdrawing her hand from Sean's grasp, Joanna smiled politely and edged toward the door. "If you'll excuse me, I think I'll go see if I can help."

When she had disappeared into the hall Sean's stunned gaze sought Matt. "*Joanna* is going to help in the kitchen?"

In the hall, Joanna heard the remark and stopped momentarily, her mouth compressing. It hurt to hear that incredulous tone in Sean's voice. Not that she blamed him. Four years ago she had been a brat. A spoiled, selfish brat.

As she continued toward the kitchen Joanna pressed her hand against her fluttering stomach, mildly surprised to realize that she was nervous. Which is just plain silly, she thought with a scornful chuckle. She'd once had a bit of a crush on Sean but that, thankfully, had died a natural death.

Joanna didn't think that Sean, or anyone else, had even been aware of her childish infatuation. At the time Sean had had his hands full with her mother's Senate campaign and had barely even noticed that she was alive.

And she, to her everlasting shame, had been too busy trying to prevent her mother from marrying Matt to actively pursue him. In the end, when Claire had withdrawn from the primary race, her staff had disbanded. "And that had been the end of that, thank heaven," Joanna muttered under her breath. "Given enough time, I probably would have made a complete fool of myself over the man."

Actually though, finding Sean there was a stroke of luck, considering the reason she'd come.

Joanna pushed through the door and walked into the huge, old-fashioned kitchen, and Claire looked up from the sauce she was stirring, a smile lighting up her face. "Hello, darling. I was beginning to wonder if you were going to make it in time for dinner."

As always these days, at the sight of her mother Joanna felt a little jolt. She supposed it was natural, under the circumstances. For no matter how often she thought about it, no matter how pleased and happy she was, it was something of a shock to see her mother—her forty-three-year-old, beautiful, elegant mother—nearly seven months pregnant.

Smiling, Joanna crossed the room and gave Claire a kiss on the cheek. "Sorry I'm late. Usually on Fridays we knock off early, but tonight Senator Hartwell kept the entire staff working till five." Joanna tipped her head toward the living room. "You didn't tell me that Sean would be here this weekend too."

"Oh, Sean can't stay for the weekend." Claire looked at Joanna, her soft gray eyes filled with wicked laughter, and added drolly, "He has a date tomorrow night."

"Ah, I see." Joanna's smile was knowing. "Still giving his little black book a workout, is he?" She washed her hands at the sink, then began to set four places at one end of the long trestle table, chuckling to herself as she recalled how she had been eaten up with jealousy every time she'd seen Sean riffling through that book. How she'd sworn that someday she would rip it to shreds.

"I think it's now a two-volume set," Claire said, rolling her eyes. "Sean's as sharp as a tack and a dear, sweet man, but he is a devil with the ladies."

Joanna chuckled and began helping her mother dish up the food, enormously pleased that now she could laugh at Sean's romantic escapades. She poured the lemon and butter sauce over the broccoli and picked up the dish to take it to the table, turning just in time to see Claire lifting a roasting pan from the oven.

"Mother! For heaven's sake! You shouldn't be lifting that," she cried, rushing over to take it from her.

Claire looked disgusted and made an exasperated sound. "I swear, you're as bad as Matt. I'm not an invalid, you know. I'm just pregnant. Besides, I like to cook, and it's about the only thing I get to do anymore."

Poor Matt, Joanna thought, smothering a grin as she set the pan on the counter and transferred the roast to a platter. Becoming a father for the first time at age forty-five was hard on him. He was both thrilled and terrified over the prospect and tended to fuss over his wife like a mother hen. The day after Claire had told him she was pregnant he had hired a woman to do all the work around the house. If Claire hadn't put her foot down, he would have hired someone to do the cooking, too.

It was amazing, Joanna thought, as she had done countless times during the past few years, how drastically her mother's life-style had changed. Though Matt was equally as wealthy as Joanna's father and grandfather had been, his family had always lived a simpler life, and Claire had embraced it wholeheartedly. She had settled in this big old rustic house and adapted to country living with astounding ease. Claire had learned to cook and keep house, even to garden. And, Joanna admitted with a smile, casting a covert glance at her mother's glowing face, she seemed to thrive on it.

When the meal was ready, the men joined them in the kitchen, and Matt sat at his customary place at the head of the table. Instinctively Joanna shied away from sitting beside Sean and chose the place on the opposite side, facing him and Claire. It was a choice she soon regretted, for every time she looked up her eyes were drawn to him like a magnet.

During dinner, conversation was general, but for the most part Joanna said little. Her reaction to Sean surprised and disturbed her. She was acutely, uncomfortably aware of him. She found herself staring, as though mesmerized, at his finely chiseled, incredibly sexy mouth. And that voice. Its deep rumble did the strangest things to her insides.

Sean was a wildly handsome man, with an appealing air of devil-may-care rakishness. Joanna told herself it was perfectly normal to be attracted to him.

But she still didn't like it.

After dinner Matt and Sean returned to the living room and resumed their discussion while Joanna and Claire dealt with the dishes. When the women rejoined them, Sean had to bite back a smile.

Claire Drummond is probably the only woman in the world who can make a pregnant waddle look graceful, he thought wryly as he watched his hostess make her way to the sofa. But then, he doubted that anything could make Claire look awkward or unattractive. Her poise was an inherent part of her, like her beauty or intelligence. It was no wonder that Matt loved her to distraction.

Four years ago he'd come close to falling in love with her himself, Sean remembered, and his soft sigh held just the barest touch of regret. But it simply wasn't meant to be. From almost the very beginning, even before they had realized it themselves, he had known that Matt and Claire belonged together.

As Claire began to gingerly lower her bulky girth onto the cushions Matt jumped up to assist her, and the smile that Sean had been so valiantly holding in check broke through. When she was settled Matt picked up her legs and slid a hassock under them. Squatting on his haunches, he slipped off her shoes and began to massage her feet.

"How are you feeling, sweetheart?" he asked solicitously.

"I'm fine, darling," Claire replied in the softest of voices, her eyes warm as she gazed down at him.

The look that passed between them brought a tightness to Sean's chest, and his amused smile faded. Suddenly, inexplicably, he was swamped with a curious mixture of gladness and envy.

Jeez! What the hell's the matter with me? Sean shifted restlessly and battled down the uncomfortable surge of emotions. It was stupid to be envious of their marriage. He was *not* the marrying kind, for Chrissake.

But then . . . neither had Matt been.

And Sean had to admit, he'd never known two people more in love, or more content with each other than Claire and Matt. Watching them, it was difficult to recall that they had once come very close to not making it.

The thought drew Sean's gaze to Joanna. He had never known what had caused the breakup between Claire and Matt four years ago, but he'd always had a sneaking suspicion that Joanna had been behind it.

Looking at her now, though, it was difficult to believe. There was a softness about Joanna, a vulnerability that hadn't been there four years ago. And the look of affectionate tenderness on her face as she watched Matt fuss over her mother clearly revealed her feelings about the marriage and the coming child.

She really is a lovely young woman, Sean mused. She'll never be the elegant beauty her mother is, but she is striking . . . in a well-bred, reserved sort of way.

"Did Sean tell you that he is being urged to run for the Senate?" Matt asked as he settled onto the sofa beside Claire and draped his arm around her shoulders. "Bob Rastin is retiring after this term and the Virginia seat will be up for grabs."

"Why, Sean! That's marvelous," Claire declared. "You'll make a terrific senator."

Abandoning his study of Joanna, Sean turned to his friends with a lazy grin. "You mean *if* I decide to run, and *if* I get elected."

"What do you mean, 'if'? You've told me for years that you want to run for office."

"Yeah, well . . . now I'm not so sure. I've been thinking lately of opening up my own public relations firm."

Claire gave him a long, shrewd look. "Well, whatever you decide, you know that Matt and I will back you. But I'm sure, once you've given it some thought, you'll decide to run," she said confidently.

"Actually, think about it is exactly what I'm *not* going to do. At least, not for a while. I've thought about it until my head is spinning, and I still don't know what I want. So I've decided to put the whole thing out of my mind for a while and concentrate on fulfilling one of my fantasies."

"I'm almost afraid to ask what that might be," Matt drawled.

Sean smiled smugly and relaxed back against the chair in his habitual indolent pose. "I've been working my tail off for the past few years and I've decided I deserve a break. I'm going to treat myself to a Caribbean cruise. Beginning next Saturday, I'm going to lie in the sun for two weeks and relax and unwind and watch pretty girls." The smile grew slowly into a wicked grin. "I may even catch a few."

Matt groaned and rolled his eyes, and Claire laughed.

No one noticed the dismayed look on Joanna's face.

The next morning Joanna hesitated before the closed door of Matt's study. Chewing at her lower lip, she wiped her damp palms down over her slender, jean-encased hips and tried to still the flutter in the pit of her stomach.

"Oh, good grief," she muttered under her breath, suddenly impatient with her own dithering. "It's no big deal. The worst he can do is say no." Joanna drew a deep breath, and with a toss of her head, flipped her long brown hair back over her shoulder and raised a hand to knock.

A deep baritone carried through the oak door. Opening it partway, Joanna poked her head around the edge. "May I speak with you for a moment?"

Surprise flickered across Matt's rugged face, but it was followed quickly by a pleased smile. "Sure. Come on in." Tossing aside his pencil, he leaned back in his chair and motioned toward the rust suede sofa opposite his desk. "Have a seat."

When she had complied Matt smiled again and raised his dark brows. "Is there something I can do for you?"

Trust Matt to get straight to the point, Joanna thought with faint amusement. He was a "take the bull by the horns" type, as different from her own father as night and day. Senator Joseph Andrews had been a born politician: diplomatic, smooth talking, clever, evasive when need be, a master at convoluted maneuvering and manipulation. Matt was direct, bold and decisive.

Which, Joanna freely admitted, was why he was such a force to be reckoned with in Washington. He knew the rules, written and unwritten, and when the occasion called for finesse, Matt could employ it with exquisite delicacy. But basically he was a mover and shaker, a man who was known for getting things done by going right to the heart of the matter.

"Yes. At least, I hope so. I have a favor to ask."

Matt's keen blue eyes sharpened ever so slightly. "Oh? What's that?"

"Well . . . uh, how do you feel about Sean running for the Senate?"

If Matt was surprised by her question he didn't let it show. Pinching his lower lip between his thumb and forefinger he tugged on it meditatively. "Actually, I think he's an excellent choice. Probably the best Newcomb and his group could have made. Sean's a good man, and he's had plenty of experience. He's a little weak when it comes to public exposure but that shouldn't be a problem. When he puts his mind to it, that Irish devil can charm the birds right out of the trees." Matt pinned Joanna with his penetrating stare. "Why do you ask?"

"Because Senator Hartwell and several others agree with Harry Newcomb. They all think that Sean should seek the nomination. The consensus is that he can easily beat the opposition's candidate. But, as you saw last night, for some strange reason Sean is being—" Joanna lifted both hands, palms up, then let them drop back into her lap "—noncommittal. Which is why I'm here. You see, Senator Hartwell thought that since you and Sean are such good friends, maybe you could persuade him to run."

"Ah, I see." The thoughtful expression on Matt's face did not alter one whit, but inside he was filled with reluctant amusement. Subtle pressure. That was the way the game was played. Though she didn't know it, he had pulled a few strings to get Joanna her job on Senator Hartwell's staff. Normally he didn't resort to such tactics, but Claire had been worried about Joanna, and to ease her mind he had used his influence. And now the Senator was pulling a few strings of his own and using Joanna to do it.

But Matt didn't give in to pressure easily.

"I don't think that's a good idea. After all, it's Sean's decision, and he's perfectly capable of making it on his own."

"Yes, of course he is," Joanna agreed quickly. "And the Senator says he is seriously considering it. But it's such a big step, I thought...that is, Senator Hartwell thought that it wouldn't hurt if he got some encouragement from you. Oh, Matt, please talk to him," Joanna pleaded. She sat forward on the sofa, leaning toward him, her face animated and full of hope. "A nudge from you is probably all he needs."

"I don't know..." Frowning, Matt braced his elbows on the arms of the chair and pressed his spread fingertips together, gazing over them out the window at the crisp winter day. The flurries of the night before had stopped, and now a thin layer of patchy snow lay like tattered fleece over the rolling Virginia hills. As Matt idly watched, one of his thoroughbred mares trotted across the near paddock, her breath coming out in puffs of white mist that trailed away in the wind and vanished.

But Matt's mind wasn't on the mare or the scenery, or even the classified papers he had been studying, but on his stepdaughter's request. Sean was well suited for politics. Matt had no doubts on that score. But he knew that it was useless to pressure him. Many people were fooled by that laid-back easygoing veneer. Few realized that behind it was a razor sharp mind and a fierce determination. Or that those slumberous black eyes could snap with temper. No, Sean Fleming was not a malleable pawn. If that was what Senator Hartwell and the others thought they would be getting they were in for a shock. Sean was his own man. When he wanted advice, he asked for it. He would listen to your opinion, weigh it carefully, but in the end he always made up his own mind. He was not a man you could prod.

Besides, even if he had been, Matt didn't believe in pressuring a man on a career decision.

Still, he hated to turn Joanna down flat. Claire was worried about her. With good cause, Matt felt. In the past three and a half years Joanna had changed drastically. Before, she had been a spoiled, self-centered brat, but at least she had been full of spirit, a vibrant, sparkling girl, filled with the zest and eagerness of youth.

Matt's eyes narrowed on his stepdaughter. They had once been enemies. Unconsciously, his jaw clenched as he remembered that time. Even now, when he thought about how close he had come to losing Claire, he felt a cold trickle of fear race down his spine. Dear Lord! Life without her would be unbearable.

But he had won, Matt reminded himself. Now he could afford to be compassionate.

Joanna's scheme to come between him and Claire had backfired on her. In the end she'd had to face a lot of unpleasant truths, perhaps the hardest being that the father she had idolized had not been the golden god she had thought him to be. Since then she had been subdued and serious—too much so for her mother's liking. His too, for that matter, Matt admitted. After that fiasco, Joanna had done an abrupt about-face. She had worked hard in college and had graduated with honors, and during the past six months, had buried herself in her job to the exclusion of everything else.

Matt cast a curious glance at Joanna's anxious face, his eyes narrowing once again. This was the first time in almost four years that she had shown even a trace of her old enthusiasm.

"Why is it so important to you that Sean run for Congress?" he asked quietly.

"Well...because I think he'd make a terrific senator, of course," she said in a voice that was just a shade too assertive, a shade too high. Not quite meeting Matt's eye, Joanna waved her hand vaguely. "He's bright and young and honest. Likeable. And as you said, he has that charismatic charm. He shouldn't have any trouble pulling in votes, and our party needs another seat in Congress."

"Mmm." Resting his chin in his palm, Matt studied her flustered face and waited for her to continue.

Joanna shifted restlessly on the plush sofa. After a while, she looked up and met Matt's steady gaze guiltily. "All right. I admit my motives aren't totally altruistic," she said with a rueful twist of her mouth. "If Sean does decide to run, I'm hoping I can get a job on his campaign staff."

Amusement tugged at the corners of Matt's mouth. "Things too dull for you in Hartwell's camp?"

"Something like that. Oh, Matt, he doesn't even come up for reelection for years yet. And anyway, he's held that office for so long he's practically an institution in his state. I'd like to be involved in something...I don't know...something with a little more challenge to it I guess."

Yes, Joanna was a campaigner, Matt recalled. She thrived on the excitement and challenge, the constant thrust and parry of a hard fought political race. Four years ago, during Claire's bid for her late husband's Senate seat, Joanna had worked tirelessly and had loved every minute of it. Claire's ultimate withdrawal from the race had been one of the biggest disappointments of Joanna's life.

Disillusionment. Disappointment. It had been a difficult time for the girl, Matt mused. Joanna was a mature, responsible, even loving young woman now, but sadly, she had had to gain her maturity the hard way.

Matt drummed a pencil against the desk top. If Sean did decide to seek the office, she would be an asset. There was no denying that. But still, even if it were possible, he couldn't in good conscience talk a man into making that kind of decision just to give Joanna's life a boost.

He was about to tell her so when Claire tapped on the door and poked her head into the room. "Is this a private party, or can anyone join in?"

The smile that wreathed Matt's features was warm and loving and heartstoppingly tender, transforming his rugged face into gentleness. "Come in, sweetheart," he said in that soft voice that was reserved just for Claire, holding out his hand to her.

An indulgent smile curved Joanna's mouth as she watched Claire give her husband a kiss, then perch rather precariously on the arm of his chair. She looped one arm across his broad shoulders. The other she placed on the turgid roundness of her protruding belly, in an unconscious protective gesture.

"So, what's going on?"

Matt reached up and tweaked one of Claire's short blond curls. "Joanna thinks I ought to persuade Sean to run for Congress. I was just about to explain to her I can't do that. I've already pointed out to Sean all the reasons why he should seriously consider running. I'm afraid that's all I can do. It's his decision to make."

"Oh, but—"

"Matt's right, Joanna," Claire said quickly, cutting off her daughter's protest. "It's his life and his future. And Sean wouldn't appreciate our interference."

Disappointment poured through Joanna. She had been hoping to get her mother's support. She knew that it was almost impossible for Matt to deny Claire anything, especially now. But it was obvious from their expressions that she was wasting her time.

Still, she wasn't going to give up. Rising to her feet, Joanna squared her shoulders determinedly. "Maybe. But someone has to talk some sense into that hardheaded Irishman. I can't just let him throw away a chance like this."

Without another word, she walked out, and Claire looked at Matt, her expression a mixture of bemusement and worry.

Matt grinned. "She wants a job on Sean's staff," he explained. "And you know Joanna. Once she's got the bit between her teeth there's no stopping her."

"Yes, I know," Claire murmured, nibbling worriedly on her lower lip. "Oh, Matt, maybe we should try. Joanna can be so headstrong. She has a tendency to just rush into things without thinking. If she angers Sean—"

"I know, I know. But, darling, you can't have it both ways. You've been wanting her to show some of her old spunk and enthusiasm. Well, now she has." A speculative gleam entered Matt's eyes as he stared at the doorway through which Joanna had just sailed, and slowly an amused smile curved his mouth. "It should be interesting, though. I've always wondered what happened when an irresistible force met an immovable object."

Chapter Two

The moment Joanna stepped on board someone called out "Smile," and a flashbulb went off. She stiffened and glared at the photographer, but in the next instant realized that they were taking pictures of everyone as they came on the ship.

Feeling foolish, Joanna handed the purser her boarding pass. Good grief, you're getting paranoid, she chastised silently. But she knew her reaction was a conditioned reflex, the result of a lifetime of having flashbulbs go off in her face. It was part of the price she had paid for having a famous mother whom the public idolized...the part that Joanna hated.

"Ah, Miss Andrews. We're honored to have you with us," the purser said as he checked the slip she'd handed him against the list on his clipboard. Glancing back over his shoulder, he motioned for the young man just behind him to step forward. "This is Riley, Miss An-

drews. He'll see you to your suite. Please let us know if
there is anything you need.''

With a smile and a quick thank-you, Joanna turned to
follow the white-jacketed young man.

They passed through what seemed like miles of carpeted passageways with literally hundreds of doors
opening off them and climbed several flights of stairs.
Within minutes Joanna was thoroughly lost...and
thoroughly intrigued. There was an air of excitement and
anticipation among the other passengers and crew
members that was infectious, and with every step she felt
a growing eagerness, a sense of adventure. Joanna had
come on this trip for a purpose, but now, for the first
time, it occurred to her that there was no reason why she
couldn't enjoy herself while she was about it.

Her guide kept up a steady chatter, pointing out the
main dining room and the shopping arcade, the gym and
the various clubs. They passed dozens of people, all
anxiously peering at the numbers on the cabin doors and
checking them against the keys they held in their hands.
A wry grimace curled Joanna's mouth as she noticed
that she seemed to be the only one with a personal es-
cort. She couldn't help but wonder if she was receiving
this preferential treatment because she had been recognized.

Her mother had grown up in the spotlight, the
daughter of one of the country's most powerful sena-
tors, and later, the wife of another. Joanna had always
detested the lack of privacy that went with her mother's
fame, and knowing that, Claire had done her best to
shield her from the constant publicity. Still, there had
been enough over the years that Joanna was often recognized. And the result was nearly always gaping stares
or fawning attention.

"Here we are," her guide announced when he finally stopped before a cabin door and opened it with a flourish.

The moment Joanna stepped inside and looked around at her plush accommodations, her uneasy suspicion faded, and she chided herself for her conceit. No doubt anyone who booked one of these luxury suites received the royal treatment.

It was gorgeous. And huge. She hadn't expected that, even knowing that there were only two of these deluxe suites on board.

She had expected round portholes. Instead, there were two large rectangular windows. Between them a tufted brown leather sofa sat along the outer wall. Flanking it were Queen Anne end tables, which held exquisite lamps made of brass and polished walnut. At right angles to the sofa were two matching brown leather easy chairs and in the center of the grouping stood an oval, marble-topped coffee table. A copper bowl in the center of the table contained an arrangement of dried flowers in autumn colors that blended with the rust carpet and draperies and the soft rust, green-and-yellow stripes in the wall covering.

Through the large windows, Joanna could see the sunlight sparkling on the waters of Miami harbor. As the steward bustled, pointing out the small refrigerator and bar and rattling off information about the temperature controls, Joanna walked to one of the windows and watched another cruise ship glide gracefully by, heading out to sea.

"And through here is your bedroom," the young man announced.

Joanna turned in time to see him throw open the double doors set in one of the side walls. Bemused, she wandered over and peeked in, her eyes widening at the sight of the king-size bed and the long vanity console. The color scheme was ivory and pale green, but this room, too, was flooded with light from two large windows.

"It's lovely," Joanna said, and the young man beamed proudly.

They heard a noise in the passageway, and he turned and headed for the door. "That's the porter with your luggage. I'll get it for you."

When he had carried her bags into the bedroom he told her there would be a lifeboat drill shortly before they got under way. "Just follow the instructions here on the back of the door," he said as he turned to leave. "They tell where your lifeboat station is and how to reach it. When you hear the announcement over the intercom just grab a life jacket out of the closet and take the forward stairs to the deck above."

As the door closed behind him Joanna stood in the middle of the sitting room, her eyes growing wide with panic. A lifeboat drill? Oh, Lord. She hadn't counted on that. She had planned to remain in her suite until they were well out at sea.

Joanna chewed worriedly at her lower lip. It was entirely possible that she might run into Sean. With a bit of discreet probing, she had discovered when she booked the cruise that his cabin was just down the passageway from hers. It stood to reason that his lifeboat station would be close by also.

Maybe I could just ignore the announcement and stay here.

"Oh, don't be ridiculous, Joanna," she muttered impatiently the moment the thought flickered through her mind. "They would just come looking for you if you didn't show up.'' She walked into the bedroom and snapped open the case that lay on the luggage rack. Scooping up a stack of frothy lingerie, she began to move methodically back and forth between the open case and the built-in dresser. "Besides," she said stoutly as her normal self-confidence reasserted itself. "With hundreds of passengers on board, surely you can lose yourself in the crowd for a few minutes."

As she hung her clothes in the roomy closet behind the mirror-covered sliding doors, Joanna glanced around at her opulent surroundings and grimaced. She hadn't planned on booking the most expensive suite on the ship, but it had been the only thing available when she'd made her reservation.

Joanna stopped in the act of hanging up a cotton sundress and giggled as she recalled her conversation with Senator Hartwell five days ago. He'd been enthusiastic about her plan, so much so that in a fit of generosity he had offered to pay for her cruise.

"It's a good thing I didn't take him up on his offer," Joanna thought, chuckling. "He'd have had a fit when he found out how much this suite costs."

She wasn't too thrilled about it herself. She could afford it easily, of course, thanks to the generous trust funds both her father and grandfather had set up for her, but under normal circumstances, she would not have booked anything so grand just for herself.

Fifteen minutes later a repetitive three-gong signal came over the ship's intercom followed by a calm voice instructing everyone to go to their lifeboat stations. Joanna's heart skipped a beat and she hesitated for an instant. Then, abandoning her half-empty suitcase, she snatched the garish orange vest from the closet and hurried out the door.

By the time she reached the stairwell the companion-way was filled with people, all wearing the bulky Mae West life preservers. Most were laughing and joking as they trouped up to the next deck. Joanna joined the throng, confident that her presence would go unde-tected in the crush.

That confidence slipped a notch, however, when she reached her lifeboat station. For there at the next sta-tion, not ten yards away, stood Sean.

With a start, Joanna ducked behind a large man whose girth almost equaled his height. She stood very still, her heart pounding wildly against her chest. After a moment, she very cautiously leaned to one side and peeked around him.

Surprise, a flicker of annoyance, then wry amuse-ment chased one after the other across Joanna's face as she stared at Sean. She had been frightened for noth-ing. He wasn't even aware of her. In fact, she told her-self with a twisted, self-mocking smile, she could probably strip naked and run up and down the deck screaming, and he still wouldn't notice her.

Dressed in navy slacks and a short sleeved pale blue shirt, Sean stood leaning over a voluptuous redhead, one arm braced against the bulkhead above her shoulder. A rakish smile curved his mouth. His handsome face wore a look of undisguised male interest: predatory, and sen-sual, his drowsy black eyes hot and sexy.

Joanna looked at the redhead and sighed. Typically, the woman was gazing up at him with a besotted look on her face, hanging on his every word.

A surge of irritation rippled through Joanna as she watched Sean throw his head back and roar with laugh-ter over something the woman had said, but she quickly squashed it. It wasn't the redhead's fault, she reminded herself. Sean always had that effect on women. It was those cleanly chiseled features, that lazy, heart-stopping smile. And, of course, that devastating aura of sheer maleness.

Plus, Sean had a secret weapon: he liked women. Genuinely liked them. And he made no secret of it. Old, young, short, tall, silly, serious. He found them all delightful and utterly fascinating. What woman could resist that? Certainly none that she knew of, Joanna admitted grudgingly. Sean managed to make every woman he met feel special, and they adored him for it.

And, as astonishing as it was, if what Joanna had heard was true, he even managed to remain friends with his former lovers.

Ship personnel at each lifeboat station began to call off the names on their rosters, and when her own was called Joanna jumped and darted another apprehensive glance at Sean before answering. But she needn't have worried. He was oblivious to everything but the curvaceous redhead.

Throughout the entire spiel on safety and emergency procedures Joanna kept her gaze trained on Sean and listened with only half an ear, torn between disgust and amusement as she watched him flirt.

At last the drill was over, and the groups around the lifeboats began to break up. Sean raised his head and glanced distractedly in her direction. Joanna doubted that he could pick her out in the crowd, but when his gaze rested briefly on her, she smiled and turned back toward the stairs.

No sense tempting fate, she told herself as she melted into the throng. A blast from the ship's whistle and a slight movement underfoot told her that they were about to get under way. Joanna was tempted to stay topside and watch, but immediately dismissed the idea. Not that it really mattered now if Sean did spot her, except that she preferred to pick the time and place of their first meeting.

Joanna? Is that Joanna Andrews? Sean stared at the brown-haired woman's retreating form and frowned. *No. No, it can't be. I must be seeing things.*

But even after the slender figure in the yellow sundress had disappeared from view he continued to search the crowds.

"Do you see the purser anywhere?"

Gloria Osborne's question finally penetrated, and Sean looked down, chagrined to realize that he'd gotten sidetracked. *For Pete's sake, Fleming! Why are you letting your imagination run away with you when there's someone like Gloria around?*

"Uh, no. Anyway, he's probably got his hands full right now. Why don't I just go find the maître d' and see what I can do?"

"Do you think he'll be agreeable to changing seating arrangements?"

"Sure. Why not? The cruise is just starting. It won't inconvenience anyone. I'll just tell him that we'd like to be seated at the same table."

Sean smiled at the hopeful expression on Gloria's face. *She really is a luscious creature,* he mused. A knockout figure, a full mouth that begged to be kissed, slanting green eyes. And she was a redhead to boot. His gaze lifted to the bright hair, and he wondered idly if it were natural. Probably not. But then, who the hell cared? Gloria Osborne was just what he needed. A worldly, uncomplicated, sensual woman, one who could indulge in a light-hearted shipboard romance with no illusions or expectations.

Reassured, Gloria toyed with a button on his shirt and gave him a sultry look from beneath her lashes. "Well, while you take care of that, I think I'll go unpack." She winked and stepped away, trailing her long crimson nails across his chest. "See you at dinner."

Sean watched her go, his smile turning decidedly wicked as he admired the provocative sway of her hips. It had been a pure stroke of luck, meeting her as they had stood in line to get their boarding passes, he decided with satisfaction. For the next two weeks he wanted to clear his mind of everything and concentrate on relaxing and having a good time. With a woman like Gloria around, that shouldn't be too difficult.

But suddenly Sean's smile faded, and he looked back in the direction the brown-haired woman had taken. Strangely, one of the things that had been on his mind lately had been Joanna. The changes in her had intrigued him and he'd thought of her often since that dinner last weekend at Claire and Matt's. Which, he told himself, is probably why you imagined you saw her.

Of course, it couldn't have been Joanna.

Hands in his pockets, Sean strolled slowly toward the purser's office.

But it had sure as hell looked like her.

Joanna entered the dining room behind two couples who were obviously together. While they identified themselves to the maître d' she adjusted the long full sleeves of her amber silk dress and casually scanned the room for Sean's dark head.

The tight feeling in the pit of her stomach was a curious mixture of anticipation and dread. How would Sean react when he saw her? Funny. She hadn't really considered that aspect until now. He would be surprised, of course. That was to be expected. But when his surprise faded, would he be angry? Pleased? Indifferent?

Joanna frowned. *Maybe I should have gone about this differently. Perhaps it would have been better if—*

"Good evening, miss. My name is Henri," the maître d' said, giving her a suave smile and a formal little bow, and with a start, Joanna realized that it was too late for second thoughts.

The urge to turn around and scurry back to her suite was strong, but she squashed it and gave him her name. *You can't spend two weeks holed up in that suite, so just stay calm and stick to your original plan,* she told herself, squaring her shoulders and falling in step behind the man as he turned to lead her to her assigned table.

Joanna felt a prickle of annoyance when she spotted the redhead sitting beside Sean. He was so absorbed in the woman he didn't even look up until the maître d' pulled out her chair. And then Joanna had to stifle a laugh. She had never seen Sean lose his blasé composure before, but the casual glance he gave her was followed instantly by a comical double take that had his jaw dropping and his black eyes bulging out as though they were on stalks.

"Joanna!"

"Hello, Sean." Joanna smiled pleasantly and took the seat across from him at the round table.

"It *was* you I saw earlier!" Astonishment and accusation blended in Sean's voice. He gaped at her as though he couldn't believe his eyes.

"Yes, I suppose it was."

"Oh, how nice," the elderly woman on Joanna's right exclaimed. "You two know each other."

Joanna turned to the woman gratefully. "Yes. Sean is an old family friend." Carefully avoiding his eyes, she pinned a bright smile on her face and introduced herself to the others at the table.

They were a good mix, Joanna noted as names were exchanged. Besides herself, Sean, and Gloria Osborne, there was another attractive single man and two married couples, one elderly, and the other so young Joanna guessed them to be on their honeymoon.

By the time the introductions were finished Sean had overcome his shock and was leaning casually back in his chair, his easy nonchalance firmly in place once again. His expression was bland and pleasant. There was even a hint of a smile curving his lips, though it didn't reach those probing black eyes. They were boring into hers like lasers.

The waiter appeared at that moment, and Sean's attention was diverted briefly as they all made their selections from the menus. But the moment the man retreated to the kitchen he focused on her again.

"I'm surprised to see you here, Joanna," he said in a drawling voice. "When I saw you last weekend you didn't mention that you were going to be on this cruise."

"Oh, it was a last minute decision. You made it sound like so much fun I decided to try it myself." Giving him a bright smile, Joanna mentally crossed her fingers that he would accept the white lie. She couldn't very well say that she was here to do a little arm-twisting. For all his easygoing charm, she had a gut feeling that Sean was not a person who would take kindly to pressure. In any case, she had learned from both her father and grandfather that the art of persuasion required subtlety and patience.

"I see. And that's the only reason?"

"Of course," she said, feigning innocence. "What else?"

Sean gave her a long, thoughtful stare, his chiseled lips pursed slightly, but he didn't comment.

"Well I think it's marvelous that you have a friend on board, my dear," Mary Wright said, patting Joanna's hand. "I imagine traveling all alone can be a bit awkward for an attractive single girl like you. And I'm sure Mr. Fleming is delighted to have your company."

Looking at those steady black eyes, Joanna doubted that. And she was quite positive that Gloria Osborne didn't share the sentiment. The redhead's face was tight with annoyance, her full lips folded inward in a thin straight line.

"You know, my dear, there is something about you that is very familiar," Mary said, gazing at Joanna intently. "I feel like I should know you."

"No, I don't think we've met," Joanna replied quickly. She looked at Sean and held her breath, expecting him to give her away, but he merely narrowed his eyes and watched her.

Turning back to the elderly woman, Joanna deftly steered the conversation onto safer ground. Within minutes she was sitting back with a smile listening to Mary explain that her husband, Charles, had just retired and that their children and grandchildren had pitched in to send them on the cruise.

Somewhere in her sixties, Mary Wright was a charming, utterly feminine little woman, slightly plump, with a cap of silver curls and faded blue eyes that still twinkled flirtatiously. Her delicate, age-spotted hands fluttered like graceful birds when she talked, and her voice was a soft, liquid drawl that conjured up visions of magnolias and mint juleps. It came as no surprise at all when Mary announced that she and her husband were from Atlanta.

Charles Wright was tall and distinguished looking, the epitome of the southern gentleman, and as quiet as Mary was outgoing. Joanna noted the fondness in his eyes whenever he looked at his wife, and she liked him instantly.

Which just shows how much your values have shifted, Joanna thought wryly, the admission stirring within her a mixture of chagrin and satisfaction. Four years of observing the love and caring that was so much a part of her mother's marriage had made Joanna sensitive to the subtle undercurrents between men and women and altered her perceptions and priorities. Now she found herself assessing a man, not by wealth or family background, or the amount of power he wielded, but by his capacity for tenderness and commitment.

The waiter returned with their food, and as they ate they gradually began to exchange background information.

Gloria Osborne was a divorcée from Dallas who worked as a buyer for a department store, and Tony Farrell was a junior partner in a New York law firm. To Joanna's surprise, Susan and Bill Adamson, neither of whom looked old enough to vote, were celebrating their sixth anniversary. Instead of appearing happy, however, they both wore a rather harried look, and Joanna couldn't help but notice the way Susan kept glancing at her watch every few minutes. They lived in Minneapolis, where Bill worked as an insurance salesman and Susan, until six months ago when she quit to have their first child, had been an elementary school teacher.

Sean was glibly evasive about his work, managing to give the impression that he was between jobs, which in a way was true, Joanna supposed, since he had recently resigned his post on the Vice President's staff.

Joanna merely said that she lived in Washington, and silently prayed that no one would make the obvious connection. She wasn't sure whether or not Sean knew about her job with Senator Hartwell, but in case he didn't, she decided to keep quiet about it, at least for the moment.

All during the meal Gloria flirted outrageously with Sean, and he responded with his usual devilish charm. He hardly paid any attention to Joanna, and by the time the meal was over she had begun to relax.

When they had finished their after dinner coffee Gloria put her hand on Sean's arm and in a sultry voice, said, "Why don't we go dancing in the Zodiac Lounge? One of the crew told me that they have a fabulous band in there."

Sean smiled regretfully and shook his head. "I'm sorry. Not tonight. There's something I need to discuss with Joanna."

Joanna wasn't sure who was more surprised, herself or Gloria. The other woman's eyes widened for an instant in outrage, but she recovered quickly and her expression grew cool and rigid. "Of course. If that's what you want," she said in a clipped voice. "Perhaps, if I'm not too busy, I'll see you tomorrow."

It was clearly a threat, but Sean chose to ignore it, giving Gloria a warm look and a wink as he rose to come around to Joanna's side of the table.

His hand closed firmly around her upper arm, and urged her, none too gently, to her feet. With a polite nod and a charming, encompassing smile for the others, he said, "You will excuse us, won't you?" Without giving any of their startled fellow diners a chance to reply, he turned and propelled Joanna toward the door.

His hand remained clamped around her arm. Joanna didn't have a chance to say a word as he hustled her up two flights of steps and out on deck. She risked a glance at him only once, when he paused to look around before marching her over to a secluded spot by the rail. His face wore its perpetual look of unshakable insouciance, but she could feel the tightly controlled tension in him.

"Now, I want an explanation, Joanna," he snapped without preamble the moment they came to a halt. "And you'd better make it good. Just what the devil are you doing here?"

Joanna swallowed hard. She had never seen Sean angry before. It had always seemed to her that he viewed life as a sort of ridiculous comedy put on for his entertainment. During her mother's campaign the strongest reaction he'd shown when things went wrong, as they invariably did, was a mild exasperation. Nothing had ruffled him. Even in the most trying situations, when others all around him had been flying off the handle, Sean had watched with ironic amusement in his dark eyes, and calmly gone about his business. But he was definitely angry now.

She widened her eyes, feigning innocence. "Why, I told you. You made the cruise sound like so much fun I decided to try it myself," she said brightly, waving her hand in a vague little gesture.

Sean spit out a searing expletive that made her suck in her breath. "Oh, come off it. Who the hell do you think you're kidding?"

Grim faced, he turned his head and stared out at the gently undulating ocean. Moonlight spilled like liquid silver over the bobbing waves and a salt-tainted breeze caressed Joanna's skin and toyed playfully with her long hair, but she didn't notice. She eyed Sean's harsh profile with trepidation and waited nervously, too stunned to even think.

Finally he looked back at her and expelled his breath in a long exasperated sigh. "We both know why you followed me on this cruise, Joanna," he said angrily.

Her heart gave a little skip. *Oh, no. He knows. And he's going to refuse.* Joanna looked at him unhappily, her shoulders slumping as her spirits sank like a rock in the ocean. But then his next words caused her to stiffen with shock.

"You're not here to have fun. You followed me because you're infatuated. You've developed a silly, schoolgirl crush."

Chapter Three

Whaaat!"

It was all Joanna could get out for a moment. She just gaped at him, her eyes growing steadily rounder.

"Infatuated! *Infatuated!* Why that's— You— You're— I'm not—"

"It doesn't take a genius to figure out why you followed me," Sean continued, ignoring her incoherent sputtering. "After not seeing each other for years, we spend one evening together, and suddenly here you are, not only on the same cruise, but sitting at the same table. It wouldn't surprise me to find out that you have the cabin next to mine. What did you do, bribe the purser?"

Heat suffused Joanna's face and neck. Against her flushed skin the ocean breeze suddenly felt icy cold, and she silently blessed the darkness. He had completely misread her motive, yet was so close to the mark otherwise that she felt absurdly guilty. Flustered, Joanna groped for a plausible excuse other than the truth. Somehow, she didn't think he'd find that anymore palatable at the moment. "I...I..."

"Look, Joanna." Though Sean's expression was still stern, his voice softened somewhat. "I don't want to hurt you. You're the daughter of one of my dearest friends. But I came on this cruise to relax and enjoy myself, and I sure as hell don't intend to spend it dodging a love-struck young girl."

Joanna gasped. Stiffening, she drew her slender body up to its full height and gave him a cool look. She was angry now. Angry and humiliated. And, recalling the crush she'd had on him four years ago, more than a little uncomfortable.

"You won't have to worry about that, I assure you. Because you're mistaken." She tried to maintain a frigid hauteur, but with every word her anger grew and her words became more heated. "I am not in the least interested in you, except perhaps as a friend, and now I'm not even certain I want to be that. Just because you think you're God's gift to women, don't expect everyone to agree with you. You...you arrogant, egotistical, insufferable—" Joanna sputtered to a halt, almost choking on her rage "—jerk! I wouldn't have you as a precious gift!"

Her hazel eyes flashed fire at him. She started to say more, sputtered again, then clasped her jaws together and stomped off.

Sean stared after her. Had he been wrong? He frowned and shook his head. It didn't seem likely. If she'd only wanted to enjoy the cruise, then why seek him out? Why choose this particular cruise?

Stuffing his hands in his pockets, Sean began to stroll toward the bow of the ship, his expression pensive. *A jerk? And egotistical? Is that how she really thinks of me?* He didn't know whether to be angry, relieved or insulted. A reluctant smile tugged at the corners of his mouth as he realized that he felt a bit of all three.

Or had her tirade just been a face-saving tactic? Then again, maybe Joanna had been right, Sean admitted with a self-deprecating chuckle. Maybe he was simply jumping to conclusions because he was an arrogant, egotistical, insufferable bastard. Maybe... but he didn't think so.

What other possible reason could she have for following me?

Sean wandered aimlessly around the ship, a jumble of thoughts running through his mind: Joanna, the uncertainty of his future, his wants, the decision he was going to have to make soon. They taunted him, bedeviled him, and no matter how hard he tried, he couldn't tune them out.

When Sean had made a circuit of the deck he was on, he climbed the stairs to the one above. As he neared the bow, the heavy, pulsating rock music pouring from the Zodiac Lounge drew him, and he went in, pausing just inside the door to look around.

The walls vibrated with the pounding explosion of sound produced by the band, and on the dance floor couples gyrated wildly. The floor looked as though it were made of thick glass. Beneath it, colored lights flashed at random in time to the primitive beat, eerily illuminating the dancers.

It could be an ''in'' spot anywhere, Sean thought with a touch of bored cynicism. Dimly lit. Frenetic. Crowded with people who were working hard at having a good time.

Short-skirted waitresses bustled between the closely spaced tables. Laughter, raised voices, the clink of glassware, all blended into a dull roar that competed with the blaring music.

Across the room Sean spotted Gloria, sitting at a table with Tony Farrell and several other people. He considered joining them, but after only a few seconds turned and left. For some reason he just wasn't in the mood for partying.

Pausing by the rail, Sean looked at the peaceful movements of the moon-drenched ocean and felt inexplicably sad. Inexplicably lonely. Which is stupid, he told himself, considering the hundreds of people on this ship. One in particular who'd be more than willing to keep you company.

But the strange discontent that he'd felt for months settled around him like a lead cape, causing a queer ache in his chest, and Sean continued to stare out at the spill of liquid silver on the heaving water. Finally, he pushed away from the rail, went inside and loped down two flights of stairs.

With his gaze fixed on the multicolored carpet, his hands stuffed in his pockets, he sauntered down the long companionway toward his cabin. "Helluva way to start a vacation," he muttered under his breath.

Joanna paced the floor of her sitting room with jerky, agitated steps.

"I don't want to spend my time dodging a love-struck young girl." Sean's words ran tauntingly through her mind. Her jaw clenched tighter and an angry sound, very much like a growl, vibrated in her throat.

"I don't believe it. I just don't believe this is happening," she muttered to the ceiling, throwing her arms wide. "He actually thinks that I'm infatuated with him. That . . . that conceited, vain . . . Romeo!"

But even as the words came out of her mouth, Joanna knew they weren't true. Though females were drawn to Sean like flies to honey, he was no womanizer. Sean admired and respected women, enjoyed them—some intimately, true—but he didn't use them. And if ever a man had a right to be conceited about his looks, it was Sean. Yet he seemed supremely unaware, or at least uncaring, that he was every woman's idea of a Greek god.

Joanna stopped by one of the windows and gazed out at the moonlight dancing on the water. She took several slow, deep breaths, and after a moment began to calm, her anger draining away. In any case, she admitted reluctantly, it wasn't really Sean's masculine beauty that made feminine hearts flutter. It was that wicked grin and those damned bedroom eyes. That faintly reckless, devil-may-care aura about him. Joanna suspected that even if Sean were ugly as sin, he could still have his pick of women.

Abandoning the view, Joanna sank down on the sofa, slipped out of her shoes and propped her feet on the marble-topped coffee table. The soft leather crackled as she leaned her head back and gazed up at the ceiling. How ironic that four years ago when she'd fancied herself madly in love with Sean he hadn't even guessed, and now that she was over all that foolishness, he was accusing her of falling for him. The ridiculousness of it made her chuckle.

When she had made her plans it had never once occurred to her that he would think she was interested in him. But in all fairness, she admitted reluctantly, looking at it from Sean's point of view, she could understand how he could have misconstrued her actions.

Somehow she was going to have to convince him otherwise. Not only was it embarrassing, it was a sure bet that as long as he thought she was chasing him she'd never convince him to run for office.

As she had done countless times in the past few weeks, Joanna wondered at Sean's reluctance to commit himself. It wasn't like him at all. In his easygoing way, he was a decisive, determined man, and according to Matt, ever since coming to D.C. ten years ago, Sean had set his sights on eventually attaining a political office. Everything he'd done, everything he'd worked for, had been with that goal in mind.

The time was ripe. Sean knew as well as she that you didn't just blithely say one day, "I think I'll run for office." You had to have backers with influence who could drop a few words in the right ears, do a little civilized arm-twisting, who had enough clout in both the public and private sectors to sway opinions and drum up the enormous amount of financial support it took to run a campaign. Newcomb and his group were offering that backing.

So why was Sean hesitating?

Impatiently, Joanna pushed aside the fruitless speculation. Unless she could convince Sean that she wasn't attracted to him romantically she didn't have a hope of finding out the answer to that question.

Joanna searched for an explanation to give Sean for being on the trip, but after wrestling with the problem for several minutes she jerked to her feet and headed for the bedroom. *The devil with subtlety. The first thing to-*

morrow morning I'm going to tell him the truth. Then maybe we can talk seriously about his political future.

But to Joanna's disappointment, Sean did not put in an appearance in the dining room the next morning. The only company she had at the table for most of the meal was Mary and Charles Wright. The entire time she was eating Joanna kept one eye on the entrance and at the same time pretended to listen to Mary's friendly chatter. But there was no sign of Sean.

As she sipped her after breakfast coffee, Tony Farrell slid into the chair next to Joanna, looking the worse for wear. Behind his fashionable glasses his eyes were bleary and bloodshot, and there was a decidedly sickly cast to his skin. Even his carefully styled hair was mussed at the sides, as though he'd been massaging his temples.

"Sorry I'm late," he murmured, reaching eagerly for the cup of coffee the instant the waiter had filled it. "Gloria and I stayed at the Zodiac until almost two this morning and it was a bit difficult to get the old bod in motion."

A curious feeling of relief flickered through Joanna. She had halfway suspected that after they had parted the night before Sean might have sought out Gloria. The chance that the woman might still be with him had been the only thing that prevented Joanna from knocking on his cabin door that morning.

When Tony had drained his cup of coffee he noted the vacant chairs at their table and glanced around the elegant empty dining room. "It looks like I'm not the only one who slept late. Either that, or everyone else chose the breakfast buffet on deck."

Joanna immediately gave herself a swift mental kick. She had forgotten all about the buffet.

As quickly as good manners would allow, she finished her coffee, excused herself and headed outside.

Stepping out into a brilliant world of blinding sunshine and vivid colors, Joanna squinted and shaded her eyes with her hand. The sky was a canopy of blue: perfect, flawless, so bright you could barely stand to look at it. The undulating ocean was several shades darker, touched here and there with frothy whitecaps. At the horizon, sea and sky blended together in a softly smudged line that made it difficult to tell where one ended and the other began. The white ship plowed sedately through the blue waters, creating more foaming waves at its bow and a wake that trailed behind like the lacy train on a bridal gown. Only the polished brass and wooden deck and the gay garb of the passengers added a dash of contrast to the great expanse of blue and white.

Smiling, Joanna breathed deeply of sun and salt air and fished in the deep pocket on her wraparound skirt for her sunglasses. There was still a line of people at the buffet table, but Sean wasn't among them. Most of the tables scattered along the deck were filled with people enjoying their alfresco breakfast, and as she strolled toward the stern of the ship Joanna discreetly glanced at each of them.

About halfway down the deck she spotted Susan and Bill Adamson, and to Joanna's surprise, Susan was holding in her lap a baby who looked to be about six months old.

"Well, good morning, you two," Joanna greeted, stopping beside their table. "When you didn't show up in the dining room I thought maybe you had made the rounds with Tony and Gloria last night."

At the sound of Joanna's voice the baby looked up and stared at her, her big blue eyes wide and unblinking. Her intent gaze did not waver even when Susan stuffed another spoonful of what looked like mashed banana into her mouth. Smiling, Joanna reached out and touched the wispy blond curl above the baby's ear. "And who is this little charmer?"

"This is our daughter, Lori," Susan said distractedly, using the side of the spoon to rake the globs of food from around the rosebud mouth and stuff it back in. "Bill's mother was going to keep her while we took this cruise, but just a few hours before we were supposed to leave she slipped on the stairs and broke her leg, so we had to bring Lori along."

"It was either that, or miss it. It was too late to get a refund on our tickets," Bill added dejectedly.

Susan looked up at Joanna with a wan smile. "Don't misunderstand. We love Lori dearly. It's just that this was supposed to be sort of a second honeymoon. Now we'll have to take turns sitting with her in the evening while the other one eats and sees the shows. We're going to try to take her with us when we go on the island tours, but if she gets too fussy one of us will have to stay on board and keep her."

"Some honeymoon," Bill muttered morosely.

"Couldn't you hire one of the crew to baby-sit for you?"

"Oh, yes. That's what we did last night." Susan wiped the baby's mouth with a napkin and handed her a bottle of milk. Lori lay back in her mother's arms and sucked greedily, her unblinking stare still fixed on Joanna. "The trouble is, we can't afford to do that very often. We had to save for this trip for years, and I'm afraid we're on a very tight budget that just doesn't allow for baby-sitting."

"That's too bad," Joanna said with genuine sympathy. "If there's anything I can do—"

"No, no," Susan cut in quickly. "We wouldn't want to impose on anyone. And don't let us spoil your trip with our problems," she added with a bright smile. "We'll work something out."

They talked desultorily for a few minutes more, but when Joanna spotted Sean leaving a table a few yards away, she excused herself and hurried after him.

"Sean! Sean, may I speak with you a moment?"

Sean turned, then groaned and looked disgusted when he saw who was calling him. "For Pete's sake, Joanna! Do we have to go through this again?"

"But you don't understand. I didn't come on this cruise to try to attract you. I—"

"Oh, Joanna, please," Sean pleaded wearily. "You aren't going to try again to make me believe that you're here just to enjoy yourself, are you? People in your set don't take cruises. They own their own yachts. Or if they don't, they have friends who do. We both know that if you got a sudden yen to cruise the Caribbean, all you would have to do is pick up the phone and call one of your jet-setting pals."

"Oh, but—"

"Joanna, I don't want to hear it. Okay? Just back off and leave me alone."

"Sean, if you'll only listen for a minute—" Joanna began again, but before she could utter another word Gloria glided up to Sean and linked her arm through his.

"There, you are. I've been searching all over for you. The calypso band is setting up by the forward pool, and one of the cruise directors is going to give lessons in island dancing. I thought maybe I could talk you into joining me." Smiling persuasively, the redhead leaned against him, pressing the side of her breast against his arm, her eyes flashing an invitation of another sort. Sean responded with a lazy grin.

"Lead the way, sweetheart," he drawled. "It sounds like fun." He turned his head and gave Joanna a pointed look. "Joanna and I were through talking anyway. I'm sure she'll excuse us."

Numbly, Joanna watched them walk away, arm in arm. Without warning a strange, aching tightness gripped her chest, and to her horror, she felt tears sting her eyes. She turned away quickly and walked to the rail. Resting her forearms along the top, she leaned against it and lifted her face to the wind, blinking rapidly. She pressed her lips together and drew a deep breath, struggling to control the wayward wobble of her chin.

This is silly, she told herself severely. For Pete's sake, there's no reason to get all teary and bent out of shape just because Sean won't talk to you? And so what if he's making time with that redhead? There's nothing new in that. Joanna stared at the smudged horizon and swallowed against the painful constriction in her throat. The stiff ocean breeze threaded through her hair, lifting and waving it like streamers of brown silk, and plastered her skirt against the front of her body. The thin cotton suggestively outlined the slender curves of hips and long shapely legs and flapped wildly behind her, snapping and cracking like a flag in the gusting wind.

Joanna held herself stiffly, her chin tilted at a proud angle, but after a moment her shoulders sagged. It was pointless to deny it: Sean's attitude did bother her. But more than his refusal to speak to her, more than his obvious preference for Gloria, what really disturbed her were his remarks about her background.

Not because they were unfair, but because at one time they would have been right on target. As recently as four years ago, Joanna admitted with lingering self-disgust, she would have looked upon this cruise as entirely too plebeian, beneath even her consideration.

Summers in the south of France or in Greece with her friend Irena or sailing the Mediterranean. Winters skiing in the Alps, and in between, flying trips to London or Rome or Madrid. That had been the pattern of her life. Her father had spoiled her outrageously. She had grown up so accustomed to having her own way she had not given a thought to the wants and needs of anyone else.

Looking back on that time, Joanna was appalled. Her selfishness had nearly cost her mother the only love and true happiness she had ever known and had driven a wedge between them. Even so, it had taken a series of shocks and disillusionments before she'd finally accepted the truth: about her father, about her parents' marriage, but most of all, about herself.

Joanna shook her head disbelievingly, her eyes full of regret. It all seemed so long ago. Sean, of course, really couldn't be faulted for his remarks. He had no way of knowing that she had turned her back on that life, that she had worked hard in school and now worked hard at a job, not because she had to but because she wanted to, that she rarely saw anyone from her old crowd.

But Joanna wanted desperately for him to know. For some reason she didn't fully understand, Sean's good opinion was important to her. If she could just talk to him, convince him to accept Newcomb's offer and then give her a job, he'd see for himself that she had changed. Somehow, she had to make him listen.

The ringing sounds of steel drums filled the air suddenly, their lilting rhythm at once soothing and stimulating. Joanna turned her head and looked toward the bow. As though drawn by a magnet, she began to stroll in that direction.

Many people were swimming or just lounging around the pool, but an equal number were standing in a semicircle around the cruise director, who was moving to the calypso beat demonstrating the steps and body movements of the dance. There was a good deal of laughter and joking as the audience tried to mimic her.

Joanna started to join the group, but thought better of it. Instead, she walked to one of the poolside lounges, stepped out of her sandals and removed her skirt. But as Joanna turned from hanging it over the back of the lounge, she found that Sean was watching her, and her stomach tightened into a knot.

It wasn't the look of annoyance on his face that disturbed her. She had expected that. It was the way his dark gaze roamed slowly over her body, taking in the brief strapless playsuit. A feathery tingle raced over Joanna's skin as his eyes narrowed and lingered on her breasts, which were clearly outlined by the elasticized top, then slid downward over her narrow waist, the gentle flare of her hips and the long, curving length of her bare legs.

Feigning indifference, Joanna stretched out on the lounge, oblivious to the admiring looks she was receiving from several other men around the pool. For the next half hour she sunbathed and pretended to doze, while watching Sean covertly through slitted eyes.

It was her intention to corner Sean when the class broke up, but she never had a chance. The moment the band stopped playing he marched over to her. Before Joanna could even struggle to a sitting position Sean bent over, braced his arms on either side of the webbed lounge and brought his face down to within an inch of hers. His beautiful mouth was stretched into a dazzling smile, but his black eyes were snapping with anger as he said in a strained but soft voice, "Knock it off, Joanna. Because I'm warning you, if you don't, I just may turn you over my knee and give you the spanking you should have had years ago. Now be a good girl and stay out of my hair."

Then he was gone. Joanna sat up just in time to see him loop his arm around Gloria's waist and lead her away. Anger and indignation welled up inside Joanna as she glared at their retreating backs. Spanking! *Spanking!* In a pig's eye!

Her eyes narrowed, and a mulish expression that her mother would have recognized settled over her face. *Damn you, Sean. I'll make you listen to me if it's the last thing I do,* she vowed.

Bristling, Joanna stood up, stuffed her feet back into her sandals, snatched up her skirt and stalked after the pair. What she had to say no longer mattered. Getting a chance to actually say it had become a point of honor.

But trying to corner Sean, Joanna soon discovered, was like trying to capture a slippery eel with your bare hands. After scouring the ship for almost an hour, Joanna finally spotted him playing volleyball, but the minute she stepped onto the court, Sean stepped off. At lunch he once again opted for the buffet on deck. When she found him, he and Gloria were sharing a table with the Adamsons, but no sooner had Joanna joined them than Sean excused himself, leaving his lunch half-finished. Later she tracked him down in the casino, but when she tried to talk to him the dealer shushed her with a black look. She retreated to the slot machines on the other side of the room to wait, but somehow Sean vanished when she wasn't looking.

It was the same story all day. Whenever Joanna got anywhere near Sean he always managed to give her the slip. But the more he evaded her, the more determined Joanna became. That evening after dinner she followed him and Gloria and waited for her chance.

They went to the Club International and watched singing idol Doug Longworth perform. After the show they moved on to the Zodiac Lounge for dancing. Finally, around midnight Sean walked Gloria to her cabin.

Feeling utterly foolish, Joanna hovered around the corner, hoping against hope that Sean would not disappear into Gloria's room for the night. To her relief, after a steamy good-night kiss, they parted and Sean came sauntering back down the companionway, whistling softly under his breath.

Joanna flew up the stairs before he could spot her and hurried straight to her suite. Leaving the door open a crack, she stood just inside and peered out, and when Sean drew close she stepped out into his path. "Sean, I must talk to you. This is important, believe me."

"Oh, for the love of..." Sean stopped, his face hardening. "All right. All right, that's it!" He looked around, then grabbed her arm and propelled her into her suite. He kicked the door shut with his foot and at the same time thrust Joanna into the center of the room. "I've tried to be patient with you, Joanna," he began grimly, advancing on her, "but you just won't take no for an answer, will you? I guess I should have known better than to expect anything else from a spoiled, self-centered brat like you."

"I am not a spoiled brat!"

"Oh yeah? You sure could of fooled me." A quick look around brought a scornful twist to his mouth. "Just look at this setup. You couldn't just book a cabin like us ordinary mortals, could you? Oh no, nothing but the luxury suite is good enough for Princess Joanna," he sneered.

"That's not the reason I booked this suite," Joanna denied heatedly, her own anger beginning to simmer.

"The point is, you're an overindulged, self-centered little girl. You're so accustomed to having whatever your heart desires that when you decide you want something you think all you have to do is reach out and grab it. Well life doesn't work that way, sweetheart, and it's about time you learned that."

Anger flared in Joanna's eyes, but before she could speak Sean continued in a warning tone. "I'm not going to become involved with you, Joanna. First of all, I'm too old for you. Secondly, you're the daughter and stepdaughter of my two dearest friends, and I'm not about to jeopardize that relationship for a roll in the hay with an immature little snit."

Joanna gasped, and Sean's expression changed to one of cynical amusement.

"Not that you're not attractive and appealing, mind you. You are, in a classy, well-bred sort of way." He stepped closer and ran his forefinger down her cheek to lightly graze the mole at the corner of her mouth. Joanna went perfectly still, her eyes widening. She couldn't have moved if her life had depended on it. "But it simply wouldn't work because, honey, I guarantee you, I'm way out of your league." At her strangled sound of protest, Sean slipped his arms around her and pulled her close. His lids dropped partway, and his eyes glinted down at her, hard and steely with purpose. Slowly, he bent his head. "And just so there's no doubt about it in your mind..."

The softly whispered words floated into her mouth as his lips claimed hers in a long, searing kiss.

Shock reverberated through Joanna. It was all sensation—sizzling fire and shivering ecstasy. There was no force, no gentle enticement: just pure seduction, bold and sure and devastating.

As his mouth rocked against hers he pulled her closer and one hand slid down her spine to press her hips tightly against his. Joanna gasped, and he thrust his tongue into her mouth, plunging deep to plunder with slow, evocative strokes that set off a throbbing heat in Joanna's feminine core.

Her heart was racing, sending blood pounding through her veins, and her chest was so tight she could barely breathe. In some remote corner of her brain, Joanna knew she should resist, protest, but her quivering body was enslaved. Years ago she had daydreamed endlessly of Sean holding her like this, kissing her like this. But those dreams faded into nothingness beside reality. This was a thousand times more potent—a shattering delight that robbed her of both strength and will.

Sean was experienced with women, and he used his vast knowledge to advantage. He knew where to touch, how to touch, and his roving hands drove her wild. When he held her close and rocked his hips suggestively she whimpered softly into his mouth and melted against him. Of their own accord, her arms lifted and her spread fingers buried themselves in his hair, the ebony strands sliding against her skin like warm silk as she clutched his head and urged him closer.

She clung to him, dizzy with the need he was so deliberately arousing, her mouth soft and fervent under his, her body aflame with sweet, hot desire. She lost all sense of time and place and purpose. At that moment nothing else in the world existed but Sean. Just Sean.

And then, suddenly, it was over. Joanna felt cold and bereft when his lips left hers. Colder still when he gripped her shoulders and held her away from him. Dazed, she stood like a rag doll between his hands, unable to respond for a moment. When at last she opened her eyes, she found Sean watching her strangely.

He stared at her in silence, his dark eyes narrowed and glittering. Then, abruptly, he released her and without a word, turned and stalked out.

Chapter Four

Joanna stared at the closed door. Slowly she raised her hand and pressed trembling fingers against her mouth. *Dear God, how could I have been so stupid?*

A sick sensation quivered through her, and she closed her eyes and let her breath out in a deep, shuddering sigh. Sean had been right all along; she was infatuated with him. She always had been. That one searing kiss had proved that.

A low moan escaped her, and she turned and walked listlessly into the bedroom. Dazed, she sank down onto the bed and stared out the window at nothing. *What a fool you are. What a complete and utter fool.*

The past few years had taught Joanna a lot about her weaknesses and her strengths. She knew that she was good at self-deception, seeing things as she wanted them to be. Typically, she had managed to rationalize her reasons for wanting Sean to run for office, and for following him on this cruise, but she knew now that the basic reason, the *real* reason, was this crazy attraction she felt for him. Firming her mouth, Joanna sighed deeply once again. No doubt, the only person she'd fooled with the weak excuse was herself. She certainly hadn't fooled Sean.

The attraction was crazy. And hopeless. Sean had made it obvious how he thought of her—a child, a spoiled brat.

And he's right, Joanna conceded unhappily. At least partially.

Flopping back on the bed, her hands balling into fists, Joanna squinted at the ceiling. "But I'm working on it," she muttered with grim determination.

Since causing so much havoc in her mother's life she had tried very hard to change. There were lapses now and then, Joanna admitted with brutal honesty. It was difficult to break the habits and attitudes of a lifetime. But she would...eventually.

Actually, viewing the situation rationally, Joanna knew she should be grateful that Sean did not share her feelings. Because the attraction was not only stupid, it was dangerous. Recalling the raw passion Sean's kiss had evoked, Joanna closed her eyes and shivered. It had caught her completely off guard and rocked her to her very soul. Even now, just thinking about it, she felt a tingling heat surge through her body.

Gritting her teeth against the disturbing sensation, Joanna rolled her head from side to side on the mattress. No, Sean was not for her. At eighteen she had been brashly confident that she could make him fall in love with her. Now she knew better. Sean was a confirmed bachelor, a man of the world. Even if they were to have a romantic relationship, the odds were that she would end up with a broken heart.

Sean had been right, she admitted with a wistful sigh. He was way out of her league.

For a few minutes she lay on the bed reviewing her foolish behavior, angry and utterly disgusted. The mental dressing down she gave herself was sharp, scathing and merciless.

But Joanna was not one to flay herself for long. She had tried that four years ago, until her mother had made her see that endless self-castigation was foolish and did no one any good. Now when she made a mistake, she admitted it, ranted a bit, then forgave herself and set about doing whatever she could to correct it.

Decisively, Joanna lunged up off the bed. Twisting her arm behind her, she lowered the zipper on her gown. The only thing to do was to make the best of a bad situation and get through the rest of the trip with as much dignity as possible, she told herself as the peach silk sheath slithered down her body and pooled around her feet. She would put the stupid infatuation out of her mind and simply relax and enjoy the cruise...and do her best to stay out of Sean's hair.

"Good morning, Mr. Fleming." The waiter poured coffee into Sean's cup as he slid into his seat at the table. "Looks like you're the only one eating indoors this morning."

Sean gave the man a lazy grin. "I'm not quite up to all that sparkling sea and sun just yet."

Aromatic steam wafted up to tantalize his nose, and Sean reached for the cup of coffee, taking a quick sip of the scalding liquid. It was the truth, up to a point, but the main reason he'd chosen the dining room over the buffet was to avoid Gloria. After the night he'd just had he wasn't in the mood for lighthearted flirting.

When the waiter had taken his order Sean settled back to wait. Broodingly, he stared at the shining surface of the coffee, a frown creasing between his brows.

Joanna. It annoyed him that he couldn't dismiss her from his mind. And, to his disgust, now just the thought of her made his chest tighten and sent a throbbing heat to his loins.

Sean shifted uncomfortably and took another sip from the cup. What the devil happened?

For half the night he had lain awake staring at the ceiling, asking the same question over and over, but he still had no answer. He had intended to teach Joanna a lesson with that kiss. Sean exhaled a rueful snort and grimaced. What a laugh! The moment their lips had touched rational thought had deserted him. It had been an explosion of pure passion, hot and raw and overwhelming. If he hadn't found the strength to end it, in another minute he'd have taken her right there.

Lord, Fleming! What the hell's the matter with you? She's just a girl, for Pete's sake. If you're not careful, you're going to turn into a dirty old man.

Yet he couldn't deny his response. She had felt exactly right in his arms, as though she'd been made for him alone. And that was what scared him. He had known many women, but never in his life had he wanted one as desperately as he had wanted Joanna.

The waiter topped up his coffee cup. Without thinking, Sean snatched it up, downed half the contents in one long swallow and gasped as the scalding brew seared his throat. Cursing under his breath, he returned the cup to its saucer just as Joanna took her seat on the opposite side of the table.

Anger, resentment and another emotion he didn't care to put a name to, gripped Sean at the sight of her. Her skin glowed and her hazel eyes were clear and direct. There were no dark circles under them, no drawn look. Dressed in a yellow sundress that left her tanned shoulders bare, her glossy hair pulled back at the sides and secured with white and yellow combs, she looked annoyingly fresh and lovely. It was obvious that Joanna hadn't spent a sleepless night.

"Good morning, Sean," she said politely.

Sean's mouth firmed, but before he could reply the waiter materialized beside her and filled her cup with coffee. When he had taken her order and disappeared Joanna folded her hands on the table and looked directly into Sean's eyes.

"Before you get angry all over again, I just want to say one thing. I'm sorry."

Surprise darted through Sean, but the only sign he gave was the infinitesimal narrowing of his eyes.

"I shouldn't have followed you on this trip. I realize that now," Joanna continued in a soft, serious voice. "But I promise you, for the rest of the cruise I'll do my best to stay out of your way."

Her discomfort was obvious, but there was determination there, too. A part of Sean admired the courage and strength of character it took to make the apology. But, dammit! He'd just spent the better part of the night agonizing over her and that damned kiss, and her freshness and composure were galling. For once, his lazy insouciance deserted him.

"Oh, sure." Sean's look was as deliberately skeptical as his tone, but Joanna met it squarely, one brow lifting.

"I'm sorry. That's the best I can do. I can't very well get off the ship in the middle of the ocean. I don't walk on water, you know."

Sean's admiration deepened, but he hid it well. "I don't suppose you'd consider getting off at St. Thomas and flying home?"

Hurt flickered in Joanna's eyes, but her steady gaze never wavered. "No, I wouldn't. But I promise I won't pester you anymore." Her chin tilted a bit higher at Sean's derisive snort, and she added with the barest trace of annoyance, "I've already asked the purser if I could change to another table, but he said it was too late. So, I'm afraid at meals we'll just have to make the best of the situation."

Sean just looked at her, his expression unyielding. After a moment she lowered her eyes. He watched her pick up her cup and take a sip of coffee. Then she folded her hands in her lap and gazed off into the distance. Only the pulse throbbing at the base of her throat betrayed her nervousness.

Her pride was evident in the tilt of her chin, in her stiff posture, yet she still looked like a defenseless waif. Even though he knew she'd brought the situation on herself, after a moment Sean began to feel churlish. Exhaling heavily, he raked a hand through his hair and let it slide down the back of his head to massage the taut muscles in his neck.

"Look, Joanna," he began, frowning, "About last ni—"

But the statement was never finished, for at that moment the Wrights and Tony Farrell arrived.

"Good morning, you two," Mary said, slipping into the seat beside Joanna. "Looks like you're the early birds."

Joanna looked up eagerly, a smile of pure relief light-ing her face. "Good morning."

Battling his frustration, Sean greeted them cordially, then settled back in his chair and watched in brooding silence.

As Charles took the chair beside his wife, Tony Far-rell chose the seat on Joanna's other side. "Hi." His gray eyes glowed warmly behind his glasses as they skimmed over her upturned face and bare shoulders. "You look terrific this morning."

"Thank you. You don't look bad yourself."

Tony flashed her a white smile that was an orthodon-tist's dream. "I looked for you yesterday. I was hoping that we could spend some time together, get to know one another. But I didn't catch so much as a glimpse of you until dinner. And afterward you disappeared again."

"Oh, Joanna had a very busy day yesterday," Sean interjected in an insinuating drawl.

When Joanna darted him a wary look he propped his chin on his fist and smiled tauntingly. Reminding her of the way she'd pursued him wasn't the gentlemanly thing to do, especially after her apology. Normally Sean wouldn't have dreamed of needling a woman—any woman—but Joanna had gotten under his skin, and for some reason he could not quite curb his irritation. Be-sides, there was something about Tony Farrell that set his teeth on edge.

Joanna turned back to Tony with a placating smile and placed her hand on his arm. "But I won't be busy today. If you'd like we could go up to the sports deck after breakfast and check out the activities."

"Great."

Sean studied them, his eyes narrowing.

The waiter brought Mary a cup of tea and poured coffee for everyone else. Gloria arrived as he was handing out the menus.

"Good morning, all," she greeted lightly as she settled in next to Sean. "I'm surprised to find you all inside on such a terrific morning." She shook out her napkin and put it on her lap, and slanted Sean a sultry, heavy-lidded look. "I looked for you on deck. For a while there I began to think you were avoiding me."

Sean looked at the red nails that were lightly scoring his forearm, then, slowly, his gaze lifted, and he studied the invitation in Gloria's slanting green eyes. After a moment he thought, *Why not? This is what you came for, isn't it?* Covering her hand with his, he leaned closer. A slow, wicked grin curved his mouth. "Now why on earth would I do that?"

It was all the invitation Gloria needed. For the remainder of the meal she flirted with Sean outrageously, and he flirted right back. He turned on the charm, his rakish smile and teasing black eyes underscoring the purring warmth in his voice, the teasing sensuality that colored their conversation.

But for all the effort he put into it, Sean was, to his disgust and annoyance, not totally engrossed in the flirtation. He was too aware of the fact that Joanna was ignoring him. Whenever he glanced across the table she was chatting with either Mary or Tony. Usually Tony. The few times Joanna's gaze met his she looked away as though he didn't exist, and when he asked her a direct question she answered him with a polite indifference that made him grit his teeth.

Joanna's low laugh drifted across the table and Sean glanced at her again. His eyes narrowed as he watched her wrinkle her nose at something Tony said. Surely she's not going to go off the deep end over that New York slick? he thought, frowning. He eyed the man's neatly styled hair, fashionable glasses, and immaculate, just right clothes sourly. He was too smooth. Too perfect. Hell, couldn't she see that? Sean's gaze dropped to Tony's well tended hands and one corner of his mouth curled disdainfully. He didn't trust a man who wore nail polish, even if it was clear.

Becoming aware of the trend of his thoughts, Sean shifted uneasily in his chair. Good grief, Fleming! What the devil do you care if the girl wants to indulge in a shipboard fling? You're not her keeper. And besides, you ought to be happy to have her off your back. Determinedly, he pulled his gaze away from the pair and turned back to Gloria with a lazy smile.

"Ready?" Tony asked a moment later.

Joanna took one last sip of coffee, then patted her mouth with her napkin. "Yes, I'm ready." With a murmured, "Excuse us," and a parting smile for the others, she rose and linked her arm through Tony's.

Broodingly, his eyes glittering slits of obsidian, Sean watched them walk away.

He was oblivious to the chatter going on around him until Gloria drew his attention with a playful rake of her long nails across the back of his hand. Stifling the unaccountable irritation that roiled through him, Sean turned his head and met her coy smile.

"Personally, I think they have an excellent idea." Gloria purred in response to his questioning look. "Why don't you and I pair off and go for a swim? I have a new bikini I'm just dying to try."

Sean stared at her, absorbing her ripe beauty, and wondered why the idea didn't hold more appeal. After a moment he impatiently thrust the thought aside and with one of his lazy smiles, drawled, "Sure. Why not?"

Suntan lotion, towel, sunglasses, paperback novel. Satisfied she had everything, Joanna added her room key to the contents of the canvas bag, pulled the door shut behind her and headed for the pool.

Her thong sandals slapped against her heels as she ran up the stairs. Rounding the landing on the next deck, she nearly bumped into Susan and Bill.

"Hi." Susan hitched Lori higher on her hip and eyed Joanna's white lace beach robe. It barely reached the tops of her thighs, and the fragile lace gave tantalizing glimpses of the cinnamon maillot beneath. "Going swimming, huh? We were just heading for the pool ourselves."

"Yeah," Bill chimed in. "It's one of the few activities that we can take Lori to. She's been swimming since she was five months old." He smiled proudly and tweaked his daughter's tiny nose. "She's a regular little water baby."

"Really?" Joanna smiled at the staring infant. "I'd really like to see that. Mind if I join you?"

"Of course not. Come on."

As they climbed the final flight of stairs together Susan slanted her a curious look. "I saw you playing shuffleboard with Tony this morning. He seemed... well... very interested. I'm surprised he's not with you."

"He's playing in a backgammon tournament," Joanna replied, biting back a smile at Susan's gentle probing. "He said he'd meet me at the pool when it was over."

"You didn't want to watch?"

"No. I'm afraid I find the game extremely boring."

Actually, Joanna had thought it wise to spend some time away from Tony. He was a nice man and pleasant company, but she didn't want to encourage him too much. There was no explaining it: he was attractive, in a smooth sophisticated way, eligible, and so far, had behaved as a perfect gentleman. But there was no spark between them—at least, not from her side.

The moment they came in sight of the pool Lori let loose with a string of ecstatic jabber, her arms outstretched toward the water, opening and closing her chubby little fists in a classic "gimmee" gesture as she bounced up and down in her mother's arms. Laughing and watching the baby's uninhibited excitement, Joanna didn't see Sean at first. When she did she stopped short.

He was sitting on a poolside lounge beside Gloria, who was stretched out on her stomach with her head pillowed on her crossed arms. The top of her bikini was unfastened, and Sean was methodically applying tanning lotion to her bare back. And if the expression on his face was any indication, he was enjoying the task immensely.

Joanna was appalled by her reaction. Pain sliced through her like a sharp knife at the sight of those tanned fingers smoothing over the woman's skin. For an instant she almost gave into the urge to turn and run back to her room. But then, as she studied the look of male satisfaction on Sean's face, her jaw tightened and she stiffened her spine. No. She wasn't going anywhere. She had told Tony she'd meet him here, and here was where she was going to stay.

Gloria's back glistened in the sun. The mingled scents of heavy perfume, coconut oil and heated flesh drifted upward from her supine body, making Sean's nostrils twitch and flare. This wasn't such a bad idea after all, he mused as he watched his palms glide languidly over her slick shoulder blades, then trail downward to her waist. The strange anger he had felt at breakfast had slowly dissipated. Smiling, he gently kneaded the soft flesh beneath his hands. This was what he needed to get his mind off things. A little sun and fun, a beautiful woman to add spice. And, he thought with pleasurable anticipation, he had a hunch that with very little encouragement, Gloria could add a great deal of spice to this vacation.

His dreamy complacency didn't last long. At that moment Sean looked up, straight into Joanna's eyes, and his hands stilled. Briefly, her cool gaze flickered over him, then she turned away and dumped her canvas bag onto a lounge. Sean clenched his jaw and cursed fluently under his breath.

Suddenly self-conscious, he finished applying the lotion to Gloria's back with a quick, impersonal touch. "There, I think that's got you covered."

"Mmm," Gloria mumbled sleepily.

Sean capped the bottle and tossed it onto the towel beside her, then moved away and stretched out on the next lounge with his fingers laced together behind his head.

Through barely slitted eyes he watched Joanna shuck her frothy little beach coat and drop it beside her bag. His eyes roamed over her, and he cursed silently once again as he felt an unwelcome surge of heat rush to his loins. The shimmering cinnamon material of her one-piece suit molded Joanna's high breasts and boldly de-

fined every hollow and curve of her slender body. Cut
daringly low both front and back, and high at the thighs,
the suit revealed a great deal of creamy skin and em-
phasized the long length of her shapely legs.

"Come on in, Joanna," Susan called from the pool.

Without so much as a glance in Sean's direction, Joanna stepped to the edge and dove neatly into the water.

For the next half hour Sean watched as Joanna played
with the Adamson's baby, who paddled with amazing
agility between the three adults. After a while they each
took turns caring for the child while the other two swam.
Sean was just toying with the idea of joining them when
Tony appeared.

"Hi. Aren't you going to swim?" Joanna asked, eyeing his cream slacks and bronze silk shirt.

"Not today. My back's still a little red from yesterday." Tony nodded toward the umbrella covered table at
the end of the pool. "Why don't you take a break and
join me for a drink?"

"Okay." Grinning mischievously, Joanna turned to
Susan and Bill. "Come on, gang, Tony's buying."

"Great!" Bill plucked the baby from the water and
urged the two women toward the side. When they had
heaved themselves out he handed Lori to her mother and
clambered out after them, and they laughingly dripped
their way around to where Tony sat waiting.

Feeling unaccountably irritated, Sean stood up and
plunged into the water. Submerged, he swam the length
of the pool three times before surfacing for air.

He was resting at the side, breathing heavily, when
Gloria jumped in beside him, feet first. She surfaced
laughing and looped her arms around his neck, pressing
her body intimately close to his. "Gotcha!" she cried
gaily. "And now you have to pay a forfeit."

Gloria tightened her arms and lifted herself higher against his body. Closing her eyes, she tilted her head back and pursed her lips invitingly.

Unable to resist, Sean glanced toward the table at the end of the pool, then looked back at the lush red mouth. Joanna wasn't watching, and it wasn't any of her business who he kissed anyway, yet he felt absurdly guilty. Determinedly Sean leaned forward, then hesitated. After a moment his mouth twisted in a rueful half smile, and he reached up and detached Gloria's arms from around his neck.

"Behave yourself," he said, smiling to take the sting out of his words. He turned the pouting woman around and gave her a little push and a playful slap on the rump. "Come on. I'll race you to the other end. I'll even give you a three-second head start."

"You're on!"

Sean watched her thrash away and shook his head. How in hell was he supposed to carry on a seduction with his best friends' daughter watching?

Chapter Five

Barefoot and makeup-free, Joanna entered the gym smiling. She wore a rose-pink leotard and lavender tights with stirrup straps that hooked under her insteps. A pair of deep purple leg warmers were slung casually over her shoulder, the ends swaying against her back with every jaunty step she took. Anticipation sparkled in her hazel eyes. Movement. Activity. It was what she needed, and she was eager to get started.

Spotting the athletic instructor across the room, Joanna altered her course. A bare six feet away, her steps faltered, and she came to a halt. In front of her, lying back on a bench with his feet braced on the floor on either side, Sean was working out with a set of hand weights.

Indecision gripped Joanna. Gnawing at her bottom lip, she eyed him warily. Should she brazen it out and ignore him, or leave? She cast a longing glance toward the instructor and the other women who were already gathering around her and sighed. It was tempting, but remembering the past few days, Joanna decided that retreat was the wisest choice.

She poised to turn, but before she could move Sean sat up and their eyes met. Anger darkened his face. With a muttered oath, he shot up off the bench and stalked to her.

"What are you doing here, Joanna?" He stood with his feet spread aggressively, hands on his hips, and growled the words in a low undertone through lips so stiff they barely moved.

Joanna was both intimidated by his anger and fascinated by his body. He wore only a brief pair of athletic shorts and tennis shoes and his bronze skin glistened with a fine sheen of moisture. Without shoes, Joanna barely reached his chin, and she found herself staring at the damp black hair that lightly furred his chest. The heat from his body hit her like a furnace, bringing with it the smell of sweat and a dizzying, tantalizing musky maleness. Helplessly, her eyes focused on a bead of sweat trickling through the band of hair that arrowed downward from his chest. At his navel it halted, then swirled around the small cavity and streaked lower, disappearing when it touched the already damp top edge of his low-slung shorts. Joanna swallowed hard.

"I . . . I—"

"I'm getting a little sick of this, you know," Sean went on, ignoring her stammered attempt at a reply. "Everywhere I go I run into you. If this is your attempt at staying out of my hair, I'd hate to see you when you're in hot pursuit."

The sarcastic comment snapped Joanna out of her sensual trance instantly. Her eyes went wide and she sucked in her breath. "Are you accusing me of following you around?"

"All I know is I can't make a move without practically stepping on you. It's only been twenty-four hours since you so sweetly promised to leave me alone, and already I've run into you by the pool twice, bumped into you in the library, the card room, the casino. Every time I go to one of the clubs or the theater you're within earshot. I'm beginning to think the only place on the ship where I can be assured of not seeing you is the men's room."

That did it. Joanna's anger soared right along with her blood pressure. She stiffened and planted her fists on her hips, unconsciously mimicking his stance. "Now just a darned minute!" she flared, glaring right back at him. "I promised to leave you alone, which I've tried my best to do, but I didn't promise to lock myself in my cabin for the duration of the cruise. I paid for my ticket, and I'm entitled to enjoy myself and to make use of all the facilities the same as you."

They stood nose to nose, their bodies stiff and vibrating with anger, unflinching hazel eyes glaring defiantly into smoldering black ones.

Across the room, the athletics instructor clapped her hands loudly and called out, "All right, ladies! Line up, it's time to get going."

With a toss of her head, Joanna broke eye contact and moved to step around Sean. "I came here to take the aerobics class," she informed him haughtily. "Now, if you'll excuse me, that's exactly what I intend to do."

Rock music exploded from the speakers on the walls as the instructor turned away from the stereo. Moving in time to the heavy beat, she faced the group of women who had spread out on the mat. "Okay, here we go.

We'll start with the hustle jog. Lift those knees! Lift! Lift! Three. Four. Five. Lift! Lift!"

Joanna scrambled to pull on her leg warmers, skipping and hopping on first one foot, then the other in her rush to join the class. When she had finally tugged them into place she found a position at the front of the group, stepped into the rhythm and threw herself into the routine with a vengeance.

"Now spread your feet, hands on hips and bend to the side! Bend! Bend! Get those elbows down! Come on ladies, reach! Reach!"

Joanna bounced downward, straining to make her elbow touch the side of her knee. Already she was breathing hard, and she could feel perspiration popping out all over her body. She glanced at Sean and found him standing where she'd left him, fists still propped on his hips, watching her. Joanna gritted her teeth and bounced harder.

Who does he think he is, glowering at me like that? Automatically following instructions, Joanna straightened, extended her arms to the sides and swiveled her shoulders in time to the beat.

Resentment bubbled up inside her as she thought of his accusations. She'd tried to avoid him. She really had. But it was impossible on a ship of this size. But did he take that into account? Oh, no. He preferred to see her as a man-chasing spoiled brat.

Joanna shot Sean a dagger-sharp glare. Up until now, every time they'd met she had either tried to make herself as inconspicuous as possible, or made an excuse and left. But no more, she decided pugnaciously. From now on, Sean or no Sean, she was going to enjoy herself. And if he didn't like it, *he* could leave.

"All right, ladies, move those buns! Get a little action in it! Shake it! Shake it! That's it!"

The music throbbed. Wild. Pulsating and primitive. Joanna's lithe body was an extension of it, moving to the heavy beat, translating it into a sinuous flow of fluid rhythm.

Her face was flushed, her hair flying. Sweat drenched her. It gathered between her breasts and streamed down the narrow trench that marked her spine, making dark blotches on her rose-colored leotard. Beneath the form-fitting garment, supple flesh and firm, feminine muscles rippled with each undulating movement, and her small, uptilted breasts swayed and bounced in unfettered abandon.

God! Sean thought a little frantically. *I've seen less erotic dances in X rated films.* He stared, unable to tear his gaze away. When the unconscious enticement of Joanna's gyrations had their inevitable effect on his body he cursed and snatched up his towel from the bench and held it in front of him, dabbing absently at his chest and arms, but his eyes remained trained on her.

Who would have thought that a leotard and leg warmers could be so damned sexy?

The neckline of the formfitting garment plunged in deep V's both front and back, but even so, it covered a great deal more flesh than even a one-piece bathing suit. Yet, somehow, its high, French cut and the bunched folds of wool that covered Joanna from ankle to knee managed to draw attention to her legs, especially the long, luscious curves of her thighs. That, in turn, led the eye irresistibly to those gently rounded hips and that tight, delectable derriere.

"Okay, ladies! Shake it out! Shake it out!" the instructor chanted. "Now bend and touch the floor! Bend! Bend! Bend!"

Legs spread and straight, her rump stuck up in the air, Joanna bent over, and with her palms flat on the floor, bounced her torso in time to the music and the instructor's chant.

Sean groaned and tightened his grip on the towel. *Christ, Fleming, don't stand here gawking like a sixteen year old in heat. Leave, for Pete's sake!*

But he didn't. He couldn't. The music pounded hotly and so did the blood in his veins. With each passing second both his excitement and anger grew. He didn't want to be attracted to Joanna, dammit!

He gave a snort of laughter at that. Want it or not, you sap, you are, he told himself in utter disgust.

Guiltily, he realized that his recent behavior was the direct result of the unwanted attraction. He'd never been deliberately rude to a woman in his life before, yet for days now he'd been glowering and snapping at Joanna every time she came near him. He'd told himself he was doing it for her own good, that sometimes you had to be cruel to be kind, but that had been pure self-defense. Just as the flimsy excuses he'd used for not becoming Gloria's lover had been pure self-deception.

Lord! This was crazy! Two weeks ago if anyone had told him that he would prefer a willowy, aristocratic girl to an earthy, sensual creature like Gloria he'd have told them they were nuts. But as he watched Joanna's sleek body move to the evocative music it didn't seem strange at all. Like a thoroughbred, she was all subtle curves and elegant lines. In comparison, Gloria's voluptuous figure seemed blowsy and overblown.

"Okay, straighten up! Kick and swing! That's it. Six. Seven. Eight. Good, ladies! Very good! Now we're really gonna move. It's time for a *Tom Jones*!"

The music throbbed on. Following the woman's lead, without missing a beat Joanna spread her legs, stretched her clasped hands above her head and rotated her hips in time to the sensuous rhythm.

Sean's breath hissed in sharply. *Dammit to hell!*

Clenching his jaw, he turned on his heel and stomped out.

From the corner of her eye, Joanna watched him go. Good riddance! she told herself firmly. She was glad he was gone. Sean Fleming could go butt a stump for all she cared.

But deep down Joanna knew that she was just using anger as a shield. Sean's attitude hurt. She hadn't expected him to fall madly in love with her, but neither had she expected him to treat her with such obvious dislike.

A surge of self-pity tightened Joanna's throat. Determinedly, she swallowed hard against the unwanted emotion and threw herself into the dance with renewed zeal.

An hour later, Joanna stood at the rail, watching as the ship glided into the harbor. Color. Serenity. She had always felt they were the two words that best described St. Thomas. The island rose gracefully from the sapphire sea in rolling green mountains. Ringing it like lace trim on the edge of a lady's full skirt were curving white sand beaches. At that distance Joanna couldn't see them, but from previous visits she knew that flowers of infinite variety and hue abounded on those verdant slopes. Ahead, the town of Charlotte Amalie spilled over the foothills and nudged the harbor, its red-roofed white buildings sparkling in the morning sun.

As the ship edged in close to the pier Joanna leaned her elbows on the railing and peered over the side and watched as the men on the dock hustled to secure the lines the seamen tossed out. She had never arrived at the island by ship before, and she was fascinated by the docking procedure.

Her grandfather had had a house on St. John. Occasionally, when she had been much younger, she and her parents had used it as a weekend getaway. Although mostly, Joanna recalled with a touch of sadness, it had been just she and her mother. On those times, though, they had always flown into St. Thomas and taken a boat across to St. John.

While they were lowering the gangway Mary and Charles Wright joined Joanna by the rail. "Isn't it simply beautiful?" the older women declared excitedly. "Oh my, I can hardly wait to get started."

Joanna smiled. "On what? Sightseeing or shopping?"

"Both. We're going to take one of the island tours and when it's over the driver will drop us off in the shopping district."

"Since this is a duty free port Mary feels honor bound to take advantage of the bargains," Charles said in a long suffering tone. "And I'm going along to make sure she doesn't 'save' me too much money."

"Oh, you." Mary gave him a poke in the ribs, but the affectionate sparkle in her eyes belied her reproachful expression. Turning back to Joanna with a smile, she said, "If you're going ashore, we'd be happy to have you join us, my dear."

As little as an hour ago, Joanna would have politely refused Mary's invitation. She had seen the island many times, and since she was fairly certain that Sean would be going ashore, she had thought it best that she stay on board, out of his way. But not now. After their run-in at the gym she'd be darned if she would curtail her movements on his account. Besides, after that strenuous early morning workout and a hot shower, she felt invigorated, eager to be doing something.

"Thank you very much. I'd like that."

Their tour bus turned out to be a stretch limo, which they shared with five other cruise passengers, one of whom was Tony. The driver, a gregarious young man in his mid-twenties named Hugo, could easily have earned his living as a comedian. As he took them around the island he kept up a running commentary, an intermingling of history, folklore and local gossip that had everyone laughing.

Bluebeard's Castle was their first stop.

"It's a hotel now," Hugo explained as Joanna and the Wrights stepped out onto the terrace beneath the old stone tower. "But in the old days it was the stronghold of Bluebeard, one of the pirates that operated in the Caribbean. This is also where he brought his wives. No one is certain just how many he had, but it's said he murdered all of them." Hugo flashed a toothy grin. "Now the Castle is a favorite place for honeymooners."

Joanna looked up at the round stone tower and shivered. Much of its rough surface was covered with ancient vines whose stems were as thick and woody as small trees. Among them scurried huge lizards, anywhere from nine to eighteen inches long. The feel of age and history about the place was intriguing, but it definitely was not her idea of a romantic honeymoon retreat.

"Brrrrr. How gruesome. Can you imagine?" Mary shuddered delicately and urged Joanna away from the tower. When they reached the low wall at the edge of the terrace her face brightened. "Well now, I'll say one thing for the old pirate. He may have been hell on women, but he sure knew how to pick a view."

Joanna laughed. "Somehow I doubt that was his prime reason for building on this particular spot."

"You're right," Tony concurred, as he and Charles joined them. "It wasn't the aesthetic appeal so much as military strategy that prompted Bluebeard to choose this spot. From here he could see any ship long before it entered the bay and blast it out of the water once it did."

The majestic three-hundred-year-old structure overlooked the harbor and the red rooftops of Charlotte Amalie. From where they stood they could see two white cruise ships docked at the pier, and another one, too large to enter the harbor, anchored just beyond the bay.

Joanna ran her fingertips over the cool surface of the ancient cannon embedded in the wall and gazed down at the blue waters. The island was peaceful and serene now, but she had no trouble imagining it as it had been all those centuries ago when pirates had ruled that part of the world.

"Say, isn't that Sean over there?" Charles said, craning his neck to see around a group of people.

Stiffening, Joanna turned slowly, but it took her a few minutes to spot Sean in the milling crowd that filled the terrace. He was with a group of people making their way toward the exit. Clinging possessively to his arm was Gloria.

When he didn't even glance in her direction, Joanna told herself that he hadn't seen her, but just before disappearing from view, Sean turned his head and looked straight into her eyes. Tilting her chin, Joanna stared right back.

The contact lasted only a second, then Sean stepped into the shadowed archway and disappeared from sight. Joanna looked back at the sapphire ocean. A mixed feeling of triumph and sadness gripped her, causing a tight ache just beneath her breastbone.

From Bluebeard's Castle Hugo took them to Drake's Seat. The lookout point high in the mountains offered a panoramic view of Magen's Bay, and as Joanna and her group climbed from the limo to view it, Sean and Gloria returned to their cab and drove away. It was then that Joanna realized they were following the same route.

Well, it could have been worse, she told herself philosophically. We could have been in the same tour group.

It was the same story at Coral World. The moment Joanna reached the bottom of the circular stairway she spotted Sean and Gloria on the other side of the undersea observation tower.

With Tony, Joanna wandered slowly from window to window and gazed out at the fantastic view of the ocean's floor. Sunlight streamed down from above, illuminating the crystal waters with a green glow. Starfish lay on the sandy bottom among the waving vegetation and goggled-eyed fish swam lazily by. At one window Joanna's heart leaped when she spotted the ghostly flutter of a stingray's wings. Even though several inches of glass separated them, she shuddered when the menacing looking creature came within inches of the window, gliding silently through the water, a restless predator in search of a victim.

A part of Joanna was fascinated and amazed by the clarity of the ocean, the myriad shapes and colors and types of underwater creatures, the grace and beauty of the plant life. But another part of her, the part she kept tucked away behind a façade of determined cheerfulness, was still smarting from her run-in with Sean.

Joanna told herself that jealousy had nothing to do with the way she felt. And for a while she almost convinced herself that it was true. But later that afternoon, when she walked into a jewelry store in the shopping district, she knew she'd been kidding herself.

Sean was just pocketing his wallet, and beside him, Gloria was admiring the gold bracelet on her raised arm.

"Oh, darling, it's beautiful," she gushed. Lifting up on tiptoes, she kissed his cheek. "Thank you so much for buying it for me."

Pain twisted in Joanna's chest. It's none of your business, she told herself. Sean is free to do whatever he wants, with whomever he wants.

Yet that knowledge did nothing to banish the feelings that were ripping away at her. Logical or not, the plain truth was—it hurt to see him with another woman. But hell would freeze over before she'd let Sean know that, and when he looked up and saw her watching them Joanna managed to hide her anguish behind a look of scorn.

To her surprise, for an instant Sean looked embarrassed, but then that easy nonchalance slipped back in place and his heavy-lidded black eyes met hers impassively.

Turning aside, Joanna gave Tony a bright smile and looped her arm through his. "Come on. Let's browse. I want to get something for my mother before we go back to the ship."

Tony grinned down at her, delighted by her sudden show of friendliness. "Blow in my ear, and I'll follow you anywhere, gorgeous," he murmured. "The North Pole. Darkest Africa. The moon." He paused a beat, then added hopefully, "Your cabin. Mine."

Joanna gave him a droll look. "The earring counter will do for now," she said repressively.

"And later?"

"Not a chance."

"Heck! I was afraid you'd say that."

Laughing at his woebegone expression, Joanna led him toward the back of the store.

Why do you still let it bother you? she thought despairingly. *You should have been over Sean long ago. By now you should be able to laugh at his little entanglements.* Joanna smiled woodenly at something Tony said and pretended to study the tray of opal earrings. *It's not fair. It's simply not fair. Infatuations aren't supposed to last this long.*

Three hours later, Joanna watched from her suite as the ship pulled away from the harbor. Slowly, inexorably, the lush green island receded, becoming smaller and smaller. When it was nothing more than a tiny dot on the horizon, Joanna sighed and turned away from the window. She dropped down onto the sofa and picked up the novel that lay open on the coffee table, but after scanning only half a page she put it down. With a sigh, Joanna stood and walked aimlessly around the room. She felt tired, but strangely restless. She needed to be doing something.

Of course, you could join the Wrights and Tony for a drink in the lounge, she reminded herself. They had invited her when they returned to the ship a half hour ago, but, pleading tiredness, Joanna had retreated to her suite.

After buying the opal and diamond earrings for her mother and a bottle of fine brandy for Matt, she had spent several hours with the three of them, browsing among the shops along the main street and those tucked away in the lush, gardenlike alleys in Charlotte Amalie's shopping district. They were nice people and Joanna liked them, but she'd had enough of their company for a while.

But still, she had to do something. Something physical. Something that required concentration. *Something that would take her mind off Sean and his redhead.*

Joanna walked back to the coffee table and picked up the printed sheet that listed the day's activities. After checking her watch, she ran a fingernail down the time column to four o'clock, and read through the choices available. "Bridge lessons, silk flower making, shuffleboard, astrology lessons, trapshooting, bingo..." Joanna's eyes backtracked. *Trapshooting!*

Her face brightened. "Perfect."

Joanna dropped the list back onto the coffee table and started eagerly for the door.

Trapshooting was done off the starboard side of the sun deck, near the stern. When Joanna arrived the ship's second mate, Mr. Ricci, and one of the crewmen were setting up the target thrower.

Joanna looked around, surprised to find she was the only passenger there. "Do you have to sign up for this in advance," she asked the officer, "or may I shoot now?"

"You may start just as soon as we get set up," he replied politely. "So far, you're the only one interested. I think everyone is tired from spending the day ashore."

When the crewman had the thrower ready Joanna paid her money and took her position by the rail.

"Have you ever fired a shotgun before?" Mr. Ricci asked, slipping two shells into the gun's magazine.

"Yes." Joanna bit back a smile. He was trying to be polite, but she could sense his uncertainty.

"Very well. You'll have eight shots altogether, two per gun. When you're ready you call 'pull' and crewman Belso will fire the thrower. While you're firing I'll load another gun for you, and after the second shot we'll trade. Are there any questions?"

"No, I understand."

Mr. Ricci worked the pump to feed a shell into the chamber and handed the shotgun to Joanna. She hefted it experimentally. Shouldering the gun, she sighted down the vent rib, testing for balance and fit. It was a plain-Jane model, but it wasn't at all barrel heavy, and it pointed perfectly. Satisfied, Joanna lowered the gun and turned to tell the officer she was ready—and froze when she saw Sean standing beside him, watching her.

"What are you doing here?" she blurted out angrily before she could stop herself.

"I came to shoot trap, the same as you."

"Since you and Mr. Fleming seem to be the only ones interested this afternoon, I suggest that you alternate shooting," Mr. Ricci put in. "A bit of friendly competition usually sharpens skills, I find."

Leaning a hip against the rail, Sean folded his arms over his chest and looked amused. "Suits me."

It had been on the tip of Joanna's tongue to refuse, but one look at Sean's face changed that. She tilted her chin defiantly and studied his complacent expression through narrowed eyes. "I'm game if Mr. Fleming is," she said finally.

"By all means." His smile deepening, Sean gestured for her to start. "Ladies first."

Joanna adjusted her stance and shouldered the shotgun. "Pull!"

The clay target sailed out from the ship, rising toward the bow. Sighting down the vent rib, Joanna swung the muzzle of the gun in a sweeping arc along the same path and pulled the trigger as the bead on the end of the barrel passed over the target. It exploded into dust at the same instant the gun recoiled against Joanna's shoulder. She pumped the gun and the empty shell ejected to the side.

"Pull!"

This time the clay disc flew out at an angle to the stern, caught a down draft and began to drop rapidly, but Joanna powdered it just before it hit the foaming wake.

She exchanged the empty gun for a full one, and without hesitation, shouldered it and called for another bird. In rapid succession, Joanna demolished the remaining six targets, clipping two and powdering the rest.

As the eighth disintegrated, she turned and calmly handed the shotgun to Mr. Ricci. Then she looked at Sean.

The smug amusement was gone from his expression. He stared at her, one brow cocked in faint surprise. Finally he dipped his head in acknowledgement and smiled wryly. "Good shooting."

"I'll say!" Mr. Ricci chimed in. "That was great!" He turned and grinned at Sean. "Looks like you've got your work cut out for you, Mr. Fleming."

Trying not to smile, Joanna stepped back and relinquished her place to Sean. As Joanna had done, for a moment he tested the gun for balance and fit, then shouldered it and called out, "Pull!"

With deadly accuracy, Sean proceeded to blast target after target, and with each hit Joanna's spirits dropped. By the time the eighth clay pigeon disappeared in a pool of smoke, she had gone from euphoric to grimly determined.

Handing the shotgun to the officer, Sean turned to her with a maddeningly polite smile and said, "Your turn, I think."

It was a direct challenge, one Joanna was more than willing to accept. Bruised feelings and a day of emotional turmoil had her nerves strung fine, and she was spoiling for a fight of some kind. For the moment, a contest of skill would do. Returning his smile with cool assurance, she stepped back into the firing position. As she accepted the shotgun she said offhandedly, "Let's make this round doubles, shall we? Just to make it interesting."

Crewman Belso emitted a low whistle as Mr. Ricci shot Sean an inquiring glance. "Very well. Doubles it is," he said when Sean nodded his agreement.

Concentrate, Joanna instructed herself, fitting the gun's recoil pad against her shoulder. *Just keep your eye on the target and stay calm. Don't rush.*

"Pull!"

Two birds sailed out over the water, one high and toward the bow, the other straight out from the side in a steady rise. Joanna swung the gun toward the first, fired, and a split second after it shattered, she pumped the action, and in a continuous motion, swung back to the right and picked off the second.

"Terrific!" Both the second mate and crewman called out in unison. Joanna let out her breath and felt some of the tension drain out of her. She traded guns and forced herself to concentrate.

Her soft voice, the shotgun blast, the metallic click and glide of the gun's precision action—for a while they were the only sounds. Steadily, repeatedly, Joanna called the terse, one-word command, fired, pumped the shotgun and fired again. When finished, she had hit fifteen of the sixteen targets.

It was not as good as she had hoped for and certainly not the best round she had ever shot, but it wasn't bad. When she turned to Sean her eyes issued a silent challenge. *Top that, if you can.*

Very quickly, it began to appear that he could. Joanna stood gripping the rail, her face calm as she watched Sean hit the first six targets without a bobble, but inside she was mentally kicking herself. *Oh, Joanna, you fool. You shouldn't have missed that last bird. And you wouldn't have if you hadn't gotten overconfident.*

The next two birds sailed out over the water in opposite directions, low and dropping fast. Sean got one, but the other splashed into the ocean just as he fired the second shot. Joanna had to bite her bottom lip to keep from cheering aloud.

The momentary exhilaration faded quickly though as he proceeded to powder the next six. Joanna didn't question why winning was so important to her. She only knew that it was. Tightening her fingers around the rail, she held her breath when Sean called for the last two birds.

He fired twice. The first clay disc shattered; the other whirled away and dropped into the ocean.

Stunned, for a moment Joanna couldn't believe it. Then a feeling of fierce satisfaction exploded inside her. She managed, just barely, to resist the urge to kick up her heels and whoop, but there was no hiding the triumph in her eyes when she turned to face Sean.

She had expected anger. Instead Sean flashed his devilish smile and looked her over in that lazily curious way of his. "Congratulations. Where the hell did you learn to shoot like that?"

"My father used to love to shoot trap and skeet. He taught me." She gave him a saccharine smile. "One of the advantages of being a spoiled rich brat."

Sean stared at her thoughtfully, but if he detected the wounded pride behind the challenging little barb, he said nothing. "How about a rematch?"

"Sorry. It's getting late, and I promised Tony I'd meet him for a drink before dinner." She started to leave, but Sean stopped her.

"Joanna... about this Tony character. What do you really know about him?"

"What do you mean?"

"Well... you seem to be spending a lot of time with him."

"No more than you are with Gloria," Joanna countered, beginning to feel the first stirrings of anger.

"Maybe. But the difference is, I'm old enough to handle a shipboard romance."

"Oh, I see. And I'm not, is that what you're saying?" Joanna was furious now. She couldn't believe his gall. "Well let me tell you something, Sean Fleming. I'm twenty-two years old, almost twenty-three, and well past the age of consent. So just mind your own business."

Sean watched her stomp away, his brows shooting upward. Bemused, his eyes traveled down her stiff back to the angry sway of her very womanly hips. Almost twenty-three. It wasn't a great age, true, but Joanna was right: she wasn't a child.

Which was exactly how he'd been thinking of her—as Claire's little girl. But Joanna was a young woman. A very attractive, very desirable young woman. Recalling the way her hazel eyes flashed with anger, the determined way she tilted her chin, Sean's mouth quirked up in a lopsided grin. She had her mother's pride and spunk, and that unbending, ladylike dignity he'd always admired.

But she's also mule stubborn and competitive as hell.

Sean discovered, to his surprise, that he found the combination very appealing.

Chapter Six

Sunrise at sea, Joanna decided, was an experience not to be missed. She leaned against the rail and watched the sky lighten from dusky blue, to mauve, to pink pearlescence. She watched the shafts of sunlight shoot out from the horizon, streaking the dark turquoise sea with gold. The world seemed to explode with color and light: silver edged clouds of lavender and crimson, dancing waves spangled with glittering sequins, an orange ball of flame rising against the deepening azure heavens. In the distance, the island of Antigua was a dark speck that grew steadily larger and greener as the ship plowed majestically through the heaving water. Enthralled, Joanna took it all in, mindless of the cool breeze or the salt spray that dewed her skin and gathered in tiny droplets in her hair.

"It's lovely, isn't it?"

Blinking, Joanna turned her head to find Susan leaning on the rail beside her. She smiled and returned her
gaze to the sea. "Yes. Yes, it is."

They stood in comfortable silence for a moment,
soaking in the beauty of the morning. "I didn't expect
to see you up so early," Susan said finally. "When you
didn't show up for dinner last night I was worried that
maybe you weren't feeling well."

"No, I'm fine. I just decided to have an early night,
so I ordered a light dinner in my suite." Actually, it had
been the prospect of facing Sean again that had kept
Joanna in her cabin, but she wasn't about to admit that
to Susan. "How about you? What are you doing up so
early?"

"I wanted to get a look at Antigua while Lori was still
asleep," Susan sighed. "Since I won't be going ashore,
that's about all I can do."

"Oh, but you shouldn't miss Antigua. It has some of
the most beautiful beaches in the world."

"I know. But we really can't take Lori. We tried it
yesterday in St. Thomas, and she got so fussy after a few
hours we were all miserable." Susan gave a fatalistic little shrug and grimaced forlornly. "Bill and I decided to
take turns going ashore."

Joanna hesitated a moment, then placed her hand on
Susan's arm. "Look, I have a better idea. Why don't I
keep Lori while both of you go ashore?"

"Oh, Joanna! We couldn't do that—"

"Of course you can," Joanna insisted, cutting off
Susan's flustered protest. "I was planning to stay on
board today anyway. Besides, I've seen Antigua. So
there's no reason why you shouldn't go. Unless, of
course, you're worried about leaving Lori with me."

"Oh, no! I'm sure—"

"Good. Then that settles it. I'll have a quick breakfast on deck, then I'll go find a steward and have a crib set up in my suite. When you're ready to leave just bring Lori to me there." Before Susan could object further, Joanna hurried away.

An hour and a half later Bill and Susan arrived at Joanna's suite loaded down with two diaper bags full of supplies and babbling their thanks. Interspersed among them was a list of last minute instructions.

Lori whimpered when she realized that her parents were about to leave her, which set off another round of doubts and protestations, but Joanna finally managed to shoo the grateful couple out, with orders that they weren't to return until it was time for the ship to sail.

When the door closed behind them Lori really started to howl. Dismayed, Joanna watched the tiny bottom lip curl pathetically and tears spill from the big blue eyes, and for the first time she began to wonder if maybe she hadn't been just a bit hasty.

"Now, now sweetheart, don't cry," she crooned. "Your mommy and daddy will be back. And you and I are going to have a wonderful day together, you'll see."

Lori's cries rose two decibels. Joanna paced the floor and bounced the child on her arm. "Come on, sweetheart. Don't cry. Please don't cry. Look! Here's one of your play pretties." She grabbed a stuffed toy from the top of one of the bags and shook it in front of Lori's face. "See, Lori? See? Isn't this nice?" Joanna squeezed the terry cloth rabbit, and it made a shrill little squeak. Lori looked away and shrieked.

The child's nose ran profusely, and her cheeks were slick with tears. As her cries took on a hysterical note her face turned a brilliant shade, somewhere between red and purple.

"Oh, baby, please, don't do that. Please don't cry."

Joanna may as well have been talking to the wall, for all the good her pleas did. She made a desperate sound in her throat and bounced harder.

Could she hurt herself, crying like that? Joanna wondered frantically. It seemed likely. At the very least she was going to make herself sick if she kept it up. *Oh, you idiot! Why on earth did you offer to baby-sit? What you know about babies would fit into a thimble, for Pete's sake.* Lori screamed harder, right in Joanna's ear. She winced and sent up a silent prayer and continued to pace.

It took a moment for the sound to penetrate Lori's shrieks but finally Joanna realized that someone was knocking on the door. She rushed to open it, reacting to the summons like a drowning man who had been thrown a lifeline. To her it meant only one thing: help had arrived.

Her hopeful expression turned to dismay when she threw open the door. "What are you doing here?" she demanded.

Ignoring her question, Sean plucked Lori from her arms, stepped inside, forcing Joanna to take a hasty step backward, and closed the door behind him. "Hey, cutie. What's all the noise about, huh? If you don't knock it off they're gonna put us off the ship, did you know that?" He hoisted the baby in the crook of his arm and tickled her tummy with his other hand. Lori's cries quietened to sharp little snubs, and she stared at him solemnly with wide, tear-drenched eyes.

"That's my girl. You don't really want to be making all that racket, do you, sweetheart?" Very gently, Sean brushed the tears from her cheeks, and to Joanna's astonishment, Lori let out a shuddering sigh, stuck her thumb in her mouth, and laid her head on his shoulder, as docile as a lamb.

"How did you do that?" Joanna demanded, wide-eyed.

Sean absently massaged the baby's back, his big hand covering her from shoulder to waist. He fixed his intent gaze on Joanna, and once more ignored her question. "The Adamsons told us at breakfast that you'd volunteered to keep Lori today. I thought maybe I'd better give you a hand."

She bristled instantly, forgetting her desperation of only a moment ago. "And just what makes you think I need help?"

"Have you had any experience with babies?"

Joanna hesitated, some of the fire going out of her. "Well, no," she admitted reluctantly. The look she gave him was part disparaging, part hopeful. "And you have, I suppose."

"I have four brothers and three sisters, all of whom are married and have large and growing families. At last count I have twenty-one nieces and nephews between the ages of two months and eighteen years," he stated calmly as he moved past her to investigate the contents of one of the bags. "I learned to pin on a diaper before I was seven."

Joanna watched him with something akin to awe as he held the limp baby on his shoulder and plucked a disposable diaper and a canister of premoistened wipes from the bag. Eight? He was one of eight children? The very thought was mind-boggling. As an only child, she couldn't even conceive of growing up in a family that size.

"Which, I'd say, is the first order of business now," Sean continued. "Part of Lori's problem is she's uncomfortable." Sitting sideways on the sofa, he laid the baby on the cushion next to him. He gave her tummy another tickle, and Lori kicked her legs and gurgled. "All that crying turned on the waterworks in more ways than one, didn't it cutie?"

With a nonchalance and expertise Joanna couldn't help but admire, within a matter of minutes, Sean had the baby stripped of the sodden diaper, cleaned and swaddled in a fresh one, and her ruffled sunsuit resnapped.

"There now, how does that feel, little one?" he said as he picked up the docile child and turned to Joanna.

Amusement twinkled in his eyes when he met her astonished stare and the corners of his mouth twitched suspiciously. "There are three things you've got to remember when taking care of babies," he drawled with just the slightest hint of superiority in his voice. "Keep 'em dry, keep 'em fed and keep 'em entertained."

Joanna sighed. "The first two I can manage. I think. But how do I do the third?"

"Go get your swimsuit on. We'll take her to the pool. Afterward we'll give her a bath and feed her. By the time we're through she should be ready for a nap."

Joanna hesitated. Accepting the plan meant accepting Sean's help, which would mean spending the day in his company. It was an appealing idea, and very tempting, but every self-protective instinct she possessed warned against it. It would be far better if she could stay angry with him, keep him at a distance. This attraction she felt for Sean was hopeless and idiotic, and the only way she was ever going to get over it was to stay away from him. It was foolish and self-destructive to even consider his offer.

Still, she reminded herself, the alternative was to cope on her own. The memory of Lori's inconsolable crying jag flashed through her mind and sent panic skittering up her spine.

Within minutes Joanna was in her bedroom, rummaging through the dresser for a swimsuit.

When she walked back into the sitting room a short while later wearing a yellow maillot and her white lace cover-up Sean's black eyes narrowed and flickered slowly over her. Joanna shifted restlessly under the silent scrutiny. "I, uh . . . I'm ready," she said needlessly.

Sean didn't hurry his inspection. The lacy top did little to obstruct his view, and his gaze slid down over her breasts and hips and the long curving length of her legs to her sandaled feet. Just as slowly, just as intently, he retraced the path. When their eyes met he smiled and tipped his head, rolling slowly to his feet.

"Why don't you gather the towels we'll need and slap a coat of sunscreen on Lori while I go change into my suit."

Lori was sitting on the floor, playing contentedly with a ring of plastic keys, but when Sean stood she looked up and grinned, flashing four tiny white teeth and crinkling her button nose. He bent and chucked her under her chin. "Behave yourself while I'm gone, princess."

Lori gurgled and shook the keys violently, whacking the floor and her chubby legs.

When he left she gave a little whine of protest. Joanna's troubled gaze went from the closed door to the wide-eyed infant, and she smiled sadly. "I know, sweetheart. He's devastating, isn't he. Even to females of your tender age."

Joanna was tense and jumpy when Sean returned, a condition that wasn't helped by the fact that he wore only a pair of rubber thongs and a tiny wine-red bathing suit that left little doubt of his masculinity. To Joanna's acute embarrassment and horror, she had difficulty keeping her eyes off his broad chest and lean, muscle-ridged belly.

With a short, "Here, you carry her," she thrust Lori into his arms, snatched up her beach bag and hustled them out the door. All the way to the pool she gritted her teeth and kept her gaze determinedly averted. Even so, from the corner of her eye, she could see his long muscular legs striding along beside her, feel the warmth that radiated from him, and she silently cursed and ground her teeth.

As soon as they arrived at the pool Joanna sat down on the end of a lounge to smooth on sunscreen. When she had finished with her legs and arms and reached around to apply the lotion to her back, Sean plopped Lori in her lap and took the bottle out of her hand.

"Here, I'll do that," he said, sitting down behind her.

The feel of his hands on her back was so shockingly pleasurable Joanna caught her breath. His palms were slightly rough and very warm. They moved over her skin in a slow, smooth glide, his fingers massaging lightly, sending shivers of delight skittering through her, making her heart race crazily. Joanna was drowning in sensations, awash with sheer bliss.

Closing her eyes, Joanna tilted her head forward until her chin rested against the wisp of blond curls at Lori's crown. She felt as though every bone in her body were dissolving. The coconut scent of the tanning lotion swirled around her, mixing with the smells of sweet baby and healthy, virile male. Vaguely, she heard the lap of the water, the hum of voices and occasional bursts of laughter, the vibrating tones of the steel drum band playing in the distance. The gentle heat of the Caribbean sun poured over her, but it was the tender abrasion of those hands on her back that made her burn.

How many times had she dreamed of Sean touching her like this? Dreamed of being with him, being the recipient of those warm looks and murmured endearments? With only a word, a glance from those dark drowsy eyes, a simple touch, Sean could make a woman feel special, cherished. It was heaven to relax and savor the feel of his hands smoothing over her back.

But the dreamy pleasure lasted only a moment before she remembered that he had performed the same service for Gloria, and with just as much care. And that the woman's face had reflected the exact emotions Joanna was feeling now.

Pain, jealousy and anger ripped through her, and she jerked away from his hands and stood up. "Thank you, but that wasn't really necessary. I'm perfectly capable of applying tanning lotion myself," she said in a sharp voice.

As she walked to the edge of the pool she felt Sean's eyes on her back but she didn't turn around. Holding the child against her chest, Joanna stepped off into the shallow end.

After a moment Sean joined them, and soon, thanks to Lori's boisterous antics, the awkwardness passed.

They splashed and laughed and cavorted with the baby for a couple of hours. Now and then they bumped into each other, or Sean would casually touch her shoulder or the small of her back as they stood close together playing with Lori. Every time, the casual contact stole Joanna's breath away, but Sean didn't seem at all affected. Disgusted, she told herself to stop acting like an idiot and kept up a determinedly blasé front. Once, when he took the baby from her, his hand accidentally brushed her breast, and Joanna felt briefly as though her whole body had burst into flame. She was appalled by the reaction but helpless to do anything about it.

Ambivalent feelings tore at Joanna. A part of her treasured this rare time of closeness with Sean and wanted it to go on and on, while another part of her longed for the sensual torment to end. That it could get worse didn't occur to her until Sean announced that it was time to get Lori out of the sun, and they headed back to Joanna's suite.

"While you bathe our gal I'll get her lunch ready," Sean said the moment they stepped through the door. He went straight to the two diaper bags and began to rummage through them. "It'll probably be easiest and quickest if you just take her into the shower with you," he added over his shoulder, pulling out a warming dish and two small jars of food.

Joanna stared at the rippling muscles in Sean's back as he leaned over the small dining table and used the curved baby spoon to scoop the contents of the jars into the dish. "A shower?" she said in a small, strained voice. She hadn't planned on that. The very idea of taking a shower while Sean occupied her sitting room, wearing nothing but a tiny strip of cloth, conjured up unsettling, wildly erotic—and admittedly exciting—images in her mind, which in turn brought a tide of color surging into her face.

But what choice did she have? It hadn't occurred to her before, but she doubted that she could bathe the baby in that tiny sink. Joanna cleared her throat and, holding Lori tightly against her chest, picked up one of the bags and began to back toward the bedroom. "Uh . . . yes. Okay, I, uh . . . I'll go do that."

The next half hour proved to be so difficult and so frantic Joanna found she didn't have time for erotic thoughts. Holding a slick, squirming little body while struggling to get both of them scrubbed, shampooed and rinsed, with only the use of one hand, was an almost impossible feat, and several times Joanna wondered suspiciously if Sean had known that when he'd made the suggestion. Holding onto Lori was like trying to hold a watermelon seed with greased fingers; Joanna was terrified that any moment the baby would squirt right out of her grasp. But finally, after much gnashing of teeth and contorting, the job was done. When Joanna emerged from the bedroom carrying her small charge on her hip, they were both dressed in loose sun shifts and smelling of baby powder.

Joanna stepped into the sitting room and looked cautiously around, only to discover that it was empty. She stood in the middle of the room, her face registering surprise, feeling both relieved and absurdly disappointed. "Obviously, he's decided he's helped enough," she muttered under her breath as she stalked over to the dining table.

The nauseating mess in Lori's dish was warm. Beside it was a bib, a wet washcloth and a baby bottle filled with milk. At the sight of the food Lori set up a demanding babble and began to bounce excitedly in Joanna's arms. "Well, sweetie, it looks like lunch is ready to be served," Joanna murmured as she set the baby in a chair and struggled to snap the bib around her neck.

Joanna felt guilty feeding such awful looking stuff to the child, but Lori ate it hungrily, at least, that portion that didn't end up on the bib or smeared all over her face. Every so often she would turn her head away and refuse the bite Joanna offered, then stretch her chubby arms out toward the bottle and demand a drink.

They were almost through with the meal when there was a light tap on the door. Before Joanna could respond, it was pushed open and Sean stepped inside. "Hi. I see you're managing all right."

At the sound of his voice Lori jerked her head around, and the bite Joanna was giving her smeared from the corner of her mouth to her ear. "Oh, just terrific," Joanna said in an aggrieved tone as she grabbed for the washcloth. "It would have helped though if you had waited until we were through to make your entrance."

Sean wore faded jeans, a red short sleeved cotton shirt and sneakers. His black hair was slicked into place, but it was still wet from his shower, and a heavy curl tumbled across his forehead as he sauntered toward them. His darkly tanned skin bore just a touch of color from its recent exposure to the sun, and as he drew near, Joanna caught a whiff of soap and woodsy cologne, and clean male. Suddenly it was difficult to breathe.

Sean hunkered down beside Lori's chair. "Hey, cutie, you're supposed to eat your food, not wear it," he said, tickling the sole of her bare foot. With a squeal, Lori curled her toes and gave his face an enthusiastic pat.

It was a struggle, but Joanna managed to shovel the last few bites into the child's mouth. Lori polished off the rest of the milk, and when Joanna had wiped her face clean Sean reached for her. "I'll go put her down for her nap while you take care of the dishes."

She wanted to tell him that he needn't bother, that she'd put Lori to bed. And if she'd had any idea how to manage it, she would have.

Joanna stared after him as he crossed the room and disappeared into the bedroom, feeling her heart pound and her chest tighten. This was crazy. Sean excited her without even trying. Being around him like this was definitely not a good idea. If he didn't leave soon she was going to wind up making a complete and utter fool of herself.

Wearily, Joanna picked up the dish and bottle and carried them into the bathroom. When she emerged a few minutes later Sean was bending over the crib, gently patting Lori's back and, foolishly, the sight made her heart contract. She tiptoed out to the sitting room, sat down on the sofa and wondered what in the world she was going to do.

A few minutes later Sean crept out of the bedroom and eased the door closed behind him. He plopped down beside Joanna, and with a sigh, leaned his head against the sofa back and stretched his long legs out in front of him. Joanna's insides began to quiver wildly.

After a while Sean rolled his head to the side and smiled that heart stopping smile of his. "I never realized before what an impulsive creature you are. What on earth possessed you to volunteer to keep the Adamsons' daughter?"

Joanna shrugged her shoulders. "It seemed like the thing to do at the time. It's only for a few hours, and Bill and Susan really need the time alone together."

"So what happens tomorrow? You can't baby-sit everyday. Even if you were willing, I'm sure they wouldn't allow it."

"I know. But I've made arrangements that will solve the problem."

"What kind of arrangements?"

"Well...I talked to the Captain this morning. His family is sailing with him this summer, and his sixteen-year-old daughter has volunteered to sit with Lori for the remainder of the cruise. In fact, she's anxious to."

"Volunteered?" Sean cocked a skeptical brow, then narrowed his eyes. "You're paying her, aren't you?"

A guilty flush crept up Joanna's neck. "Well...yes, I am," she admitted reluctantly. "But that's just between Maria and me. The Adamsons need never know. Maria's going to come by our table tonight and beg them to let her keep Lori while they visit the islands." At Sean's admonishing look Joanna tilted her chin. "I know I'm interfering, but where's the harm? Susan and Bill can enjoy their second honeymoon, and Maria is delighted to be earning some extra money. And I can certainly afford to pay for a few hours of baby-sitting."

After a moment Sean's stern look faded and his eyes grew warm. "That was a very nice thing to do, Joanna." His voice was deep and soft, caressing her like warm velvet, making her skin tingle deliciously. "And it was very nice of you to keep Lori today."

"No, actually I was being selfish." Joanna glanced at Sean and her mouth twisted wryly. "I needed the practice, since I'm going to have a new baby brother or sister in about six weeks or so."

Sean studied her intently, then sat up straight and turned sideways on the sofa. Stretching his arm out along the back, he played idly with the spaghetti strap on her white terry cloth sun shift. "You're really pleased over this baby, aren't you?"

"Yes. Yes, I am." The smile that tilted Joanna's mouth was soft and dreamy, full of pleasure. "Matt adores my mother, and she him. It seems only right that a love like that should produce a child. And besides, it's what they both want.''

"And what do you want, Joanna?" Sean asked softly, running his forefinger up the gentle slope of her shoulder to her neck.

A shiver rippled along Joanna's skin. She swallowed hard. Turning her head, she looked at him with wide, dazed eyes. "Wh—what do you mean?"

"I mean you've changed. The Joanna I knew four years ago never had a thought for anyone but herself. It would never have occurred to her to help out a young couple, to saddle herself with a rambunctious child just so they could enjoy themselves for a few hours. Or to be gracious and attentive to a sweet old couple like the Wrights." His fingers trailed fire over her skin and caused goose bumps to spring up all over her as they moved up the side of her neck and tugged gently at her lobe. Joanna could barely concentrate on his words. "And my guess is," he continued in an even softer voice, "that Joanna would have been resentful, possibly even outraged by her middle-aged mother having a baby."

Joanna tilted her head, trying to evade those tormenting fingers. Lord! Didn't he know what his touch did to her? "We . . . we all grow up eventually."

"True. But you've done it so beautifully." His fingers slipped from her ear into the thick, still damp hair at the back of her head. With his other hand he cupped her chin and drew her face around. She found herself staring into his dark eyes, and her heart began to flutter wildly at what she saw there. "So very beautifully," he murmured huskily as his gaze dropped to her mouth, and his head began its slow, purposeful descent.

Joanna thought she was going to faint. Her heart was chugging like a runaway train. When his lips settled softly over hers its speed almost doubled. Her eyes fluttered shut and her breathing stopped completely. Every cell, every molecule in her body tingled with vibrant awareness, almost unbearable excitement. She was afraid that at any second her whole system would go on overload.

The kiss was warm, tender, tentative. His lips caressed hers with a gentleness that was devastating. Rocking slowly back and forth. Nibbling. Rubbing. Joanna sat there motionless, her insides aquiver, her chest tightening with a sweet, sweet ache.

He nipped her lower lip with gentle savagery, and her inner quakes became an ecstatic shudder she couldn't hide. Immediately the kiss grew bolder.

Seeking became hungry demand as his lips grew firmer and his tongue probed the soft barrier of her lips. Without thought of denial, Joanna opened her mouth to grant him entrance and sighed helplessly as he tasted the honeyed sweetness with deep, evocative thrusts.

The hand that cradled the back of her head tightened. Grasping her hip with his other hand, Sean rolled her toward him, bringing her closer. The heat of their bodies combined, and the mingled scents of woodsy cologne and baby talc rose between them.

Joanna was almost afraid that she was dreaming. Only this was so much more wonderful than any of her dreams. Years ago she had spent hours trying to imagine Sean kissing her with tenderness and passion, how it would feel to be held in his arms, but now all those foolish fantasies faded into nothingness. They had been paltry, insubstantial things that had not even come close to the exquisite pleasure of reality.

As Sean's mouth rocked hungrily over hers the hand at her hip slid around and cupped her buttocks, squeezing the firm flesh while pressing her even closer. One of Joanna's hands clutched at his shirt front, the other crept up over his chest to his neck, and her fingertips tentatively stroked the side of his jaw.

Sean's mouth left hers, and Joanna's head tilted back as he trailed a line of kisses along her jaw and down the side of her neck. "Oh, Joanna. Joanna. You're so sweet. So very sweet." His warm breath dewed her skin as he murmured the words in a voice that was husky with passion. He nipped her lobe, then his tongue bathed away the tiny pleasurable pain and moved on to trace the graceful swirls of her ear.

Joanna shuddered, then drew in a deep breath. With it came a measure of reality and caution. This was wonderful, sheer heaven, but the tiny kernel of fear deep inside her would not let her ignore the danger. Very gently, she pushed at his chest. "Wh—what are you doing, Sean?" she finally managed breathlessly.

She felt him smile against her neck. "I would think that's obvious."

"Don't toy with me, Sean. Please."

He grew still, and slowly, he pulled back far enough to look at her. Her lips were slightly puffy and rosy, her face flushed, but the glaze of passion was fading from her troubled eyes. He remained silent, but Joanna knew by his expression that he understood.

"I...I'm very attracted to you, Sean. But...well...you could hurt me very badly. You must know that."

Sean released her completely, and Joanna sat up straight and stared at her hands, twisting them together in her lap. Feeling like a fool, she chewed at her inner lip, but after a moment she looked back at him. "Things could never be just casual between us, we both know that. There's your friendship with my parents. And your career. Plus I'm not...that is...I don't..."

Sean put his hand over hers, stopping their frantic writhing. "I understand, Joanna," he said with a tender smile that somehow made her spirits sink even lower. "And you're right. I shouldn't have kissed you. I, uh...I guess I just got carried away for a moment there."

He gave her hands a squeeze, then stood up and wandered aimlessly around the room, his fingertips stuck in the back pockets of his jeans. Feeling wretched, Joanna watched him, and when he paused and gave her a determinedly friendly smile she tensed, knowing what was coming but dreading it all the same.

"Look, I'm sure you can manage fine now on your own. Lori will probably sleep for two or three hours, and by then her folks will be back. So I think I'll go up on deck. I may even go ashore for a while."

Joanna stood up and mustered a smile. "Of course. Go right ahead. I shouldn't have any problems." When he reached the door she added in a stiff little voice, "And thank you, Sean, for all your help. I really appreciate it."

With his hand grasping the door handle, he paused and looked back at her. "Are you all right?" he asked with soft concern.

"Of course. I'm fine."

Her determinedly bright smile faded with the click of the door. She stared at it for several long seconds, and fought against the urge to cry. Why had she been so damned honest? Why couldn't she have just taken what he'd offered? At least she would have had something. A few memories.

But even as her mind voiced the protest, Joanna knew, despite the pain, that she had done the right thing, the only thing for her. She simply wasn't the kind who could survive on memories.

Grim faced, Sean strode down the companionway, silently cursing himself. *Of all the stupid, reckless things to do! God, Fleming! All right! So she's lovely and you're attracted. That's no reason to lose your head. Hell, you're a thirty-six-year-old man who ought to know better, not some randy teenager. What the hell's the matter with you, you stupid ass?*

With angry motions, Sean unlocked his cabin door, stepped inside and slammed it behind him. He paced the confines of the small room like a caged tiger and called himself ten kinds of fool. But what really bothered him, what made him feel like a thorough bastard, was the fact that it had been Joanna who had had the sense to call a halt. "You were too aroused to even realize you were about to step off a cliff," he spat out in a scathing voice.

What he felt for Joanna was more than just lust, and deep down, Sean knew it, but instinctively he shied away from the thought.

He knew that Joanna had been right: a casual affair between them would never work. And he certainly didn't want to hurt her. Even if he were ready for a permanent relationship—and that was something he wasn't at all sure about—he was too old for Joanna.

But straight talk and common sense helped little. Desire still clawed at his gut. Not for just any woman, but for a willowy, hazel-eyed beauty, a young girl he knew he had no business wanting.

Chapter Seven

Joanna entered the dining room with her head held high and a sick sensation in the pit of her stomach. She paused just inside the door to look across the room at her table, and the feeling grew worse. The others were already there, including Sean.

The temptation to return to her suite was strong, but she gritted her teeth and battled it down. She refused, absolutely refused, to play the coward two nights in a row.

Clutching her small evening bag in a death grip, Joanna drew a deep breath and started across the room.

As she approached the table the others were busy either talking or studying their menus, and Joanna slipped into her chair almost before anyone spotted her. "Good evening, everyone. Sorry I'm late." Smiling, she glanced around the table, being careful to avoid Sean's gaze.

"Joanna, my dear, there you are," Mary greeted warmly. "We were beginning to wonder if you were going to join us tonight."

"Yes, we certainly were," Susan chimed in. "In fact, Bill and I were beginning to worry that maybe Lori had worn you out."

"Oh, no. Lori was no trouble at all." Involuntarily Joanna's glance found Sean, and her pulse fluttered when she discovered him watching her steadily. Quickly, she turned back to Susan. "And anyway, I...uh...I had help. Sean stayed on board and gave me a hand."

"I wondered what happened to you," Gloria said, giving him an arch look. "I searched all over for you this morning. I even went by your room, but you weren't there." Sean frowned, and immediately her voice softened. "I was hoping that we could see Antigua together."

"Sorry." Sean's flat tone dismissed the woman's complaint, and without further explanation he turned his attention back to Joanna.

The Adamsons looked stricken. "Oh, Sean, I'm sorry," Susan wailed. "We didn't mean for you to give up your vacation time to baby-sit our daughter. I feel just terrible."

"Nonsense. I enjoyed it. We both did. Like Joanna said, Lori was an angel." He flashed her his most devastating smile, and Joanna watched Susan melt under its persuasive power.

Quickly, Joanna turned to Mary and asked how she and Charles had liked Antigua, and as hoped, the older woman launched into a detailed description of the tour they had taken, effectively changing the subject.

Though Joanna was tense and uncomfortable, the meal passed without incident. Several times she caught

Sean staring at her, but he never spoke to her. Except for a few remarks directed to everyone in general, he talked mostly with Gloria. When she heard him agree to the woman's suggestion that they go dancing after dinner, Joanna kept her eyes on her plate and stoically battled against the ache in her chest, telling herself it didn't matter.

They had reached the after dinner coffee stage and Joanna was trying to think up an excuse to leave when Tony surprised her by saying, "You know, Joanna, while I was at the beach today one of the passengers said the strangest thing. She wanted to know what you were like, and how it felt, having the daughter of such a famous woman at our table. Before I could ask what she meant her husband told her to mind her own business and dragged her off."

"Of course! That's it!" Mary exclaimed excitedly, clapping her hands together. "I knew your face was familiar. You're Claire Andrews' daughter!"

There was stunned silence, and Joanna cringed inwardly as everyone at the table stared at her. Instinctively, she glanced at Sean for support, but he merely grimaced and gave a fatalistic shrug, his look telling her that she should have expected it.

"Are you? Are you really?" Tony asked, at first with something akin to awe, then with growing excitement.

Joanna hesitated, but after a moment exhaled a small sigh of resignation. "Yes, I am. Only mother is Claire Drummond now."

The admission brought gasps and exclamations, which were quickly followed by a babble of questions. What was it like, having such a beautiful, famous mother? Were she and her mother close? Did Claire miss being actively involved in politics? Was she happy in her new marriage? Pleased about having another child at forty-three? They were the kind of prying questions Joanna had been asked all of her life and she was used to them, but she still found them amazing, and irritating.

Her maternal grandfather had been a powerful U.S. senator. So had her father. Yet it had always been Claire who had fascinated the press and public and been the object of their insatiable curiosity. Never more so than in the past five years since both her husband and father had perished in the crash of their private plane.

It wasn't her mother's fault. Joanna knew that. Early on, her grandfather had recognized what a political asset he had in his only child, and he had deliberately enhanced and promoted that special appeal she seemed to hold for the American people. Claire had grown up in the spotlight, admired, envied, often idolized, and always the object of curiosity and speculation. Sometimes people acted as though she were public property. Claire didn't like it any more than Joanna did, but a lifetime of coping and a more patient personality allowed her to accept the situation with good grace.

With the possible exception of Gloria, Joanna liked her table companions, but as she listened to their barrage of questions she wanted to tell them all to mind their own business. Instead she forced herself to do what her mother would under the circumstances. Smiling stiffly, she answered them as noncommittally and with as much charm and brevity as she could manage.

Sean finally took pity on her and diverted their attention by casually mentioning that he had been Claire's campaign manager during her aborted bid for the Senate.

Relieved, Joanna sent him a grateful look and settled back in her chair, content to let him field their questions. With his glib Irish tongue and easygoing charm, Sean was a master at handling awkward situations and inquisitive crowds. Many times during her mother's campaign Joanna had seen him hold his own with a whole room full of aggressive reporters.

"Well, I think this is just marvelous," Mary gushed. "I can hardly wait to tell my friends back home. Imagine! All this time we've been rubbing elbows with a celebrity and didn't know it."

"I'm hardly that, Mary," Joanna began, but a squeal from Susan cut off her self-conscious protest.

"Oh, my gosh!" Susan put her hand over her mouth and looked appalled, her eyes huge. "It just hit me! Joanna Andrews, Claire Andrews' daughter, baby-sat with *our* daughter! No one's ever going to believe it. Unless—" she looked at Joanna hopefully "—maybe you could...that is...would you let me take your picture holding Lori?"

"Yes, of course," Joanna agreed pleasantly, but inside she was saddened by the difference in Susan's attitude. Only that morning they had been friends, equals.

Tony caught her eye and gave her an ingratiating smile. "Joanna, I just want you to know that I've always admired your family. Your father and grandfather were true statesmen, the kind this country needs more of. And your mother, well, everyone admires Claire Andrews. She's not only beautiful, she's a great lady."

The others were quick to voice their agreement, even Gloria. Gritting her teeth, Joanna thanked them, hating the fawning and the insincerity.

"I'm delighted, that we met," Tony added, leaning closer. "And I'm hoping that we can stay in touch after this trip is over, maybe even get to know each other better. It's not all that far between New York and Washington. You could come up for a weekend and we could take in a play, or I could come to Washington and you could show me the sights."

"Perhaps," Joanna replied noncommittally.

She had been wondering how she could escape without appearing rude, but now she didn't care what they thought. She had to get out of there. "If you'll excuse me, I'll say good-night," Joanna announced quickly, pushing back her chair. Before anyone could move or protest she stood and headed for the door.

Instinctively, Joanna sought the uppermost deck and fresh air. As she climbed the outside stairs the wind whipped her dress, plastering it against her body like a second skin. When she reached the top its full force hit her, and she had to lean forward and strain for every step.

The sea was growing rougher. Dark clouds scudded like tattered banners across the sky, occasionally blocking out the moon. The threatening squalls had discouraged the fainthearted, and as she struggled forward Joanna found that she had the unsheltered deck all to herself.

When Joanna reached the bow she grasped the rail with both hands and stood with her head high, face to the wind. It clawed at her upswept hairdo with rough, maniacal fingers, tearing several silken tresses from their moorings until they trailed out behind her and whipped the air in a frenzied dance. Joanna raised one hand and removed the useless hairpins and, one by one, tossed them into the ocean. With her hair flying wild and free, her white silk Grecian style gown molded to her slender curves, she stood motionless and stared moodily at the storm-tossed sea.

That was how Sean found her. Small, proud, defiantly lovely—facing the elements and the night in brooding silence, like a ship's figurehead from days long past.

Joanna started when he came up beside her and leaned against the rail, but she didn't move except to slant him a sideways glance. "What are you doing up here? I thought you were going dancing with Gloria."

"I changed my mind." Joanna returned her gaze to the turbulent sea, and for a moment Sean studied her elegant profile in silence. "The question is, what are you doing up here?"

"I wanted to be alone."

"I can understand that, but you picked a bad spot. It's about to rain and these decks are slick when they're wet. It's not safe. Come on, I'll take you back down."

As he spoke the first drops began to fall, fat globules that splattered against their skin with an icy sting. Not waiting for her assent, Sean grasped Joanna's arm and hustled her back to the stairs. The wind at their backs pushed them along, aiding their retreat, and before the downpour began in earnest they had clattered down the two flights to the shelter of the covered Promenade deck.

Farther down the dimly lit deck there were a few other people, but most of those were going indoors. Heedless of the fine mist that blew in under the shelter, Joanna moved over to the rail and watched the fierce deluge lash and merge with the surging waves.

"What's wrong, Joanna?" Sean asked as he came to stand beside her. "Does it bother you that they found out who you are?" At her nod he frowned. "Why? I've never known you to be publicity shy. You campaigned for both your father and mother."

"That's different. I don't mind working for a goal or a cause. That's not on a one-to-one basis. But being well-known can ruin your personal life."

"How so?"

"Oh, Sean. Didn't you notice how they changed? How the minute they realized who I was, or rather, who my mother was, they started to gush and fawn? I've always hated that. Thank God all that adulation from mother's public only spills over me occasionally. But just imagine how she must have felt all those years. You never know whether someone likes you for yourself, or because of who you are."

"Mmm. I see what you mean. That's rough." He paused, then added, "But all this does prove my point."

"What point?"

"Don't you see? That's just all the more reason for you to keep away from guys like Tony. Involvement with Claire Drummond's daughter would give his career a boost, and you can damn well bet that he knows it."

The words hit her like a slap in the face. She gasped and stared at him with wide wounded eyes, hurt pouring through her. The only defense against it was anger, and that came surging to the surface quickly. "Oh, thank you very much! First I'm a spoiled brat who's pursuing you, and now you as much as say that the only reason a man would be interested in me is because I happen to be Claire Drummond's daughter!"

Sean winced, his expression chagrined. "Aw, Jo-anna, I didn't mean it like th—"

"Don't touch me!" Joanna snapped, slapping his hands away when he reached out to grasp her shoulders. "Just stay away from me." Shaking her head, she backed away a step. "All right! All right! Maybe I am spoiled and headstrong and . . . and all the other things you've accused me of being. And I realized a long time ago that I'm far from being your ideal woman. But, believe it or not, Sean Fleming, there are some men who like me just the way I am.''

Her voice broke on the last word and she had to fight hard against the emotions that clogged her throat and threatened her composure. *I will not cry,* she vowed silently. *I will not!* Joanna glared at him, her chest heaving, unaware of the revealing pain that swam in her eyes.

"Joanna, listen to me, please. I—"

But she'd had enough. Ignoring his entreaty, Joanna turned on her heel and stalked away, calling back over her shoulder, "From now on you can keep your opinions and your advice to yourself. I don't need them.''

"Joanna! Joanna, wait! Let me explain! Oh, hell!'' Sean hurried after her.

Farther down the deck Joanna jerked open the door and rushed inside. Five seconds later, he did the same, and immediately barreled into an elderly, overweight woman, sending her staggering backward, arms flailing. Her purse hit the floor with a thud and a lipstick and several coins flew out of it and went rolling across the floor.

"Oh, I'm sorry. Are you all right?'' Sean asked distractedly, taking hold of the woman's upper arms. Over her shoulder Sean caught a glimpse of a slender figure in a white silk dress scooting around a small clutch of people in the passageway. Silently cursing, Sean ground his teeth.

"Oh, my. Really, young man, you should be more careful,'' the flustered matron admonished. "You almost knocked me down!''

"I'm sorry. I really am. But I'm in a bit of a hurry.'' Sean steadied her quickly, then retrieved her purse from the floor, scooped up her things and crammed them back inside, and stuffed it back into her hand. ''Please excuse me, ma'am.'' Ignoring the woman's outraged gasp, he rushed off in the direction Joanna had taken.

She was nowhere in sight. Sean sprinted along the passageway, hastily apologizing as he darted around people. When he reached the first stairway he came to a halt and grabbed the rail, his chest heaving. He looked down, and cursed vividly when he spotted a flash of white silk on the deck below. He'd never catch her before she made it to her suite.

Grimly, Sean loped down the stairs after her anyway. Though he knew it was useless, when he reached Joanna's suite he stopped and knocked on the door. ''Joanna? Joanna, I know you're in there,'' he said as loudly as he dared. He paused and waited, but still there was no answer. ''Joanna, we have to talk. You're taking this all wrong.''

A woman emerged from her cabin farther down the passageway and gave him a strange look. With a muttered oath, Sean turned away and stalked the few yards to his own cabin. He stormed inside, slammed the door behind him and marched straight to the phone. When he'd punched out Joanna's extension he stood glaring at the ceiling, his jaw growing tighter as he counted off the monotonous rings at the other end of the line. On the tenth one he slammed the receiver down on its cradle. ''Damn pigheaded female!''

Sean shucked out of his dinner jacket and flung it onto the chair. He flopped down onto the bed, shoes and all, and stretched out on his back with his hands clasped beneath his head. He stared stonily at the ceiling, his expression growing even grimmer as he recalled the hurt look on Joanna's face just before she had bolted. *Hell,*

I tried to explain, didn't I? But she wouldn't even give me a chance. What more can I do?

Nothing. Not a damned thing, he decided angrily. If she wouldn't listen, he'd just let her nurse her hurt feelings.

Sean tried to maintain his righteous anger, but his conscience continued to prick him, and after a moment he exhaled a deep sigh. He sat up and swung his legs to the floor, propping his elbows on his spread knees as he bent his head and wearily rubbed the back of his neck. "No, you won't," he muttered to himself. "You hurt her with your clumsy meddling, you idiot, and you owe her an apology. And the first thing tomorrow morning you're going to give it to her."

It was a vow that was easier to make than to keep, Sean discovered.

Joanna didn't show up for breakfast. When a quick search of the ship failed to locate her he went to her suite. He found the room steward there cleaning, and the man told Sean that Joanna had gone ashore as soon as they had docked in Barbados that morning. "With Mr. Longworth," he added with a sly grin that stopped Sean in his tracks.

"You mean Doug Longworth? The singer? The one who's starring in the show in the International Lounge?"

"Yes sir."

Without another word, Sean turned and started slowly down the passageway toward his own cabin, a distracted frown drawing his brows together. Joanna with Doug Longworth? Lord! The very thought set his teeth on edge.

Didn't she know the man was the worst kind of skunk when it came to women? Of course she did. Everyone, both inside and outside show business, knew that Longworth used and discarded women like Kleenex.

Sean let himself into his cabin, and stood in the middle of the floor, pulling thoughtfully at his bottom lip as he stared out the porthole at the Barbados dock. *Maybe I ought to go find her.*

Don't be an ass, Fleming. It's none of your business what she does. And like the lady said, she is past the age of consent.

Still, Claire and Matt wouldn't want to see her hurt. As their friend, the least I can do is watch out for her. Absently, Sean stripped out of his clothes, put on bathing trunks, then pulled his jeans and shirt back on over them.

No. No, I can't do that. No matter how you rationalize it, it's still butting in. Slinging a towel over his shoulder, he left the room. *Joanna has the right to do whatever she pleases. Even if it is a mistake.*

But it wouldn't hurt just to keep an eye on her. Make sure that Longworth doesn't get out of line.

No, dammit! I'm not her keeper. Besides, that's not my style.

All the way down the gangway the silent battle waged, but an hour later, after scouting three beaches, Sean found himself sitting on the sand, grimly watching Joanna.

"All right! Way to go, baby!" Doug Longworth shouted when she dropped to her knees and brought both fists up under the volleyball just before it hit the sand, sending it skimming back over the net.

Sean watched Doug reach down and help Joanna up, his jaw tightening when the singer's hands lingered at her waist. Joanna responded to his whispered comment in her ear with a chuckle and a saucy look and stepped away.

Eyeing Doug Longworth darkly, Sean tried to figure out just what it was about the man that women found so fascinating. As far as he could see he was just another flashy punk with blue eyes, a perpetually surly expression and bleached blond hair that was about four inches too long. With a minimal amount of talent he'd managed to turn out a few hit records, but as far as Sean was concerned he was purely second-rate, as a man and as an entertainer.

Joanna threw herself into the spirited game with the same zeal and determination she gave to aerobic dancing and trapshooting. Sean suspected it was how she approached everything. She lunged and leaped and put her all into every effort. And the whole time she flirted madly, not just with Longworth, but with Tony Farrell and several others. Sean, she ignored, though he knew perfectly well she was aware of him watching her.

Despite Joanna's efforts, her side was losing. Mainly, Sean decided sourly, because her teammates couldn't take their eyes off her. Not that he could blame them. In that tiny white bikini she was a sight to tempt any man. Even him, Sean admitted grimly, cursing under his breath as he felt the stirring warmth in his loins. Her lithe body was firm and supple, her flesh tanned a delicate apricot, and she moved with a natural, unselfconscious grace that mesmerized, drawing the eye to those slender curves, those lovely, endless legs.

Most of the men were content to just look, but Doug Longworth never missed a chance to put his hands on her. Watching him through narrowed eyes, Sean felt a savage urge to ram his fist through the jerk's face.

Sean stood up and edged closer to the field of play, but Joanna studiously pretended he wasn't there. Finally, when one of the men on her team dropped out, Sean stepped in and took his place. He subtly maneuvered around the other players until he was standing just behind Joanna and Doug. A moment later the ball came sailing over the net in their direction and Sean called out "I've got it," and stepped between them, spiking it back.

"Hey, watch it, fella," Doug sputtered when he bumped into him.

For a few seconds, they slammed the ball back and forth across the net, and during the fast and furious play Sean ignored the other man's glare. Finally Sean smashed the ball with such power it hit the sand before anyone could touch it. While their side prepared to serve he turned to Doug, his black eyes as hard as stone, and said in a soft, strangely threatening voice, "I intend to."

He turned and met Joanna's indignant glare and murmured, "I want to talk to you."

For just an instant Sean glimpsed uncertainty and vulnerability in Joanna's eyes, but almost at once the coolness returned. Without a word, she stepped around him, and grabbing Doug's hand, began to drag him toward the water. "Come on, Doug, I'm tired of playing. Let's go cool off with a swim."

He complied with alacrity, pausing only long enough to send Sean a smirking look over his shoulder before racing hand in hand with Joanna toward the water.

Oblivious to the scrambling efforts of the others to keep the volleyball in play, Sean stood stock-still and watched the pair splash into the surf, his narrowed eyes a glittering obsidian.

The mood in the Zodiac Lounge was gay, convivial. The dreamy music the band played blended pleasingly with the murmur of conversation, the occasional bursts of laughter.

Outwardly Sean appeared his usual carefree self. He sat relaxed in his chair with a forearm braced against the edge of the table, the tips of his fingers lightly touching the rim of his glass, rotating it slowly. A languid smile of anticipation curved his mouth as Bill Adamson drew out his humorous tale. When he delivered the punch line Sean laughed along with everyone else at the table, but inside he was seething.

As conversation flowed between the Adamsons and the Wrights, Sean lifted the squat glass of bourbon and took a sip. Over its rim his eyes once again sought the couple on the dance floor.

Hell, you'd think they'd be tired by now, Sean thought as he watched the blond singer sway to the dreamy music with Joanna locked tightly in his arms. *They've been out there for the past half hour. And he's holding her so close they look like they're glued together.*

Beneath the table Sean's hand closed into a tight fist as he watched Joanna lean back in Doug's embrace and smile seductively. All day he had watched her flirt with Longworth and Farrell and several others. Whenever he had tried to approach her she always managed to slip away. This was the closest he'd been to her since she'd left the volleyball game that morning.

Watching Longworth grin at something Joanna said, Sean's eyes narrowed ominously. When the little creep's hand slid down her spine and brazenly cupped her bottom, something inside Sean snapped. He made a harsh sound and slammed his glass down on the table with a thud. The others jumped and stared in astonishment as he lunged out of his chair and headed for the dance floor with long purposeful strides.

Reaching around, Joanna grasped Doug's hand and returned it to its former position at her waist. "Uh-uh, none of that," she scolded lightly. Her tone was teasing, but her hazel eyes flashed a steely warning.

The corners of Doug's mouth twitched upward in cynical amusement. "Sure, baby, sure." He pulled her closer and whispered in his sexiest voice, "I can wait."

Joanna sighed. It was her own fault. She shouldn't have agreed to accompany him to the beach, much less flirt with him the way she'd done. Doug Longworth was accustomed to having his pick of women. That the evening would end any way other than the two of them going to bed together would simply never occur to him. And why should it? She certainly hadn't done anything to make him think otherwise.

Joanna knew her behavior had been reckless and totally out of character, but darn it! She had *felt* reckless. Reckless and angry and insulted. Sean couldn't have made it clearer; he didn't want her, nor could he imagine that anyone else would. Did he have any idea how much that had hurt? It had been foolish, perhaps even childish, to encourage Doug, but she had needed to feel desired, to feel that someone found her attractive, no matter how fleeting or shallow that attraction.

Joanna sighed again and gazed sadly over Doug's shoulder. Lord, it was awful to be attracted to someone who didn't want you. Unrequited feelings made you do the dumbest things.

Worrying over how she was going to handle the scene that was sure to take place later, she didn't see Sean until the instant before he tapped Doug on the shoulder.

The expression on his face caused her heart to give a little leap, but there was no time to head off the confrontation.

"I'm cutting in, Longworth," he announced flatly.

Doug looked at him as if he had lost his mind, then grinned nastily. "Not a chance."

"Let her go, Longworth, or in three seconds you're going to be eating those pretty capped teeth."

Surprise, then anger flashed across Doug's face. For an instant it appeared as though he were about to argue, but a closer look at Sean's smoldering eyes changed his mind.

"Now, look here. Who do you think you are?" Joanna protested as Sean pulled her from Doug's slackened embrace.

"Shut up, Joanna." Placing both her hands on his chest, he wrapped his arms around her and brought her tightly against him. When she tried to wedge some space between them he gave her a painful squeeze and commanded sharply, "Stop that!"

Joanna was so astounded by his harsh tone she stopped struggling and lapsed into silence, automatically moving with him to the romantic music. This time she had pushed him beyond mere anger. He was incensed. Absolutely furious. She could feel it in the coiled spring tension of his body, the thunderous beat of his heart against her palm. Though he held her in a lover-like embrace she had the disquieting feeling that what he really wanted to do was throttle her.

She could hardly believe it. Sean, laid-back, devil-may-care Sean, was so enraged he was about to blow apart. It was frightening . . . and thrilling. Joanna stared over his shoulder, intensely aware of his freshly shaved jaw against her temple, the strength of the arms that surrounded her, the scent and the heat and the feel of his body, pressed so intimately to hers. Her insides were quivering wildly, and she didn't know if it was due to fear or his nearness.

They danced in strained silence, and when the music ended Sean clamped his hand around her upper arm and marched her toward the exit. Joanna started to protest, but one glance at his set face and those burning black eyes changed her mind. Out on deck he led her to a secluded spot by the rail and turned her to face him. Joanna braced herself and raised wary eyes.

"Just what the devil is the matter with you?" he demanded. "Don't you have any better sense than to get involved with a creep like Longworth? Lord, I'm beginning to think you need a keeper."

Joanna sucked in her breath. Trepidation gave way to shock, then anger. "Now wait just a min—"

"And as if that weren't bad enough, you were flirting with half the men on the beach. They were following you around with their tongues practically dragging in the sand."

"So what?" she shot back. "It's none of your business."

Sean's eyes narrowed dangerously, and Joanna's angry defiance fizzled as a shiver rippled its way down her spine. She took a step backward. "Now, Sean," she cautioned nervously when he matched it, and backed away another step.

"Then I guess I have to make it my business," he said in a low, purring voice that made the fine hairs on her arms stand on end.

"Sean, please, this is—"

He hooked an arm around her waist and pulled her up against him. With his other hand he cupped her jaw and tilted her face up. Beneath half-lowered lids, fire smoldered in the dark depths of his eyes as they fastened on her mouth.

"Shut up, Joanna."

Chapter Eight

His mouth closed over hers with the firm demand and possessiveness of a man staking his claim. This time there was no tentative seeking. It was a bold kiss, an explosive release of frustrated desire, an admission of needs too long denied. His lips were warm and devouring, almost brutal.

For a moment Joanna was too stunned to react, or even move. She just stood there with her heart booming, her hands clutching his shirt, while her knees threatened to give way beneath her. But soon exquisite sensations began to penetrate the barrier of shock, and she responded to the rough embrace with a matching hunger. She felt as though her body was suffused with heat, glowing like a molten ingot. Pressed against the hard wall of his chest, her breasts were achingly tight and tender.

In some remote corner of her mind Joanna knew that this was foolish, futile, that she should end it before she was hurt more, but it was no use. The feelings she had tried so hard to deny burst free, and her yearning heart overflowed with love—a love that craved this moment of bliss at all cost, that recklessly welcomed the passion that flamed between them.

She was aquiver with longing, greedy in her need. Straining closer, she ran her palms up over his chest and shoulders and buried her hands in the thick ebony strands above his collar, her spread fingers learning the shape of his head, urging him even closer. Her mouth opened to eagerly accept the deep bold thrusts of his tongue as her own darted and entwined, luring him to taste his fill.

A growl rumbled from Sean's throat. He wrapped both arms around her, tightening his hold. Shifting his stance, he thrust one of his legs between hers. Joanna caught her breath.

He was hard. And warm. So very warm. His heat seared her, melted her, made her burn. As his tongue embedded itself in her mouth once more, his hands cupped her buttocks and held her tightly to him. Joanna felt his hard virility pressing against her, felt her body flower and throb, and a soft moan sighed from her mouth into his. The desperate little sound brought an answering groan from Sean.

The last thing Joanna expected was for him to stop, but suddenly he thrust her from him and turned away. Dazed, she found herself swaying unsteadily on legs that felt like rubber, shaking uncontrollably, and she groped for the rail. The cool breeze off the ocean felt icy against her aroused body. She stared at Sean's stiff back, confused . . . frightened . . . hurting.

"Wh—why did you stop?"

"I'm sorry, Joanna. That shouldn't have happened."

"What is this, Sean?" she demanded in a voice raw with hurt. "Some kind of game you're playing? Are you trying to teach me a lesson? Punish me? What?"

Sean spun around, his face a tight mask of anguish. "No! I'm trying my best to see that you don't get hurt." Raking a hand through his hair, he sighed heavily. A look of self-disgust made his expression grim. "And not doing a very good job of it, I'm afraid."

"But . . . but I don't understand. If you . . ." Joanna paused and swallowed around the painful constriction in her throat. " . . . if you aren't . . . attracted to me, then why . . . why did you kiss me?"

"Not attracted!" Sean snorted, his mouth twisting in a bitter little grimace. "Good Lord, Joanna! How could you think I'm not attracted to you? Oh, I've tried to deny it. I even had myself halfway convinced that I was merely looking out for a friend's daughter . . . until today." His face hardened as he remembered the sheer torment of the past twelve hours. "I've been eaten alive with jealousy, watching you with that creep, Longworth," he admitted with angry resentment. "Every time he touched you I wanted to smash his face in."

A great uprush of joy and hope filled Joanna's chest. *Sean cares. He really cares.* She wanted to throw herself into his arms but an inner voice urged caution. Something was wrong. She could see it in the grim look on his face. "If . . . if you feel that way, then what's the problem," she asked shakily.

"Isn't it obvious? I'm too old for you, Joanna."

"Too *old?*" Joanna gave an astonished little laugh. "You call thirty-six too old?"

"For you, yes."

"Oh, Sean, please. Be reasonable. So there's almost fourteen years between us? So what? It's not that big a gap. And it's not as though you're old enough to be my father."

"No. I'm not," he agreed. Watching her, he added softly, "Nor do I intend to be a father substitute."

"What's that supposed to mean?"

"Look, Joanna, everyone knows that you were the apple of your father's eye. He doted on you, spoiled you rotten, and you adored him. And now he's gone, and you miss him. It doesn't take a genius to figure out that you're unconsciously seeking an older man to take his place." Reaching out, Sean ran the backs of his knuckles down her jaw. His voice lowered and softened. "It's understandable, honey, but that's not a role I want to play."

Hurt and wounded pride shone from Joanna's eyes. She tilted her head back, freeing herself from his touch. Turning away, she grasped the rail and stared out at the phosphorescent glow of the white-capped waves. Her chin was high, her expression closed. "You don't have to worry about that, I assure you," she informed him coolly, though not quite able to control the quaver in her voice. "I've been through that once already. I admit that I usually have to learn life's lessons the hard way, but once they're learned, I never make the same mistake twice."

Sensing the distress behind her words, Sean stared at her proud profile, and after a moment asked softly, "Would it help to talk about it?"

Joanna sent him a sidelong glance, then looked back at the sea. For a moment he thought she wasn't going to answer.

"It . . . was while I was in college," she began finally in a diffident little voice. "Shortly after Mother married Matt. I had just found out some things about my father. Not . . . very complimentary things." She bit her lower lip and glanced at him again. "I guess . . . I guess I was feeling cheated. I wanted what I had lost; someone to idolize, to look up to. Someone to whom I would be...I don't know...special, I guess. Of course, I didn't realize that at the time." Her self-derisive chuckle floated out over the ocean. "I thought I was madly in love."

"Who was he?"

"Arthur Spelling, one of my college professors. He was in his forties—sophisticated, intelligent, distinguished. All the females on campus, students *and* faculty, were wild about him. When he singled me out I thought I was the luckiest girl in the world. I gave him my innocence and my heart, and for six months I lived in a daze of sheer happiness." A bitter little smile tilted Joanna's mouth, and she looked at Sean with sad, world-weary eyes. "You know what they say: ignorance is bliss. One day I caught him with another girl and I thought I would die. Later I found out that he was known as the campus Don Juan. While he was having an affair with me he was also seeing two other girls."

Sean spat out a vivid curse and gripped the rail tightly. All the while her tale had been unfolding he had felt a growing sense of outrage. Now he was filled with anger and an aching sympathy for the disillusioned, vulnerable girl she had been. But most of all, he was filled with a searing jealousy. *Damn that bastard to hell,* Sean thought venomously. *If I could get my hands on him I'd break him in two.*

"Oh, don't be upset on my behalf," Joanna said. "Actually, I got over it all very quickly. That's when I realized that it wasn't so much heartbreak that I had felt, but disillusionment that once again my idol had turned out to have feet of clay. I knew then that I had just been looking for someone to take my father's place."

"That doesn't excuse him," Sean argued. "The bastard still took advantage of a young girl. He ought to be horsewhipped."

"I think we took advantage of each other, really. Anyway, it's over, and I learned from it, so I guess it wasn't a complete waste."

Looking into her sad hazel eyes, Sean fought a silent battle with the fury that burned in him. More than anything in the world he wanted to shield her, protect her, cherish her. If it were in his power he'd wipe out her past hurts, erase from her mind all memory of other men.

The thought brought back the clawing jealousy, and before Sean could stop himself he reached out a hand and cupped her face. "Joanna, it's none of my business, and you don't have to answer if you don't want to, but . . . since then . . . has there been anyone else?"

He hated himself for asking. He knew it did not deserve an answer, and no matter what it was it wouldn't change the way he felt. Yet he held his breath and waited for her reply.

Staring solemnly into his eyes, Joanna shook her head slowly, and a fierce gladness exploded in Sean's chest. "No, no one," she murmured. "No one else interested me . . . until now."

Sean's breath caught once again, and the joyous ache beneath his breastbone became so intense it was almost pain. He tried to subdue it. He told himself that it didn't change anything. Even if Joanna was truly attracted to him, he was still too old for her.

It didn't work. All the common sense and self-chastisement in the world couldn't banish the feeling of elation, nor stop the tender smile that slowly curved his mouth. Emotion shimmered warmly in Sean's dark eyes, and a fine tremor shook his other hand when, as if compelled, he lifted it to her face.

For several moments he just stood there with her lovely face cupped between his broad palms. She was a delight to his senses. With every breath he inhaled her sweet womanly fragrance, mingled with just a hint of floral perfume. The tips of his fingers were buried in the silken hair at her temples, and against his palms he could feel the downy softness of her cheeks, warm and satin smooth. Through the scant inches that separated them he could feel the heat of her body, sense its slight quivering.

He searched her features one by one, taking in the lush mouth, the elegantly sculpted nose and cheekbones, the gracefully winged brows and wide smooth forehead. With his thumb, he touched the enticing little mole at the corner of her mouth. *She's so lovely,* he thought wistfully. *So young. And so very vulnerable. You can hurt her badly, and you know it. If you have any decency in you, Fleming, you'll let her go, end it now.*

But as their gazes met and held he knew both joy and despair, for the hope and longing in her wide hazel eyes struck an answering chord in his heart and made dust of his good intentions.

"Oh, Joanna." He sighed her name in helpless surrender. The husky tone held uncertainty and a lingering touch of resistance, but the current of emotions that pulled them together was too strong. "Joanna," he whispered again, and as his head slowly lowered her eyelids fluttered shut in anticipation.

It began as the tenderest of kisses, soft, adoring, a warm melding of mouths that made hearts pound and knees tremble. But the feelings between them were too intense to be held in check for long. Passion flared, hot and intense, and with a groan Sean wrapped his arms around her and pulled her close.

Joanna responded eagerly, all the pent up longing of years surging to the surface. She melted against him and looped her arms around his neck, meeting the demanding kiss with an ardent hunger that matched his own.

The heated kiss went on and on until finally, the need for air tore them apart. Joanna cried his name weakly and clung to him. When she attempted to recapture his lips he cupped the back of her head and pressed her face against his chest. Eyes closed, his chin resting against the top of her head, he held her tightly and rocked her back and forth, and struggled to bring his raging desire under control.

"Easy. Easy, sweetheart," he crooned softly when she made an agitated move. He ran his hands soothingly up and down her back and rubbed his chin against her hair, feeling the silky strands catch on his faint beard stubble. Gradually their labored breathing quieted, the thunderous beating of their hearts slowed, but for several moments they remained as they were, each giving and drawing comfort from the embrace. The only sounds were the splash of the waves against the ship's hull and the soft sighing of the wind.

"All my chivalrous instincts and common sense tell me to call a halt to this now, before it's too late," Sean murmured after a while. Joanna stiffened and grew very still, not saying a word, and he knew she was waiting for him to continue. Sean hesitated. He stared out at the dark ocean, his face filled with pained indecision, but finally he exhaled a long sigh. "Oh, hell. We both may live to regret this, but will you spend the day ashore in St. Croix with me tomorrow?"

Joy exploded inside Joanna like a starburst, and she closed her eyes against the sweet pain. She wanted desperately to say yes, but like Sean, she was leery of allowing things to go further. Despite the longing that tugged at her heart, Joanna could not forget that scores of beautiful women had come and gone in Sean's life. The thought that she might end up like they had, just another name and phone number in his little black book, made her feel sick.

She pressed her lips tightly together as the emotional tug-of-war raged within her, but in the end need won over fear. With her cheek still pressed against his chest, she whispered unsteadily, "Yes. Yes, I'd like that."

He grasped her shoulders and held her away from him. Her face was flushed with passion, her lips slightly puffed, and all that she was feeling was there in her luminous eyes for him to see. Sean felt his heart turn over. At that moment he wanted, more than anything, to carry her to his cabin and make love to her until neither of them could move, but he stubbornly refused to listen to his body's urgings.

He brushed her mouth with a feathery kiss and tucked her against his side. "Come on, sweetheart. I'll take you to your suite."

Neither spoke until they reached her door. When Sean unlocked it and handed her the key Joanna licked her dry lips and looked at him with a hesitant smile. "Would...would you like to come in?"

He sighed, his wry grin tinged with regret. "Oh, I'd like to. But I'm not going to."

His smile turned tender when he saw the mingled relief and disappointment in her eyes. "I don't want to rush into anything, Joanna. Not with you."

This time when his lips met hers it was with the merest touch. Softly, almost reverently, he skimmed her mouth with a warm moist caress that made her tremble, and she clutched at the sides of his lean waist for support. Her lips parted in sweet invitation and their breaths mingled, but he made no effort to deepen the kiss. Gently, with exquisite sensuality, he rubbed his mouth against hers, until Joanna thought she would faint from the tender torment.

Finally he lifted his head and smiled into her bemused eyes. "Good night, Joanna," he whispered.

Feeling as though she were walking on air, Joanna entered the suite and drifted toward the bedroom. Halfway there she stopped and hugged herself, then twirled around, arms outstretched, and sent a beaming smile toward the ceiling. She was so happy she was tempted to pinch herself to see if she was dreaming.

Yet, strangely, when Joanna did get to sleep her dreams were disturbing and disjointed, a phantasmagoria of blondes, brunettes and redheads with blank faces, all laughing tauntingly; thousands of little black books swirling through the air, trapping her in an ever narrowing vortex; Sean's face, looming eerily, floating and wavering like fog, his sexy eyes and wicked smile alternately soft and beckoning, or filled with amused scorn.

When Joanna awoke her euphoric mood was shattered. "What have you let yourself in for?" she fretted as she dressed for the day ashore. "You're just asking for trouble. You know perfectly well that Sean doesn't expect or want permanence in a relationship.''

Joanna paused in the act of adjusting the spaghetti straps on her pink sundress, her eyes going slightly out of focus as she thought about her mother and Matt, about the love and tenderness that flowed between them, their total commitment to each other. She sighed wistfully. It was what she wanted. What she needed. Joanna knew she couldn't settle for anything less.

But Matt had been a confirmed bachelor too, before he fell in love with Claire.

Her heart gave a little leap at the stunning thought, but Joanna quickly tamped down the flare of elation. She shoved her feet into a pair of flat white sandals and stomped to the mirror. ''Sean isn't Matt,'' she told her reflection severely. ''And you'd do well to remember that.''

The whole time she dressed, and later, while toying with the croissant she had ordered for breakfast, Joanna vacillated between despair and an almost desperate hope. By the time Sean arrived she was so worked up she was certain that the day could only be a disaster.

Even so, when his knock sounded she rushed to the door, opened it and went perfectly still.

They stared at each other in breathless silence, feeling the strong pull of attraction, the nervous uncertainty its newness caused.

Everything about Sean assaulted her senses. He was freshly showered and shaved, and she could smell soap and woodsy cologne, the faint hint of starch in his crisp blue cotton shirt. Tiny droplets of moisture still clung to the errant black curls that fell over his forehead, and to the sparser thatch visible in the V opening of his shirt. Joanna stared at his bronze throat and remembered the warm resilience of his skin beneath her lips, the slightly salty taste of it.

Slowly, Sean's gaze skimmed over her, taking in her bare shoulders, the enticing curves beneath the soft material of the pink sundress, then traveled down over her long legs to the white sandals on her feet. When at last his eyes returned to hers they glittered warmly.

"Good morning," he murmured with husky intimacy, and dropped a soft kiss on her mouth that sent shivers down her spine. "Ready to go?"

Joanna nodded and stepped out the door. Her heart drummed with excitement while her stomach churned with doubt. *We'll probably end up in another fight before an hour passes,* she thought miserably as they started down the passageway.

She couldn't have been more wrong. It turned out to be a perfectly glorious day, the best Joanna had ever known.

Hand in hand, Joanna and Sean poked through the quaint shops facing the Christiansted harbor, looking at everything from jewelry to T-shirts. After an hour of wandering through the tiny town they traveled across the island to Fredriksted in one of the van taxis, which they shared with three other couples.

Like St. Thomas, there was a lushness about St. Croix, a soft-edged beauty that Joanna found entrancing, almost too perfect to be real. The verdant, sloping mountains at the north end of the island gave way to a wide sweeping vista of cultivated meadows and white sand beaches. A profusion of tropical flowers abounded, dotting the island with splashes of brilliant color, while overhead pristine white clouds floated in the cobalt sky. The pace was relaxed, easy, the mood serene. It was quietly lovely, paradise on earth.

Or maybe I just think so because I'm here with Sean, Joanna admitted to herself wryly. Taking the path of least resistance, the road followed the dips and rises of the rolling plain past sorghum fields, banana plantations and sheep farms. Sean sat with his arm draped across the back of Joanna's seat, and when the taxi driver pointed out things and places of interest he leaned across her to peer out the window. The feel of his chest pressing against her side, the heady aroma of clean, healthy male that surrounded her, sent delicious tremors quaking through Joanna, and she found herself wishing that the trip never had to end.

In Fredriksted they spent the first hour wandering through the old fort that overlooked the harbor. Afterward, opting for lunch, they bought sandwiches and soft drinks and carried them down to the pier where several sailboats were tied up.

Tiny waves lapped at the pilings, making slapping, sucking noises. The water level was only about a foot lower than the dock, and so clear Joanna could see the sandy bottom, littered with shells and pieces of coral and an occasional starfish.

The moment they sat down on the wooden dock Sean took off his shoes and rolled up the legs of his jeans. As he dipped his feet into the cool water he leaned back on his hands and sighed with pleasure.

"Ah, this is great. Sun, sea, tropical breezes. I think, with half a chance, I could easily become a beach bum."

"You?" Joanna smiled skeptically and handed him a roast beef sandwich. "Somehow I doubt it." For all Sean's deceptive, laid-back air she knew he was ambitious and hard working.

Sean grinned and took a healthy bite out of his sandwich. He stared thoughtfully at the horizon while he chewed and swished his feet in the water. "Naw, I guess you're right," he conceded. "The work ethic is too deeply ingrained."

He delved into the sack that contained their lunch, pulled out two soft drinks and popped the tops off before handing one to Joanna. Tipping his up, he swilled half the contents in one long swallow, then wiped his mouth with the back of his hand and flashed her a rueful grin. "Anyway, my old man would never stand for it. He may be seventy, but if one of his offspring so much as thought about dropping out he'd kick their tail from here to Canada."

"Really?"

"You'd better believe it. Thorne Padriag Fleming doesn't tolerate slackers." Sean took another bite of sandwich and washed it down with more cola. "Dad came to the States from Ireland when he was seventeen," he continued reminiscently. "He had twenty dollars in his pocket. It was tough, but he worked at any job he could find, and even managed to take a few night classes. When he was old enough he joined the police force and became one of New York's finest. He retired a few years back as a captain."

"He raised eight children on a policeman's salary?" Joanna asked in astonishment and awe.

Sean looked at her intently. "We didn't have much money, but we kids didn't know that. We were happy, well-fed and loved. Anyway, everything is relative. Compared to what he had in the old country, Dad feels well-to-do. He's proud of what he's achieved and the fact that he's raised eight kids to be solid citizens. To his way of thinking, he's a living example of the American dream."

The censorious note in Sean's voice brought a vivid flush to Joanna's face and neck. *Oh, Lord. When will I ever learn?* "Sean, I'm sorry. I know how snooty that must have sounded, but I didn't mean to insult you," she insisted anxiously. "Honestly, I just—"

"That's okay. I guess, considering the life you've had, it must be hard for you to understand."

Feeling miserable and horribly embarrassed, and unable to think of a thing to say, Joanna watched Sean polish off the last of his sandwich and drink, then toss the wrapper and can into the sack.

When done, he leaned back on one palm, propped a wet foot on the pier and draped his arm across his knee, squinting his eyes against the light reflecting off the water. Joanna half expected him to suggest that they return to the ship, but after a moment he picked up the conversation again.

"I guess the point is, Dad believes that with hard work and determination you can be whatever you want to be. He encouraged all his children to set their goals high and reach for them." Sean shrugged and smiled crookedly. "In addition to loving his adopted country he's fascinated by the way the system works, and I suppose some of that rubbed off on me, which is why I got involved in politics."

"How about your brothers and sisters? What do they do?" Joanna asked hesitantly.

"Mike—he's the oldest—followed in Dad's footsteps and became a policeman. Kathleen is an attorney, and Dennis will be, just as soon as he passes the bar exam. Bridget is a social worker, Ryan's in med school, and, let's see... Colin just graduated from college and is starting out in sales, and Meghan..." Sean's face softened and his eyes grew tender. "Meghan's the baby of the family. It's hard to believe that she now has a baby of her own."

Sean looked at Joanna, and she could see in his face the deep affection he felt for his youngest sibling, plus a trace of sadness that she had left the innocence of childhood behind.

"She's the mother of the two-month-old nephew I told you about. Both Meghan and her husband work and go to school part-time. They're as poor as church mice, and it's a constant struggle for them to make ends meet, especially now with the baby, but they refuse to take help from anyone," he said with a frown, both irritation and pride evident in his voice.

"My goodness. No wonder your father is proud of his children. I'm sure your mother is, too."

"Oh sure," Sean said with a chuckle. "Although I think the fact that seven of her eight offspring are happily married and producing grandchildren means more to her than anything else. Mom's never happier than when she's got her whole brood gathered around." He rolled his eyes eloquently. "Lord, you ought to see us during holidays and family gatherings. It's pure bedlam. There's thirty-eight of us, for Pete's sake."

"I can—" Joanna stopped and laughed, shaking her head wryly. "I almost said, 'I can imagine,' but I really can't. It certainly sounds interesting, though."

"Oh, it is. It is."

Enthralled, as only an only child can be, Joanna listened as Sean related several anecdotes about his family. Some were hilarious, some poignant. To Joanna they were all fascinating. She was well aware that Sean, with his Irish gift of gab, had probably embroidered and embellished the tales, but she didn't care. It thrilled her that he was sharing them with her, giving her a glimpse of that private part of his life. Somehow, she knew instinctively that it was a privilege he didn't afford many people.

Joanna laughed so hard after one particularly funny tale that she had to dig into the trash sack for a napkin to dab the tears from her eyes. "Oh, Sean, that was pr-priceless," she choked weakly, mopping at her wet cheeks. "Your nephew actually shaved off all the other kids' eyebrows?"

After a moment, when Sean didn't reply, she peered over the napkin and found that he was watching her, his face serious, intent.

"You really are a lovely woman," he said quietly. Leaning closer, he caressed her cheek with his fingertips, and Joanna felt her heart begin to pound. "I wonder why I didn't notice that years ago?"

"Probably because I was a pushy, arrogant brat," Joanna said on a weak laugh.

Sean grinned. "Yeah, you're probably right. But you've changed," he murmured, growing serious again. "And I find that I like the new Joanna very much." Slowly, he trailed his fingers down the side of her neck, across the gentle slope of her shoulder and down her arm to her elbow, then back up. Joanna closed her eyes and shivered delicately. "Very much," he repeated in a husky whisper.

His breath feathered across her skin, and Joanna lifted her heavy lids to find that he had moved closer still, and that his gaze was locked on her mouth. The meandering hand slid back over her shoulder and cupped around her nape. With gentle but firm pressure he urged her forward until their lips met.

It was the softest of kisses. With the merest pressure, his lips rocked against hers in a slow seductive motion.

The tip of his tongue slid enticingly back and forth between her barely parted lips, tasting, tempting. But for all its gentleness the kiss was filled with heat and power. Joanna trembled beneath its sweet hot touch as a shimmering flame raced through her and her skin prickled deliciously.

Their lips clung, then parted. His black eyes glittering with leashed passion, Sean pulled back just inches and studied Joanna's glazed look and flushed face. He drew his hand from her nape and cupped her jaw, smiling tenderly as his thumb swept over her trembling lips and touched the tiny beauty mark at one corner.

"I think we'd better go back to shopping or sightseeing, before I forget we're in a public place and do something to embarrass us," he whispered roughly, half teasing, half serious.

The lambent flame in his eyes filled Joanna with sheer joy. How many times had she dreamed of him looking at her in just that way? Of hearing that husky, intimate tone? It was a fantasy come true.

So was the rest of the day. Flushed with happiness, Joanna strolled with Sean through the Fredriksted's narrow, picturesque streets. In an interesting, tucked away alley paved with cobblestones and lined with unusual shops, they discovered a sidewalk cafe, where they enjoyed piña coladas beneath a huge poinciana tree and talked endlessly of nonsensical, inconsequential things. But with every look exchanged, every touch, they communicated on a far deeper, more basic level.

They returned to Christiansted and the ship late that afternoon. It was almost sailing time, and they decided to watch the ship get under way from the sun deck. When they reached the bow, however, they both stopped short at the sight of Gloria and Tony standing in the shallow end of the pool, locked in a passionate kiss.

Cautiously, Joanna looked at Sean. "Does that, uh . . . upset you?"

"No, not a bit," Sean said with casual indifference. Then his eyes narrowed. "Why? Does it bother you?"

"Me? Why should it bother me? Tony and I aren't romantically involved." Joanna shot him an accusing glance, then tilted her chin disdainfully and sniffed, "Certainly not to the point where I would allow him to buy me a gold bracelet."

A dawning light appeared in Sean's eyes and he grinned slowly. "Ah, so that's it. Well this may be hard for you to believe, but I bought that gold bracelet for Gloria because I felt guilty for *not* having an affair with her."

"Oh, please. You don't really expect me to believe that, do you?"

"It's true. Oh, I intended to. But somehow I just couldn't work up any enthusiasm." Sean picked up a handful of her hair, rubbed it experimentally between his fingers and thumb and gave her a look that caused her insides to flutter wildly. "Someone else kept occupying my thoughts."

"Oh." Delight percolated through Joanna, and she beamed up at him foolishly.

"Yes, oh." There was a hint of teasing in his voice, but his eyes were very serious. "So you see, I'm not in the least upset about those two. I'm perfectly happy with the status quo. How about you?"

"Oh, yes," Joanna agreed softly. "I'm very happy."

Chapter Nine

Excitement and anticipation tingled through Joanna like the fluttering, whispering wings of a thousand butterflies.

On stage the dancers were performing a strenuous, precision tap routine to the band's rousing rendition of "Yankee-Doodle Dandy." It was an excellent show. Every member of the troupe was talented and professional, and Joanna watched them with every outward sign of enjoyment. But for all that her mind was on the performance they might just as well have been left-footed hippos in tutus.

Sitting beside Sean in the dim theater, their clasped hands resting on his thigh, Joanna could think of nothing but him—the day that had just passed, the night that was to come.

The theater seats were actually love seats, arranged in curving rows around the stage, and sharing one with

Sean, Joanna could feel his heat, the tensile strength of him, all along her side from her shoulder to her knee. Against her bare arm his coat sleeve felt rough, slightly scratchy, wonderful. Her gaze dropped to their clasped hands and a smile played about her lips. The contrasts were marked: large to small, strength to fragility, dark to pale, rough to smooth. Yet, somehow, they looked so right together. And it felt so natural to be touching him.

The dance number came to an end, and all around Joanna the audience broke into enthusiastic clapping, snapping her out of her sensuous study. The Wrights were seated in the row in front of them, and when Joanna's gaze fell on Mary's silver head the hovering smile grew. Other than exchanging knowing glances, no one had seemed surprised earlier when she and Sean had arrived for dinner together. Shrewdly noting the warm look in Sean's eyes and the way his hands had lingered on Joanna's shoulders after he had pushed in her chair, Mary had merely leaned close and whispered in her ear, "It's about time," and then had laughed delightedly at Joanna's startled look.

Gloria had allowed herself one hostile glare before resuming her flirtation with Tony, who had seemed delighted with the situation.

Apparently everyone else was aware of our feelings before we were, Joanna thought wryly. At least...before Sean was.

"Ready?" Sean asked, and Joanna looked at him in surprise, blinking as the lights came on, only then realizing that the show had ended.

As they inched their way up the aisle in the midst of the crowd Sean walked just behind Joanna with his hands resting lightly on either side of her waist. Smiling, Joanna savored the feel of his body brushing against her back and hips, the blatant possessiveness of his touch.

"How about a walk in the moonlight?"

Sean's warm breath filling her ear sent a tingle racing over Joanna's skin. He nipped her lobe gently, and against her neck she felt him smile as a shudder rippled through her. Joanna could only nod.

They eased out of the crowd at the first exit and stepped out onto the Promenade deck. By silent mutual consent, they took the outside stairs up to the next deck, which was open to the star-sprinkled sky. Hands clasped, fingers laced together, they strolled toward the stern, their footsteps making soft measured thuds on the teak decking.

The warm night air flowed against their skin like a lover's breath, caressing, arousing. Resembling a misshapen silver disc, an almost full moon hung in the dark sky, bathing everything in its gentle glow.

Joanna felt as light as a feather, as though she would float away were it not for Sean's anchoring hand. She was drunk on happiness and the romantic atmosphere, the sheer magic of the night. Unlike the effects of alcohol, the emotional high did not dull her awareness, but made it sharper. As though her sensory perception had been fine tuned, she was acutely conscious of every nuance of feeling, every tiny detail around her: the slight salt tang of the air, the surprising calluses that ridged Sean's palm, and the wonderful warmth of it against hers, faint sounds of music and laughter floating up from the lounges on the deck below, silk drifting against her legs as the softest of breezes toyed with the handkerchief hem of her gown, lovers lurking in the shadows, whispering, embracing, the trembly feeling in her lower belly, resulting from the sure knowledge that they were about to reach a new turning point, one that would alter their relationship forever.

The hint of a smile hovering around Sean's mouth told her he was aware of her anticipation and shared it. His pulse throbbed beneath her fingertips, its rhythm exactly matching the heavy thud of her heart, and the occasional burning looks he cast her way made it beat even stronger and flooded her body with heat.

They walked in silence, their deceptively lazy steps marking off the sluggardly passing of time. A heady tension crackled in the air around them like invisible heat lightning.

The shadows at the stern enveloped them, and they stopped by the rail to look out at the sea. With no wind stirring it was calm as glass, except for the phosphorescent froth of the wake that trailed behind the ship. Joanna stared at it, waiting, the trembling expectancy growing to a tormenting, delicious agony.

Beside her Sean turned, and she sensed his gaze drifting over her profile.

"Joanna." He uttered her name in a low voice that wasn't much more than a whisper, a sigh, yet the sound was filled with longing and entreaty.

With her heart kicking against her ribs, Joanna turned slowly and looked up at him. In the shadows Sean's face was barely discernible, but she could sense the intense emotion that gripped him. It mirrored her own.

Never taking his eyes from her, Sean lifted the hand he still held and pressed her palm to his mouth. With the tip of his tongue he traced a wet circle on the tender flesh. The contact sent a bolt of fire zinging through her, straight to the heart of her femininity, making it pulse and liquefy. "Oh, Joanna, what have you done to me?"

he asked in a rasping whisper, moistening her skin even more with the dew of his warm breath.

"I... What do you mean?"

"I've never felt this way before. Never been this obsessed with a woman before." Back and forth, he rubbed his lips against her palm. "I haven't been able to think of anything but you since we left Florida."

"I have the same problem," she said throatily, shivering.

"Do you? Do you have any idea how much I want to hold you? Love you? It was all I could think about all day while we were ashore. And tonight during dinner." He grimaced, his face twisting in remembered frustration. "And that show. Lord! I thought it would never end."

Beyond speech, Joanna could only nod her understanding, then close her eyes helplessly as his teeth nipped the soft pads at the base of her fingers.

Sean's gaze roamed over her rapt face. The most delicate lids he had ever seen shuttered her hazel eyes, sweeping the lavish fringe of lashes across her cheeks like dark fans. Unable to resist, he laid her hand against his chest and bent forward, placing a feathery kiss on each one.

As though weighted with lead, Joanna's lids lifted slumberously. She gazed up at him with all that she was feeling plainly visible in her face, in her eyes. Even in the shadows Sean could see the emotion swimming in their hazel depths. Lord, he thought a bit desperately. She looks so fragile, so vulnerable, so very lovely.

Once again Sean experienced a pang of guilt, but he pushed it aside. It was far too late to be noble; he no longer had the strength to walk away. He wanted to kiss her senseless, to pull her to the deck and ravage that sweet mouth and body, but even more, he didn't want to frighten her. Controlling his raging impulses, Sean brought her other hand to his chest, slipped his arms around her and tenderly gathered her to him.

With an urgent little sigh, Joanna pressed closer and slid her hands up over his shoulders, burying her fingers in the silky hair at his nape. The tiny evening bag that hung from her wrist bumped gently against his back. As the soft globes of her breasts flattened against Sean's chest a moan of animal pleasure rumbled from him, and his head descended.

"Dear Lord, you're lovely," he whispered achingly against her lips. "So very lovely."

Sean kissed her with a depth of emotion that surprised even him. Hungrily, a bit desperately, he rocked his lips over hers. He wanted to devour her, absorb her, until they were one in mind, body and soul.

Joanna's instant, ardent response made his heart leap. Any lingering doubts Sean had about her maturity vanished as she kissed him back with a woman's passion, a woman's needs.

Desire flamed between them, and the kiss became hotter, more intense. Sean's tongue plumbed the sweet depths of her mouth. His hands roamed her slender curves. Joanna groaned and burrowed closer, her fingers clutching his hair in a desperate grip.

With an effort of will, Sean tore his mouth from hers and buried his face in the fragrant hair at the side of her neck. "Oh, God, Joanna. If we don't stop now I'm not going to be able to," he gasped.

Joanna made a strangled little sound, and he straightened and clutched her tightly against his chest. Tilting his head, Sean rested his cheek against her crown and rocked her back and forth. He was afire. Burning.

He wanted Joanna more than he had ever wanted any woman in his life, but he knew it wasn't just physical. He hungered desperately for something more. It was a deep, gut-wrenching need he'd never experienced before. It clawed at his soul and made him tremble.

Shakily, he held Joanna away from him and stared down at her with feverish eyes. He knew, just as surely as he knew that tomorrow would come, this would not be a casual fling he could enjoy for a while, and then walk away from. And, to his surprise, he found that he was glad. "I want you, Joanna," he said in a voice roughened by passion. "I need you." His fingers tightened on her shoulders and he looked at her intently. "Will you come back to my room with me?"

Joanna's heart stopped for a millisecond before it took off at a gallop. Joy exploded inside her, creating such pressure in her chest she could barely breathe. Her body yearned for his touch, and her heart urged her to say yes, but even so, she could not shut out the niggling doubts. He could hurt her badly. The pain she had suffered after that ill-considered little affair in college would be nothing in comparison. And yet . . .

Joanna hesitated, hope and fear, longing and wariness warring within her as her emotions told her one thing, her common sense another. But it took only a moment for her to realize that there was really no choice to make. She loved Sean. It was as simple as that.

Looking up at him with her heart in her eyes, she drew a deep breath and smiled tremulously. "Yes. Yes, I'll go with you."

Something hot and wild flared in Sean's eyes. "You won't be sorry. I promise," he vowed in a rough whisper. He bent and kissed her hard, then tucked her against his side and started back the way they had come.

Every nerve in Joanna's body quivered like a plucked string. Sedately, their arms around each other, they strolled across the deck, down the stairs and along the passageway, all without speaking. They stopped at Sean's door, and he smiled warmly into her eyes while fishing in his pocket for the key without relinquishing his hold on her. As he fumbled to fit it into the lock with his left hand Joanna stared at his intent profile, her heart thumping as doubts of a different kind assailed her.

She was so inexperienced. What if she didn't please him? Sean had known many women. Beautiful, glamorous women. Women like Gloria. Joanna thought about her own plain brown hair, her slender, girlish body, her small breasts. Would he be disappointed? What if...

The door opened and Sean's encircling arm urged her into the cabin. When he turned to hang out the Do Not Disturb sign she stepped away and stood in the middle of the floor, her body rigid with apprehension.

It was a small cabin, not even as big as the bedroom in her suite. The room steward had already removed the spread and turned down the covers on the double bed that sat flush with one wall. As she stared at it, Joanna felt a quivering in the pit of her stomach and quickly looked away.

Next to the bed a low chest of drawers sat beneath the porthole. On the opposite wall were two doors, which she presumed led to the bathroom and closet. The only other furnishings were an upholstered chair, a tiny table and a TV.

Sean moved away from the door, and she turned to him with a determined smile. But some of her anxiety must have shown on her face, for when he stopped just inches from her, his expression was infinitely tender. His hands settled lightly on her forearms and glided upward to cup the rounded curves of her shoulders, the feathery touch leaving a trail of goose bumps on her skin.

"Oh, love," he whispered, pulling her closer. "There's no reason to be nervous. It's going to be wonderful. You'll see." His dark eyes glowed with sensual promise, and his slow smile made her heart thrum. His gaze roamed her face, lingering lovingly on each feature. When it stopped at her mouth, his lids dropped halfway and his voice became even huskier. "I've never felt this way about a woman in my life, Joanna. Never. Something this special just has to be right."

Joanna drew in her breath as, like magic, his words swept away all her misgivings, all her fears. She had needed so desperately to know that she was more than just another in the long list of women who had fleetingly held Sean's interest. She stared at him with wide, luminous eyes, hope unfurling inside her with all the fragile tenacity of a flower blooming in the desert. He hadn't said he loved her, and maybe he didn't yet, but surely, surely, given time, he would. Emotion clogged her throat and her shining eyes brimmed with tears. As they trickled over and streamed down her cheeks, she smiled tremulously.

"Oh, Sean." His name came out in a broken whisper, a soft sigh of adoration that told him all he needed to know.

Lovingly, Sean enfolded her in his arms and covered her mouth with his. The kiss was a tender ravishment that set her soul aflame. She quivered within the embrace, her heart overflowing with love as his lips moved against hers with a slow, heated fervency. Giving. Savoring. Sweetly devouring.

Joanna's mouth flowered open, and Sean's tongue dipped into it repeatedly, drinking from her sweetness like a man dying of thirst. "Lord, you taste heavenly," he said, as he rubbed his mouth back and forth over hers. "I'll never get enough of you. Never."

Joanna's tiny purse dropped to the floor with a soft plop. She clung to him, her hands clutching at the lapels of his dinner jacket while his worked their drugging magic, smoothing over her bare shoulders, her waist, the rounded curves of her bottom. When he lowered the zipper at the back of her dress and brushed the thin spaghetti straps from her shoulders she obediently lowered her arms. The garment slid down her body and fluttered to the floor in a billowing cloud of silk chiffon.

The fully lined dress required no slip, and when he eased her away she stood before him in only a wispy triangle of lilac silk and a wickedly sinful ecru lace garter belt and stockings. Sean looked at her, his black eyes glittering hotly, his chest heaving. His handsome face, distorted by desire, was rigid and flushed.

His gaze drifted hungrily down over her belly and silk covered legs, then returned to stare at her pert, uptilted breasts. As though mesmerized, he slowly circled one dusky pink nipple with his index finger, and something flared in his eyes as it tightened into a hard bud. He cupped the soft globe in his palm. "Your skin is like satin," he murmured hoarsely. "So smooth and warm." He raised his eyes to hers. "I can feel your heart beating."

Joanna quivered under that hot look. Her breasts felt heavy and feverish, and when he bent and touched his tongue to the aching tips she gasped and clutched at his shoulders. "Oh, Sean! Sean!"

Just as her knees started to buckle he groaned and snatched her back into his arms, burying his face in the silky curls at the side of her neck. "Oh, God, sweetheart! You're so beautiful. Just the sight of you drives me wild."

"I . . . I . . ." Coherent speech was beyond Joanna.

The scrape of cloth against her sensitized nipples was almost painfully erotic. When Joanna began to fumble with the buttons on his shirt Sean went perfectly still, then eased back a fraction to allow her better access. In her haste, her movements were jerky and awkward, but she finally managed the task, then snatched the shirt free of his trousers. Frantically, she pushed wide the gaping front sections of the garment and burrowed close, making a soft sound, somewhere between a moan and a sigh, as her breast flattened against his furred chest.

A violent shudder rippled through Sean, and his arms tightened around her convulsively. He held her close for a moment, but when her soft hands tunneled beneath his dinner jacket and the loose shirt to move searchingly over the taut muscles in his back, his control snapped. With decisive quickness, he swept her into his arms and carried her the few steps to the bed. He placed her on the soft, fragrant linens, and Joanna's breath caught as his fiery gaze blazed over her.

Then, methodically, he set about removing her few remaining articles of clothing.

Two soft plops sounded, one after the other, as he slipped the high heeled sandals from her feet and dropped them to the floor. With shaking fingers, he unhooked her garters and peeled the sheer silk stockings from her legs. As though unable to help himself, he bent and kissed the strip of flesh between the top of her bikini panties and the lacy garter belt. His teeth nipped her satiny belly. His nimble tongue swirled a wet circle around her navel, then speared into the tiny cavity, withdrew, and plunged again. Her hands helplessly clutching the sheet on either side of her, Joanna moaned and writhed beneath the delicious torment.

Sean raised his head and smiled. "I'm going to love all of you. Every beautiful inch of you," he vowed in a raspy whisper.

He hooked his thumbs beneath the top of her panties, drew the lilac silk slowly down over her legs and tossed it to the floor. The wisp of ecru lace followed. His dark gaze sizzled over her again. "Oh, babe, I burn just looking at you."

Straightening, Sean stripped off his shirt and dinner jacket at one time, tossed them into the chair, and went to work on his trousers. Within moments he was naked, his discarded clothes strewn haphazardly over the chair and floor, and he was stretching out beside her, pulling her urgently against his heated flesh.

The kiss was a hungry outpouring of unleashed passion. His tongue delved into her mouth, stroking, probing, plundering sweetly.

With barely restrained urgency, his hand smoothed over her body, exploring the long, exquisite line of thigh and hip, the inward curve of waist, the gentle flare of ribcage. In a feather-light touch, the back of Sean's knuckles grazed the underside of her breast. Then his large hand cupped around the warm fullness, and Joanna shuddered as his thumb swept back and forth over the rosy crest.

Sean rained kisses down Joanna's neck and shoulder, the underside of her jaw, her collarbone, down into the scented valley between her breasts. As his hand moved downward over her quivering belly, he drew the engorged nipple into the wet warmth of his mouth and drew on her with slow, rhythmic suction.

"Oh, God, Sean!" Joanna cried out in surprise, tangling her fingers in his hair and urging him closer as the tugging pressure set off little incendiary explosions within her body that sent liquid fire racing to the core of her femininity, making it tighten and throb.

Sean lavished the same loving attention on the other breast, and the delicious agony became almost unbearable. Joanna whimpered and writhed in restless passion, her nails digging into the taut muscles in his back.

The whimper became a low, long moan of pure ecstasy when Sean's hand slipped between her thighs and probed the delicate petals of her womanhood.

Sean lifted his head and looked at her. His handsome face was flushed, his eyes a burning black. Silently, he questioned, and just as silently she answered. Obeying the tugging of her hands and the urgent plea in her eyes, he moved into position between her thighs. Braced on his palms, he remained poised above her for a second, his intent gaze locked with hers. Then with a slow, sure stroke, he made them one.

He thrust deep, sheathing himself completely in her velvety warmth, a slight smile curling his mouth as he watched Joanna's eyes grow smoky with passion. Watching her still, he began the smooth, rocking movements of love, and a look of fierce satisfaction tightened his face as her rapture grew.

"You feel wonderful. You are wonderful," he murmured.

Joanna gazed up at him languorously, her eyes swimming with love and sensuous pleasure. With a soft, beguiling smile, she ran her hands up his arms and linked her fingers at his nape. "Come to me, my love," she urged in a breathy whisper. "Come to me."

"Oh, God, yes!" Sean cried as he lowered his chest over the soft globes of her breast and felt her long limbs enfold him.

The pressure built. Their pleasure grew to breathtaking proportions. It swelled within them, around them. It pushed the breath out of their lungs and filled their hearts to bursting. Bodies grew taut, straining, movements rapid. The sweet agony built and built until it became too much for mere mortals to bear.

Then the explosion came—a fiery conflagration that consumed them.

Long minutes after their hoarse cries of completion died away, they lay without moving, clinging to each other, utterly replete. As their labored breathing gradually slowed, Joanna stroked her hands over Sean's damp body and drifted on a sea of languor, savoring his closeness, his pressing weight, the musky scent of satisfied male.

At last, Sean stirred. Raising himself up on his forearms, he toyed absently with her silky hair spread out on the pillow and looked down at her, his expression serious, a bit uncertain. "You okay?"

"Yes. Yes, I'm fine." Smiling, she lifted a hand and ran her finger over one heavy black brow, loving the wiry satin texture of it.

"No regrets?"

"No, none. That was wonderful, Sean. The most beautiful experience of my life." Her smile faded a fraction. "What about you? Are you sorry?"

"Hardly." The worry left his face as his slow smile grew. The sight of it made Joanna's insides flutter. "What we just shared happens to be the greatest experience I've ever had also. I've known a lot of women intimately, Joanna," he added when she frowned doubtfully. "And I enjoyed making love with every one of them. I won't lie to you about that. But it was never like this. I've never felt this...this...joy before."

"Oh, Sean." Tears filled Joanna's eyes, and she reached up and framed his face tenderly between her palms. It wasn't a declaration of love but it was very close, especially for Sean. It was more than she even dared to hope for this soon, and her heart felt as though it were about to burst with sheer happiness. It was all she could do to keep from blurting out her love for him. "I'm so glad," she whispered in an emotion-choked voice. "So very glad. I . . . I couldn't have stood it if you had regretted making love to me."

The sensuous smile that tugged at Sean's mouth held just a touch of devilment. "Does this feel like regret?" he asked lazily.

"Sean!" Joanna gasped, her eyes going wide as she felt his body stir within her. "So soon? How can you...I mean, I thought..."

He chuckled wickedly and nibbled at the tender skin just behind her ear. "Easy. I've been going out of my mind wanting you ever since this trip started. It may take all night to satisfy my hunger." His lips trailed moist kisses over her throat, across her cheek. His tongue flicked maddeningly at the corner of her mouth, and Joanna turned her head, blindly seeking. "In fact," he whispered huskily against her lips. "I don't think I'll ever get enough of you."

Joanna moaned a little sigh of ecstasy as his lips closed possessively over hers. Looping her arms around his neck, she returned his kiss with all the fervent love that swelled her heart and gave herself up to the spiraling passion he so easily aroused.

Much later, as she drifted off to sleep in Sean's arms, spent and satiated, Joanna's last drowsy thought was, *Who says dreams don't come true?*

Chapter Ten

The ethereal lavender light that heralds the coming of sunrise seeped in through the porthole. Joanna smiled and blinked languorously, watching the misty glow ease the shadows from the cabin. As sweet memories came creeping in with the dawn she sighed in utter contentment.

Sean lay beside her, his head on her pillow. She could feel his deep, even breathing against her shoulder, the heavy weight of his arm draped across her waist, the radiant heat from his body. Closing her eyes, she savored the tactile pleasure.

Sean stirred, mumbled something and hooked his leg over hers. Smiling, Joanna rubbed her silky smooth limb back and forth against his calf, delighting in its hairy roughness.

She rolled her head on the pillow and gazed at him, and felt her heart give a little bump against her ribs. His face was softened in sleep, his lips slightly parted and slack, making him look endearingly vulnerable. Overnight beard stubble created a bluish smudge along his jaw and upper lip, and his hair was mussed and untidy, lying across his forehead in tousled ebony curls. Pleasure came washing over Joanna at his nearness, at finding herself there, where she had never thought she'd be. He was so handsome and so male . . . and she loved him so.

Waking up in bed with a man was a new experience for Joanna. Because Arthur had insisted they keep their relationship secret, the time she had spent with him had been brief—furtive little meetings stolen now and then, that had lasted only an hour or two at most. Joanna had not liked the situation, but Arthur had claimed that it would jeopardize his position with the college if it got out that he was involved with one of his students. It wasn't until later that she'd realized it had merely been a clever means of keeping his various girlfriends from learning about one another.

That all seemed so long ago, Joanna thought with lazy contentment, feathering her fingertips over the silky hair on Sean's forearm. So unimportant now.

The circle of sky beyond the porthole changed to crimson and gold. Seconds later a splinter of sunshine beamed across the carpet like a tiny spotlight. As much as she hated to, Joanna knew she ought to return to her suite before the other passengers began to stir. It would be a bit awkward if anyone she knew saw her sneaking in at dawn, still dressed in her evening gown.

She lifted Sean's arm from her waist, eased her leg from beneath his and scooted gingerly over to the edge of the bed. Cautiously sitting up, she swung her legs to the floor, but the soles of her feet had barely touched the carpet when an arm hooked around her midriff and hauled her backward.

Joanna uttered a soft cry and slumped back against Sean's bare chest.

"Going somewhere?" he inquired in her ear. He nuzzled aside her hair and nipped at her neck with tender savagery.

"I...I... Back to my suite."

"Wanna bet?" His tongue bathed her flesh with loving strokes. "You're staying right here. Where you belong."

Joanna shivered as he trailed a line of nibbling kisses down her neck and over her shoulder, then back up to that sensitive spot behind her ear. Playfully, he drew a wet circle with his tongue and warmed it with his breath. "Ah...Sean...stop...I have to...have to..." Joanna's faltering thought processes shut down when Sean moved sensuously against her back. The feel of silky chest hair feathering across her skin set off a delicious tingle, and Sean chuckled wickedly when he felt her shiver.

"Have to what?"

"To...to..."

"Whatever it was, forget it." His free hand came around her and cupped her breast. He fondled it gently, testing its shape, its weight, its softness. "All you have to do is stay here with me. In bed."

"Oh, darling, I—" She gasped as he grazed his palm slowly over the tips of her breasts. "I can't...I have to go back to my suite to change clothes," she protested breathlessly.

His arms tightened around her midriff, and with a jerk, he rolled with her, bringing her over him and onto her back. Braced on his forearms, he grinned down into her startled face. "You don't need clothes for what I have in mind."

His tone was teasing, but his dark eyes smoldered with desire. Despite the night they had just spent together, the look kindled fires deep inside Joanna and brought hot color flooding into her cheeks. "And just what is it you have in mind?" she asked, striving for lightness.

"Oh ... a good morning kiss, a room service breakfast—" he lowered his head and nuzzled the tender underside of her jaw "—a leisurely shower, together if we can both fit into that cubicle..." Joanna gasped as excitement shot through her, and she felt him smile against her neck, but he continued with his list of activities in the same casual tone. "... a little talking, a lot of loving, maybe a nap later." He raised his head and gave her a slow, sexy smile. "Not necessarily in that order, you understand."

Simmering heat flooded Joanna's body and pulses throbbed. "You have a one-track mind, Sean Fleming," she scolded with mock indignation, but her voice was low and husky, not quite steady.

"Uh-hmm," he admitted with such cheerful relish Joanna couldn't help but laugh.

But her laughter faded quickly as Sean's sensual gaze grew more intense. His night-black eyes roamed over her face, touching her lips, her flushed cheeks, the silky arch of her brows, before finally meeting hers. Joanna felt her bones melt beneath that hot, hungry stare.

"Don't go," he urged in a low, raspy voice. "Spend the day with me, darling."

Love welled up inside Joanna, swelling her chest with a sweet pressure. How had she ever gotten this lucky? she wondered. Placing her palms in a light caress along his cheeks, she rubbed her thumbs over his chin and the corners of his mouth and smiled tenderly when she felt the rasp of whiskers against her skin. "There's nothing in this world that I want more," she vowed in the softest of voices. "But first, I really must go back to my suite. I'll just be gone a few minutes."

Sean looked as though he were about to argue, then his gaze dropped to her mouth. "All right. But first I get my good-morning kiss."

Joanna saw the determined glint in his eyes. "Now, Sean, I don't think—"

He silenced her weak protest with his mouth. The kiss was warm and firm and deeply arousing. With exquisite, gentle insistence, Sean's lips moved back and forth over hers, stoking the fires, coaxing, expertly building her passion to a fever pitch. Soon Joanna was moving restlessly, breathing hard, her hands clutching at his shoulders.

All thought of leaving fled.

Sean's mouth left hers to trail a line of kisses downward. "Your breasts are so beautiful," he murmured against the pearly flesh. "So white and firm."

"They're...they're too small," Joanna gasped in weak denial and shuddered as his tongue lathed the rosy crest and left it beaded in desire.

"No, they're perfect. They just fit my hand," he insisted, curling his fingers around the satiny swell to prove his claim. His mouth closed around the rosy crest and he drew on her with a slow, sweet suction.

Clutching his hair, Joanna moaned and arched her back. She blushed hotly all over as he lavished attention on both her breasts, but his whispered accolades filled her with pride and joy.

The loving torment continued as his hand swept down over her abdomen and smooth, slightly concave stomach to the triangle of silky curls at the apex of her thighs. Without hesitation, he homed in on his target. "You're lovely here, too." His stroking fingers underscored his words. "So moist and warm and welcoming."

He made her feel beautiful. Womanly. Desired. Unselfishly, he adored her with his fingertips, his eyes glowing as he noted what pleased her, what made her eyes go soft and smoky. With exquisite care and tenderness, he stroked her feminine portal, giving her untold pleasure, sending her to the edge of mindless passion.

Joanna shuddered, her fingers digging into the taut muscles in the back of his neck and shoulders as he found the core of her womanhood and kneaded it gently with his thumb.

"Oh, Sean. Sean. Sean." His name was a breathless chant on her lips. A plea. A command. A siren's song. Obeying its call, Sean moved over her, taking her mouth in an ardent kiss as he fitted his hips to hers, his firmness to her pliancy.

Joanna wrapped her long legs around him, her soft cries of love filling the room, as with long loving strokes, he took her to that glorious realm she had known only in his arms.

The end came quickly, an explosive burst of rapture that left them both spent and trembling. Eyes closed, Joanna held Sean close and ran her hands languidly over him, absently brushing away the sheen of moisture from his back. Their hearts thundered in unison. Their lungs labored for air.

After a moment Sean summoned the energy to move and rolled from her onto his side. Draping an arm possessively across her waist, he closed his eyes and kissed her shoulder. "Mmm, what a heavenly way to say good morning," he mumbled drowsily.

"Uh-huh. And a very effective method of getting your own way," Joanna scolded.

She tweaked the hair on Sean's chest, but he merely grunted and burrowed deeper into the pillow, neither admitting nor denying her accusation. Smiling, Joanna watched him, her eyes tracing lovingly over his handsome face, exulting in its nearness. She felt saturated with happiness, utterly content.

For a time Sean did not move or speak, and Joanna thought he had fallen asleep until suddenly he emitted a long, agonized sound.

"What is it? What's the matter?"

"I just thought of something."

"What?"

"Matt's going to kill me," he groaned.

"Matt?" Joanna's amused chuckle held surprise and skepticism. "Don't be silly. Why should Matt care?"

"Because you're part of his family now, and Matt Drummond takes care of his own." Sean opened his eyes and looked at her quizzically. "Didn't you know that?"

Joanna shook her head. "But ... but I'm his stepdaughter, not his daughter."

"To a man like Matt, there's very little difference. And men tend to get a bit paranoid and protective where their daughters are concerned. Hell, if he'd known about that lecherous professor of yours he'd probably have given the man the beating he deserves."

Joanna raised up on one elbow and gazed at Sean with eyes as round as saucers. "Really?" It stunned her to think that Matt would be that fiercely protective of her. Would her own father have resorted to physical violence on her behalf? Joanna doubted it. Oh, he would have sought revenge by some covert method, but he would not have actually soiled his hands on the man.

"Yes, really," Sean assured her, smiling at her astonished expression. "Matt happens to be very fond of you. When you graduated from college with honors he was as proud as punch. He even cut short a meeting with the Secretary of State to make it to your graduation ceremony."

Dazed, Joanna fell back on her pillow and stared up at the ceiling. She and Matt had made their peace with each other years ago. Since that time she had come to admire and respect him, to like him as a person, but for some reason their relationship had never developed beyond a sort of cautious, polite friendship. Certainly she had never suspected that Matt harbored any paternal feelings for her.

But, as Joanna thought about it, a pleased smile began to grow on her face. She found that being regarded as a cherished daughter by a man like Matt Drummond was very pleasant indeed. It gave her a warm feeling she hadn't known since her father's death.

"Why are you so surprised?" Bracing on his elbow, Sean propped his head in his hand. With deep absorption, he watched his other hand chart the long curve of her hip and thigh.

His intent gaze made Joanna suddenly aware of her nakedness. Though she knew it was ludicrous, all at once she felt painfully shy. Rising partway, she reached for the sheet to cover herself.

"Oh, no you don't." Sean chuckled wickedly and pushed her back down onto the pillow with gentle but firm pressure. "It's too late for modesty now, my sweet. Besides, there's not an inch of that beautiful body I haven't already seen. Or kissed." Holding her gaze, he smiled a slow, devilish smile and skimmed his hand up over her waist and the gentle flare of her ribs. "Now go ahead, answer my question."

"Matt . . . Matt and I got off to a bad start four years ago," Joanna replied unsteadily. She drew several deep breaths and struggled to ignore that marauding hand, the heel of which was now pressing rhythmically against the side of her breast. "We, uh, we worked it out, and we get along fine now, but, well . . . I, uh, I guess I just never expected him to care all that much about what happened to me."

"It's not really so surprising, when you consider how much he loves your mother. You're Claire's daughter, a part of her, and in Matt's book that makes you a very special person." Sean abandoned his sensual teasing and touched her chin with his fingertips, turning her head toward him. Smiling tenderly, he looked at her in a way that made Joanna's breath catch and said in a low, husky voice, "And I happen to agree."

He placed an infinitely soft, lingering kiss on her mouth, then pulled her close and settled her head on his shoulder. Joanna nestled against him with a happy sigh. Feeling utterly content, she absently threaded her fingers through the forest of black hairs on his chest, and after a moment a pleased smile began to build on her face. "Matt is crazy about Mother, isn't he?" she said, in dreamy satisfaction.

"Yeah, he is that," Sean agreed drowsily.

"It's amazing when you think about it. Matt knew Mother for over fifteen years and to tell you the truth, I don't think he even liked her. Then all at once they fell head over heels in love and got married." She chuckled at the memory. "That really knocked some people for a loop, especially the Washington social leaders. For years

Matt had been D.C.'s most eligible, most elusive bachelor.''

"Well, your mother is a special lady. She's beautiful, she's bright, she's nice and just about as classy as they come. It's easy to understand why Matt fell so hard." Sean's chest shook, and beneath her ear, Joanna heard the soft rumble of laughter before it left his throat. "Hell," he admitted with a little snort of rueful amusement, "I came very close to falling in love with Claire myself."

Joanna went perfectly still. Her heart began to pound with slow, painful thuds and a sick sensation curled in the pit of her stomach. Sean? In love with Claire? Oh, God!

A quivering hurt started deep in the center of Joanna's being and spread outward, encompassing every cell, every molecule. Suddenly she felt cold and achy and very fragile. She had to get out of there. Now! Before she shattered.

"Hey. Where are you going?" Sean asked in surprise when she firmly eased out of his embrace and sat up.

Joanna blushed when she saw her dress. The fluttery silk chiffon creation lay on the floor where she had stepped out of it the night before, like a circular puddle of pastel flowers. Beside it lay her bikini panties and her tiny gold mesh evening bag. The lacy garter belt and stockings were draped wantonly over the chair, just as they had landed when he stripped them from her and tossed them aside.

Keeping her back to Sean, Joanna picked up her panties and stepped into them, then hastily drew on the wrinkled chiffon gown. "I've got to go back to my suite," she said over her shoulder, struggling to keep her voice calm. "I told you that a while ago."

Sean exhaled a resigned sigh. "Okay, honey, if it'll make you feel better, go ahead. I'll take a shower and order breakfast while you're gone. What would you like?"

"Anything. It doesn't matter." After retrieving her purse from the floor, Joanna snatched up her garter belt and stockings and rolled them into a tight ball. With hurried, jerky movements, she stepped into her shoes and headed for the door. She was reaching for the knob when Sean's arms encircled her from behind.

"Hey, not so fast," he chided huskily in her ear. "You're not getting out of here without telling me goodbye." He kissed the sensitive spot he had discovered on her neck and playfully batted her lobe with his tongue. Moving closer, he settled his middle more firmly against her derriere.

Through the thin chiffon of her gown, Joanna could feel his manhood pressing against her. He had come to her naked, and his warmth and his male scent enveloped her. She closed her eyes briefly, swamped with conflicting feelings of despair and longing.

His splayed hands were gliding caressingly over her midriff and abdomen. Joanna grasped his forearms to stop the tantalizing motion. "Sean, please," she scolded with a feigned lightheartedness that required a great effort of will. "If you don't stop that I'll never get out of here."

"Promise?"

"Sean!"

"Oh, all right."

He reached up to turn her face to the side for his kiss. His muscular forearm fit snugly between her breasts, against her skin above the low cut gown. Their lips clung sweetly in the softest of kisses that served to increase her inner trembling. When he lifted his head Sean looked deep into her eyes and whispered, "I'll see you in a half hour. Now go, before I change my mind."

Unable to speak, Joanna nodded and fled.

Magnificently naked, Sean stood in the middle of the floor for several seconds after the door closed behind her, a bemused smile tugging at his mouth. Feet apart, hands on his hip bones, he threw his head back and chuckled at the ceiling, a soft masculine rumble of amused self-derision. Joanna. Joanna Andrews. If anyone had told him, even a week ago, that she would become the center of his world he would have said they were crazy. Yet, that was exactly what she was. She had gotten under his skin, become as necessary to him as food and drink, as breathing. Even now he had to stifle the urge to stomp out after her and drag her back.

God, Fleming. You've really got it bad if you can't bear to let her out of your sight for only a few minutes. Shaking his head, he turned and started for the shower.

All the arguments he had given her for not getting involved were still valid, he reminded himself as he adjusted the water and stepped beneath the spray. He was too old for her. Too experienced. Their backgrounds were totally different. Though not exactly poor, he certainly wasn't in her financial bracket. And Claire and Matt would probably have a walleyed fit when they discovered that he and Joanna were lovers. Sean rubbed the bar of soap over his chest and shoulders, creating mounds of creamy lather. His face wore a pensive smile. Hell, Matt would probably get out his shotgun.

It was a daunting list of negatives, but this morning they just didn't seem all that important. He squirted shampoo into his palm, closed his eyes and scrubbed his ebony curls until they squeaked. If he was going to have breakfast delivered before Joanna returned he would have to hurry. Sticking his head under the shower spray, he hummed happily as the bubbles streamed down over his face and sleek, wet body.

Damn, I feel terrific!

Joanna felt wretched. Confused, sick at heart, she paced the floor of her sitting room. Though she tried to banish it, Sean's casual comment played over and over in her mind. *"I came very close to falling in love with Claire myself."*

How close was close? A mild attraction? An infatuation? A burning passion? What?

Joanna stopped by the window and stared out at the ocean gliding by. They were cruising leisurely toward Jamaica. This was a day at sea, a day she should be enjoying with Sean, not hiding out in her room harboring these nasty suspicions. But she couldn't help it. They gnawed at her unmercifully.

Looking back, a lot of things were clearer now: the long, hard hours Sean had devoted to Claire's senatorial campaign four years ago—hours that had kept him in almost constant contact with her, the way he had been so protective of Claire when Matt had walked out on her, the fondness in his eyes whenever he looked at her mother. At the time Joanna had merely thought that he was an extremely good and conscientious press secretary, doing his job. Instead, it was unrequited love.

Recalling the crush she'd had on Sean then, Joanna gave a bitter little laugh. She crossed her arms over her middle and gazed, unseeingly, at the sky. Lord! No wonder Sean hadn't even noticed that she was alive. He'd only had eyes for Claire.

Not that she blamed him. Her mother was, then and now, a beautiful woman. She was also intelligent, articulate and very strong, yet she possessed that soft femininity that fascinated and charmed both men and women.

Joanna knew perfectly well that there had never been anything between her mother and Sean, and that whatever Sean had felt, he had kept to himself. Claire was totally, passionately, irrevocably in love with Matt. Yet, every time Joanna thought of Sean loving her mother she felt a spurt of anger that terrified her.

Making a harsh sound, Joanna turned away from the window and raked both hands through her silky hair, slicking it back away from her face and pressing her palms flat against her temples. Lord, she didn't want to feel this way. Especially not about her mother. It had taken a long time and a lot of growing up on Joanna's part for her to appreciate Claire. In the past few years they had developed a close and loving relationship, and Joanna didn't want anything to jeopardize that.

She wanted very much to believe that Sean really cared for her, that what they had shared the night before had been special, but she couldn't help but wonder if she had just been a substitute for her mother. If the love that Matt felt for Claire could be extended to include her, then why couldn't Sean's?

Tormented by the thought, Joanna paced faster. With every circuit of the room her movements grew more and more agitated. "I will not run the risk of being used," she muttered forcefully, fighting back tears of despair. "Nor will I allow myself to be eaten up with jealousy. I *won't!*"

The vow had barely left her lips when the telephone rang, making Joanna jump. She swung around and stared at it as though it were a coiled snake about to strike. It shrilled repeatedly, but Joanna made no move to answer it. She knew who was calling.

When the insistent ringing finally stopped, Joanna walked to the sofa and sat down. As she had known he would, within seconds Sean knocked on the door.

"Joanna? Joanna are you in there?" She didn't reply, and after a few seconds he knocked again, harder this time. "Joanna?"

He tried several more times and though she could detect the growing note of concern in his voice, she remained still and quiet. When at last the pounding stopped Joanna leaned her head back against the leather sofa and closed her eyes. Tears squeezed from between her lids and her chin quivered. Her heart felt like a lead weight in her chest.

Joanna stayed in her room for the remainder of the day. Hiding. Hurting. Sean knocked on her door and called several more times, but she gritted her teeth and ignored him. She paced and cried. She lay on her bed and cried. She stared out at the sea and thought and cried. Over and over she told herself she was doing the right thing, but it didn't help.

Lunch time came and went and Joanna didn't notice, but by evening her empty stomach was beginning to protest. Briefly, she considered ordering dinner in her suite, but quickly dismissed the idea. They would be cruising for another week yet. Sooner or later she was going to have to face Sean.

Deciding that there was no point in prolonging the inevitable, she bathed her puffy eyes in cold water, applied her makeup carefully, donned a confidence-building strapless yellow voile dress and headed for the dining room.

Hoping that Sean would not make a scene in front of the others, she deliberately arrived late. It was a futile hope, for he bounded up out of his chair the moment he saw her. His expression held not even a trace of his usual nonchalance.

"Where the hell have you been?"

"In my room."

"In your room!" She couldn't have shocked him more if she had said she'd been on the moon.

"Yes." Joanna gave him a cool look and slipped into her chair, leaving him standing there simmering impotently. As she calmly shook out her napkin and draped it across her lap she could feel his incredulous gaze raking over her.

"I knocked on your door several times, and I called your room every half hour. Why the hell didn't you answer?"

"Sean, please, don't stand there shouting. People are beginning to stare."

"I don't give a good—" He bit off the profane curse he was about to utter and glanced around at the avid expressions on the faces of their table companions. A muscle rippled along his clenched jaw. With barely controlled violence, Sean flung himself back into his chair and leaned close to Joanna. "If you're worried about me making a scene, then you'd damn well better give me some answers, and fast. Why didn't you answer your door or your phone? For that matter, why the hell didn't you come back to my cabin like you were supposed to?"

"Sean!" Joanna turned a deep pink and cast an anxious glance at the others.

"Answer me."

"I had a headache. I didn't feel like talking."

"And you couldn't have picked up the phone and told me that? Dammit, Joanna, I spent the whole day searching this ship for you. I've been frantic. I was beginning to think you'd fallen overboard."

"I'm sorry, but I really don't feel that I have to explain myself to you or anyone. Now, if you don't mind, I'd like to order dinner. I'm starving. I haven't eaten all day."

Sean seethed. Joanna could feel the fury radiating off him in waves, and she held her breath, sure that he was going to explode at any moment. Apparently so did the others, for no one moved or spoke.

After what seemed like a small eternity, Sean said tightly between clenched teeth, "All right. We'll have dinner. But afterward you and I are going to have a talk."

The silence around the table was so tense it fairly hummed. At first Mary tried to make small talk but everyone was so ill at ease, after a while she gave up. Despite a day without food, Joanna's appetite was non-existent, and she did little more than move her food around on her plate. Sean didn't even pretend to be interested in eating. Throughout the meal he merely watched Joanna through narrowed eyes and sipped from the glass of bourbon beside his plate. The close scrutiny twanged her nerves like a plucked string.

The others finished quickly and began to excuse themselves. When Mary announced that she and Charles were going to the show in the Caribbean Lounge, Joanna made a last-ditch attempt to avoid the confrontation that was brewing between her and Sean.

"That sounds like fun. Do you mind if I join you?" she asked ingenuously, rising to her feet as they did.

Mary and Charles exchanged dubious looks, but they were spared the necessity of a reply when Sean said succinctly, "I mind."

Joanna sputtered, but before she could voice an objection he rose and clamped his hand firmly around her arm. With a nod and a terse, "Excuse us" for the Wrights, he turned and all but frog marched Joanna from the dining room.

Without a word, he led her down the stairs to their deck. She shot him a cool glare when he stopped outside the door to her suite. "You surely don't expect me to invite you in?"

"We need someplace private to talk. It's either this or my cabin. The choice is yours."

Joanna gritted her teeth in silent frustration, but after a moment, dug into her purse for her key.

"All right, now I want to know just what you think you're doing," Sean demanded the moment they stepped into the room, and the door clicked shut behind them.

"I don't know what you're talking about," Joanna replied haughtily.

"I'm talking about this little game of hide-and-seek we've been playing all day. What the hell was that all about?"

"I'm not playing a game."

"Then what do you call it?"

"I told you, I had a headache."

Sean's one word reply was blunt, to the point and crude.

Joanna sucked in her breath. "All right! That's it!" she huffed. "Just get out. This discussion is over."

Spinning around on her heel, she started to march toward the bedroom, but Sean grabbed her wrist and whirled her back. Momentum sent her stumbling forward until she collided with his chest. Sean's arms encircled her, and he thrust his furious face so close to hers their noses were almost touching.

"That's what you think," he growled. "You're not going anywhere, Joanna, until I have some answers. Last night we became lovers, and this morning you pull a disappearing act and now you're giving me the deep freeze treatment. I want to know why!"

Joanna braced her forearms against his chest and strained to break his hold, but she only succeeded in bringing their lower bodies into even closer contact. Though Sean's face remained stern the glint in his eye told her he was aware of the intimacy and enjoying it. After the miserable day she'd had, that was the final straw. Joanna's temper shot up like a Roman candle on July Fourth.

"All right! I'll tell you why," she all but shouted. "I decided that I don't want to be a substitute for another woman, that's why!"

"Another... Substi... What the hell are you ranting about? What other woman?"

"My mother, that's who."

Sean's arms fell away from her, and he took a couple of staggering steps backward. Mouth agape, he stared at her in blank shock. Then, to Joanna's utter astonishment, he threw back his head and roared with laughter.

Chapter Eleven

Don't you dare laugh at me, Sean Fleming!"

"I ca...I ca-can't...help it," Sean choked out between the deep, rumbling guffaws.

Joanna was torn between anger and hurt, but anger soon won out. She blinked furiously to keep the tears at bay, and stuck her chin out at a pugnacious angle, though it still quivered uncontrollably. "There's nothing funny about this situation."

Finally, either her irate tone or the wounded look on her face got through to Sean. With a struggle, he managed to control his mirth, but remnants of it were still visible in his twinkling eyes and twitching mouth. "*You* are what's funny, sweetheart. Good grief, Joanna, where on earth did you get the idea that I'm in love with Claire?"

"From you."

"*Me!*"

"Yes. You admitted as much this morning. When we were talking about how strange it was that Matt and Mother fell in love, after knowing each other for years, you said that you had come very close to falling in love with her yourself."

"So, because of that innocent comment, you think that I've been carrying a torch for Claire all this time?" The amusement faded from Sean's face, and a tiny frown tugged between his brows. A hint of sadness touched his expression. "And because I couldn't have her, I settled for you, is that it? You actually think I'm the type of man who would do that?"

Joanna wilted and heaved a dispirited little sigh as some of the fight went out of her. "Oh, not consciously," she said, with a forlorn twitch of her mouth. "But unrequited love can drive us to do strange things. I ought to know. I followed you on this cruise on the flimsiest of excuses."

Leaning back against one of the leather easy chairs, Sean crossed his arms over his chest and smiled crookedly. "So, you admit to that now, do you? And do you realize that you've as much as admitted that you're in love with me, and have been for a while?" Sean tipped his head to the side and cocked one brow. "Did you have a crush on me four years ago, Joanna? Was I too blind to notice?"

"Sean, please, don't tease me," Joanna pleaded, giving him a desperate look and blinking against a fresh rush of tears. "Not now."

"Ah, sweetheart, don't cry." Sean crossed the space between them and took her hands. As he searched her unhappy face his expression was a mixture of tenderness and exasperation. "Joanna listen to me. I am *not* in love with Claire. Almost falling in love is one heck of a long way from actually falling in love.''

"But you were attracted to her, weren't you?'' Joanna wanted to kick herself for asking. It was like probing a sore tooth with your tongue: you knew it was going to hurt but you couldn't resist doing it.

Sean sighed heavily. "Yes, I was. Claire is one heck of a woman. And yes, I'll admit that *if* things had been different, *if* there hadn't been Matt, and *if* your mother had been attracted to me, it might have happened. But, darling, those are all very big if's. I haven't been pining away from unrequited love for the past four years. It never went that far. The truth is, I'm glad things turned out as they did. Matt is my best friend, and your mother runs a close second. I'm happy for them.''

Catching her bottom lip between her teeth, Joanna looked at him worriedly. A lingering trace of doubt mingled with the hope and longing in her hazel eyes. "Are you sure?''

"Positive.''

Sean raised his hand and traced the elegant line of her cheek and jaw. Then he threaded his fingertips through the silky hair at her temple. His thumb skated lightly back and forth over the tiny mole at the corner of her mouth. "Oh, Joanna, you goose. I can't believe you've put us through this miserable day over that one offhand remark. After what we shared last night, how could you possibly think that I was in love with another woman?''

Covering his hand with hers, Joanna pressed her cheek against his palm and closed her eyes wearily. "I don't know. I...I guess I still can't quite believe that this is happening. Us, I mean. I suppose, deep down, it seems too good to be true, and I keep expecting something to go wrong.''

Sean felt his heart constrict. An overwhelming tenderness gripped him as he studied the fragile beauty of her face, the delicate sweep of dark lashes against pale skin. Lord, she was so sweet, so guileless. He couldn't remember ever feeling such a strong desire to protect a woman, to cherish, to claim her for his own.

Sean slipped his thumb beneath her chin and tipped her head up. "Joanna, look at me," he commanded, and Joanna's lids drifted open. She gazed up at him with soft, luminous eyes filled with love, and he felt as though his insides were melting. "There is only you," he said in a soft, rough whisper. "There will be only you. Here, on this ship, and when we return home to Washington. You're the only woman I need. The only one I want."

It was more of a commitment than he had ever made before, but strangely, with this woman, it just wasn't enough. He wanted more. Wanted to give more. "Joanna, I . . ." He hesitated, his chest aching with a yearning pressure as he stared down at her. She was waiting, watching him with her heart in her eyes, and suddenly his own widened. "I love you." He said the words slowly, as though stunned by the discovery, his face blank with amazement.

And then, softer, surer, in a voice deepened by awe, "I love you."

Joanna sucked in her breath. For a timeless moment she stared up at him, her eyes slowly filling with tears. "Oh, Sean," she choked out unsteadily through quivering lips. "Do you mean that? Please don't say it unless it's true. I—"

"Shhh. Shhh, sweetheart." He placed his fingers over her mouth to stop the anguished flow of words and looked at her tenderly. "I mean it. It took me by surprise, but I do love you, Joanna. Very much."

"Oh, Sean." She struggled valiantly to contain the tumultuous storm of emotion that buffeted her, but it was impossible. Her mouth and chin wobbled as tears spilled over and trickled down her cheeks, and with a joyous little cry she flung herself against him, burying her face against his chest and wrapping her arms tightly around his lean middle.

Sean held her close and rocked her gently. With a tender smile, he rubbed his chin against the top of her head as she laughed and cried at the same time. "I'm going to assume that you're crying for joy. Otherwise my ego is going to take a hell of a beating."

Joanna sniffed and hiccuped. Leaning back within his embrace, she laughed self-consciously and wiped at her cheeks with the back of her hands. "Of course I am. Oh, Sean," she said in an emotion-packed voice, looking up at him with melting eyes. "I've loved you for so long, but I never really believed that you would ever love me back. You never seemed interested in a serious relationship, even though there have been many beautiful, glamorous women in your life—"

"Hey." He stopped the flow of words with a quick, breath-stealing kiss. When it ended he smiled into her eyes. "That's all over now. I was never serious about any of them, because I didn't love them. I do love you, Joanna. Very much."

She cupped his face between her palms. "And I love you, darling," she whispered tremulously.

Their lips met in a slow, sweet kiss. Joanna twined her arms around his neck and held him close, her heart swelling with a pleasure so intense it was almost pain. Sean's arms enclosed her, binding her gently but firmly to him, flattening her breasts against his chest. His hand splayed over her buttocks, pressing her feminine cradle tight against the hard ridge of his arousal. Heat sizzled between them. Their aching bodies throbbed. Taut muscles quivered. And still the tender kiss went on and on.

When Sean's lips left hers to trail moistly over her cheek Joanna stroked her hands over his shoulders and neck and tunneled her fingers in the thick hair at his nape. A shudder rippled through her when his tongue wetly traced the delicate swirls in her ear, and she sighed. "Oh, darling, this seems too wonderful to be true. I'm terrified I'm going to wake up and find it was all a dream."

"This is no dream," he murmured, nibbling a wet path down the side of her neck. "This is real. I intend—" his lips pressed against the pulse at the base of her throat "—to show you just how real."

Sean's mobile mouth blazed a tormenting trail back up over the arch of her throat, lingering a moment to nuzzle the tender skin on the underside of her jaw. Then his lips claimed hers again in a slow, drugging kiss that made her senses swim, her knees go weak.

Breaking the thrilling contact suddenly, Sean scooped her up in his arms. He paused, holding her high against his chest, his dark, fiery gaze searing over her flushed face with a possessiveness that made Joanna's skin tingle. "It may take me all night," he said huskily.

Joanna looped her arms around his neck and smiled. "I hope so."

Sean growled, and his mouth came down hard on hers. Without breaking the thrilling contact, he headed for the bedroom with long, purposeful strides.

The next few days passed in a haze of sheer happiness. They were so perfect, Joanna still had trouble convincing herself she wasn't dreaming it all.

In the evenings after dinner they went dancing or saw a show in the main lounge, or just strolled the decks, arm in arm, before returning to either Joanna's suite or Sean's cabin. Their nights were filled with passionate loving so intensely beautiful it left them both shaken and awed, but their hunger for each other went beyond the physical. For hours, lying in each other's arms while the ship rocked gently beneath them, they talked quietly, sharing secrets, hopes, joys and disappointments.

The daytime hours were spent ashore on the islands. Together, Joanna and Sean explored Ochos Rios and toured Jamaica's heavily cultivated coastal lowlands and valleys and the inland limestone plateau. On Grand Cayman they visited a turtle farm and strolled hand in hand for hours down the beautiful seven-mile beach.

The ship's next port of call was Cozumel, where Joanna and Sean spent the morning strolling through the quaint shops before succumbing to the lure of the beach. With rented snorkeling equipment, they explored the turquoise water for over an hour. Then, like two children, they indulged themselves in a boisterous game of tag, splashing and dunking each other mercilessly. Finally, exhausted, they hauled themselves out of the water and collapsed on the large towels they had spread on the sand.

Sean flopped down on his back and flung his forearm over his eyes. "Whew! I may never move again. Keeping up with a sweet young thing like you is tough on an old man."

Joanna dropped onto her knees beside him and began to towel dry her hair. "Oh, come on, you're not that old. Don't tell me a little shopping and swimming has you tuckered."

Rolling his arm up a quarter turn, Sean gave her a long, sizzling look and drawled, "It's not so much the shopping and swimming, as all those strenuous nights."

"Complaining?" Joanna asked with a sultry smile.

Sean's face softened, and he reached out and lifted a drop of water from the end of her nose with his fingertip. "Hardly," he said huskily.

Joanna took his hand and brought it to her mouth. Holding his gaze, she kissed the end of his finger tenderly.

"Ouch!" Sean yelped when she nipped the pad, and Joanna laughed throatily, the sound full of delight and mischief and sensual promise.

"You little devil, you—"

"Oh, look," Joanna cried, cutting him off as she sprang to her feet. "There's someone selling ice-cream cones." She looked at him eagerly and began to search through her terry cloth beach bag for some money. "You want one?"

Sean's smile was indulgent. "I think I'll pass. But you go ahead."

"Okay. I'll be right back."

Rolling to his side, Sean propped his head against his palm and watched her trot away toward the vendor's stand. Subtly, his smile changed to one of masculine enjoyment as he admired her narrow, tapered back, the cute derriere, the firm lithe curves of her legs.

Sean was still amazed by the feelings that swamped him every time he looked at Joanna: love, pride, jealousy, a violent possessiveness. He'd never felt like that about a woman before. He'd liked many, been fond of several. A few he had even thought he loved, but it hadn't been like this. Never like this.

For the past few years a vague feeling of discontent had been slowly growing in him. As little as three weeks ago he had been besieged with doubts, and had felt restless and unsettled, unsure of what he wanted out of life, personally or professionally. No longer.

He knew now exactly what had been missing from his life: love, commitment, having that one special someone to share your triumphs and defeats, your joys and griefs. And there was no doubt in his mind or his heart that for him, that someone was Joanna.

Neither was there any longer doubt about which direction he wanted his professional life to take. The long-term goals he'd been working toward for years were still worthwhile. And now that he'd found what he'd unconsciously been searching for, he was eager to pursue them.

Joanna had her ice-cream cone and was strolling back at a leisurely pace. Sean smiled as he watched her pink tongue lick the fast melting sweet. His eyes ran down her slim, willowy body, deliciously revealed in the skimpy bikini, noting the way her hips swung with unconscious provocation, and he felt his body tighten, his heart flood with emotion. She was innocence and sensuality, youthful eagerness and gritty determination, girlish appeal and womanly allure.

And she was his.

At least, she would be soon if he had anything to say about it.

Joanna dropped down beside him and waved her cone under his nose. "Wanna bite?"

"Umm, but not of ice cream," Sean drawled, dropping his gaze to the soft swells of her breasts above the bikini bra. His black eyes glinted with drowsy sensuality, and as the flush spread up over Joanna's neck and shoulders his smile grew wicked.

"You're insatiable."

"Complaining?" he asked, in the same intimate tone she had used.

Joanna forgot all about her embarrassment as heat suffused her. When Sean looked at her that way she felt all tingly and weak. Her gaze went soft, and her voice dropped to a warm velvet pitch. "No. Not in the least." Holding her cone out to the side, she leaned close. "Since I can't do anything about that appetite of yours right now, maybe this will hold you until we get back to the ship."

Her mouth met his, open, sweet, soft. It was the gentlest of caresses, a mere touch, a delicate rubbing of flesh to flesh, yet its sensual impact was staggering. At the first touch Sean's heart slammed against his ribs and began to beat with a painful, heavy thud. Her tongue darted into his mouth, rubbed his and darted out again, and he shivered. She tasted of ice cream and salt water and woman. Of Joanna.

It was a taste he was becoming addicted to. Hungrily, he sought more. Over and over, without increasing the pressure of the kiss, he delved into the honeyed sweetness, plumbing the silken depths of her mouth thoroughly, slowly.

His hand slid up her braced arm to her shoulder, her neck. Lightly, he touched her jaw with the tips of his shaking fingers, then sank them into the damp hair behind her ear.

A squealing child ran by, followed by a yapping dog. They didn't hear them, or the faint swish of waves tumbling gently against the shore or the dry rattle of tatter

palms overhead. Their lips nibbled softly, rocked back
and forth, clung. Their breaths mingled. The sun beat
warmly against their damp flesh, but they felt only the
heat of passion that surged so hotly between them. Tor-
tuously, the soft kiss went on and on as taut muscles
quivered against the tender restraint.

Joanna's fingers crushed the waffle cone, and the
melting scoop of ice cream plopped to the sand.

Abruptly, Sean ended the kiss. Their gazes locked,
and for a moment they stared at each other in heated silence. A few strands of Joanna's hair lifted in the gentle
breeze. Their chests rose and fell as they drew in long,
shaky draughts of air. With every breath they inhaled the
smells of sand and sea, of warm flesh, of coconut-
scented tanning lotion.

A muscle twitched along Sean's jaw. Without warning, he grabbed Joanna's wrist and stood, dragging her
up with him. "Come on," he commanded in a tight,
strained voice, snatching up the towels and her beach
bag. "We're going."

"Where?" Joanna cried. He marched across the sand
with long, ground-eating strides, and she stumbled along
beside him.

"Back to the ship. This beach is too damned public
for what I have in mind."

In the taxi that took them back to the harbor they sat
on opposite sides of the seat, stiff and silent, looking
straight ahead, only their clasped hands touching. The
air between them was thick with awareness. Their bodies throbbed with anticipation.

When they boarded the ship there was almost no one
around. It was early afternoon, and most of the passengers and crew were still ashore. As they walked down the

long, deserted passageway it seemed to Joanna that they would never reach her suite.

The moment the door clicked shut behind them they were in each other's arms.

"Oh, Lord, sweetheart, I can't get enough of you," Sean panted in between tumultuous kisses.

"I know. I know," Joanna agreed breathlessly.

Her clutching hands roamed frantically over his back, before they slipped beneath the waistband of his swimsuit and grasped his firm buttocks. Sean growled and grabbed the string tie of her bikini top.

In a frenzy of snatching and tugging, they worked to rid each other of their skimpy beachwear. Within seconds Joanna's bikini bra went sailing across the room. It landed on a lamp shade and dangled provocatively. As their lips met in a long hungry kiss Sean's fingers worried the string ties at Joanna's hips. When they wouldn't budge he growled in frustration and gave them a sharp yank, and with the sound of popping thread, the ties tore away and the tiny scrap of material dropped to the floor to join the pile of towels at their feet.

With her thumbs hooked under the top edge of Sean's brief trunks, Joanna bent her knees and pushed them downward. Dropping lower, she scattered frantic kisses over his chest, his abdomen, his lean belly. Her teeth nipped at his protruding hipbone, and a violent shudder rippled through Sean. "Oh, God, Joanna," he groaned and clutched her hair with both hands as her tongue traced a wet line down his thigh.

Desperately, he bent and lifted her to her feet. For a taut instant they looked at each other in silence. Then she melted into his arms, and their soft moans of pleasure blended together as warm flesh met warm flesh. Their mouths melded in a searing kiss. Joanna raised up on her tiptoes and coiled her arms around his neck, shuddering at the gentle rasp of his chest hair against her tight, aching nipples.

Sean's hands roamed freely over her slender curves while he kissed her with a hungry passion, his tongue thrusting slowly, ardently, into the sweet darkness of her mouth.

A few feet away the bedroom beckoned, but neither could wait. With their mouths still fused together, they sank to the carpeted floor. There was a wild hunger raging in both of them. We're like greedy children, Joanna thought, and briefly she wondered at her own wantonness. But it didn't matter. Nothing mattered but their love, and the delicious pleasure it brought them.

They touched and explored and stroked until they could not stand it a moment longer. "Dear heaven, you make me wild," Sean declared huskily, as tremors wracked his body.

Clutching at his shoulders, Joanna urged him to her and sobbed, "Now, darling. Oh, please, now." and Sean moved between her thighs and slid into her. He thrust deep, loving her with a ferocity that should have frightened her, but didn't. Instead she matched it, and the compelling rhythm built, faster, stronger, spinning out of control, until there was a vast, ecstatic explosion that sent them hurtling into space.

And then they were falling . . . falling . . . falling. . . .

Joanna had no idea how long she floated in that delicious sea of languor, but all too soon Sean was nudging her. "Come on, sexy. That floor is okay in the throes of passion, but if you fall asleep there you'll be too sore to move later."

"But Sean," she groaned in protest as he hauled her to her feet. "I'm so sleepy."

"There's a perfectly good bed in the next room to nap on. But first we hit the shower."

Too lethargic to protest further, Joanna allowed him to bundle her into the shower stall. She was thoroughly scrubbed and shampooed, and after she returned the favor Sean backed her against the tile wall, and there beneath the warm spray, they made love again. Slowly. Deliciously.

A half hour later, curled against Sean's side in the king-size bed, Joanna smiled drowsily and ran her fingers through the mat of hair on his chest. She felt content, sated, complete. Settling her head more comfortably on his shoulder, she sighed with sheer pleasure and wondered if anyone else had ever been as happy as she was at that moment. Sean loved her. After all this time it seemed a miracle, and she clutched the knowledge to her like a coveted treasure.

Sean's arm encircled her, holding her close, his hand absently massaging her hip. He stared at the ceiling as he nuzzled her forehead with his chin. Tipping her head up, Joanna gazed at his handsome face, pensive now in repose, and smiled. "What are you thinking?" she asked quietly.

He looked down at her and smiled with his eyes. "Oh, I was just wondering if you would be happy as the wife of a senator," he said, so casually it took a moment for his words to register. Even then she wasn't sure she'd heard him right.

Her eyes grew wide and her heart began to pound. "Wh-what do you mean?"

Sean's grin flashed at her confusion, and just as quickly his expression grew serious. "I've decided to run

for that Senate seat, Joanna, and I want you by my side.
As my wife.''

Joanna's heart soared with joy. She looked at him in
amazement, her eyes slowly filling with tears as emotion choked her. "Oh, Sean," she managed finally in a
wobbling voice and reached up and touched his cheek
with her fingertips.

Capturing the hand, Sean brought it to his lips. The
teasing smile returned to his eyes as he lazily nipped her.
"Does that mean yes?"

Laughing and crying at the same time, Joanna flung
herself across his chest and covered his face with wet
kisses. "Yes! Yes! Yes!"

Sean laughingly accepted the exuberant smacks, but
after a moment he caught her head between his palms
and brought her lips down to his for a hard, searing kiss.
When it was over he eased her back and looked deep into
her eyes. "I love you," he said with such depth of feeling that Joanna almost started crying again.

Love filled her heart and overflowed, spilling like a
warm tide through her body. She blinked and gave him
a melting look. "And I love you, my darling," she said
with a tremulous smile. "Very much."

He wrapped his arms around her and pulled her
against his chest. For a long, soul-satisfying time they
held each other tight, absorbed in the wonder and beauty
of the moment.

"You never answered my question about being a senator's wife," Sean said after a while, idly rubbing his
hand up and down her back. "I want to make a bid for
the nomination, Joanna, but not if it's going to make
you unhappy."

Joanna's eyes popped open wide and she caught her
breath. Good Lord! She had been so wrapped up in

Sean, she hadn't even thought about the Senate race in days. Senator Hartwell would have a fit if he ever found out that she hadn't even brought up the subject.

She raised up on her forearms and looked at him. "Sean, I love politics. I'm delighted that you've decided to run. I don't mind campaigning. In fact, I love it. And I told you, I don't object to publicity, as long as it's for a good reason and isn't taken to an extreme, like it always has been with my mother."

"I was hoping you'd say that," Sean said, heaving a relieved sigh.

Tilting her head to one side Joanna looked at him quizzically. "When did you make up your mind about the race? And what caused you to accept? You seemed undecided a few weeks ago."

"Actually, I have you to thank for that."

"Me!"

Her astonished look drew a chuckle from Sean. "Yes, you. I came on this trip so I could put the whole thing out of my mind for a while, give it a rest, so that maybe I could put it into better perspective. With you on board, I was able to do just that." He lifted his head and planted a quick kiss on her mouth. "I haven't been able to think of anything but you since that first night."

Which, Joanna thought, thoroughly chagrined, *is exactly the opposite of what I was supposed to accomplish.*

"When I fell in love with you I realized that it was not my career, but the emptiness of my personal life that had been causing my dissatisfaction all along." His fingers stroked the side of her neck and played idly with the velvety rim of her ear. "Now that I have you, running for the Senate seems like a terrific idea. I'm itching to get back and get things rolling."

Joanna was deeply touched. And as she leaned down to kiss him she told herself that it was probably for the best that Sean had reached the decision on his own.

Chapter Twelve

Leaning close to the mirror, Joanna twirled the mascara wand over her lashes. When finished she brushed the merest touch of blusher across her cheeks, smoothed a deep bronze pink lipstick over her mouth, stepped back to survey the results and smiled. Without conceit, she knew that she looked better than she ever had in her life. Her eyes sparkled, and she glowed from within. Even her hair seemed to have taken on an extra shine. Love, Joanna decided, was the world's most fantastic beauty aid.

A glance at the travel clock beside her bed sent her scurrying to the closet. Sean would be back in a few minutes. A smile tilted Joanna's mouth as she riffled through the selection of evening wear. If she met him at the door in her robe they probably wouldn't make it to dinner at all. It was a tempting thought, but she resisted it and pulled out the bronze silk chiffon gown. Holding it in front of her, she twirled around to face the mirror.

The asymmetrical neckline draped low in the front and still lower in the back, the soft folds gathering together at her right shoulder with a rhinestone clip. Below the nipped-in waist, a full, floating skirt swirled around her calves like a misty cloud. It was a deceptively simple dress that managed to be both elegant and alluring.

Still, it wasn't very colorful, and Sean had liked that blue crepe she had worn the other night. He seemed to have a preference for blue. Cocking her head to one side, Joanna frowned at her reflection.

She was still debating a few minutes later when a knock sounded on the door.

"Oh, Sean, why couldn't you be late for once," Joanna moaned, tossing the dress on the bed, but her face was alight with eagerness as she hurried through to the sitting room.

"Sean, you said—" she began as she pulled open the door, only to come to an abrupt halt when she saw the uniformed young man standing there. "Oh! I'm sorry." Joanna pulled the lapels of her robe together and tightened the sash. "I thought you were someone else."

"This just came for you, Miss Andrews." The young man smiled and handed her an envelope, then disappeared down the companionway before she could do more than offer a stammered thank you.

Shutting the door, Joanna stared curiously at the envelope, turning it over in her hand. As she opened the flap and drew out the folded sheet of paper she crossed to the sofa and sat down. It was a radiogram, and when her eyes darted down to the name at the bottom of the page Joanna winced. It was from Senator Hartwell.

EXPECTED REPORT BEFORE NOW stop
PERSUADED FLEMING YET stop DO WHAT-
EVER NECESSARY stop MUST CONVINCE
HIM TO ACCEPT BACKING stop TIME IS
RIGHT stop CALL IN REPORT IMMEDI-
ATELY stop

SEN HARTWELL

Joanna sighed heavily. She should have expected it.
Her boss was not the most patient of men. She would
have to call him. But not tonight. There would be plenty
of time in the morning.

Reading through the message once more, Joanna felt
a pang of guilt over the rash plan. She realized now that
it had been incredibly arrogant and presumptuous of her
to even try to influence Sean. Still, she couldn't regret
coming on this trip.

Actually, everything turned out for the best all the way
around, she assured herself. Senator Hartwell and the
others were going to be pleased with Sean's decision, and
it was one he had come to all by himself.

Three sharp raps on the door brought Joanna's head
up, and her eyes began to sparkle. With a smile growing
on her lips, she hurried to answer the summons, stuffing the radiogram into the side pocket of her robe on the
way.

"Hello, darling. As you can see, I'm not quite ready,
but it won't take but a minute to put on my dress."

"No problem." In a smooth, languid move, Sean
stepped inside, closed the door and reached for her.
"Mmm, you smell good," he murmured, nuzzling his
face against the side of her neck. He mouthed the tender skin behind her ear. "And taste good." One hand

slid down her back and cupped her buttocks, bringing her tightly against him. "And feel good."

The satin robe molding her curves was an erotic enticement, and his hands glided over her back and hips in a sensuous caress. His touch worked its magic, filling her with a quivering heat. Already Joanna could feel her body going weak and malleable.

"Oh, no you don't," Joanna chuckled weakly, pushing against his chest when his nibbling kisses edged toward her mouth. "If you don't stop, we'll never get out of here, and I'm starving. Now behave yourself, and let me get dressed."

"Spoilsport," Sean growled, but when he lifted his head a devilish smile played around his mouth and his black eyes were gleaming.

It was a look that almost made her relent. Before she could succumb to its sensuous promise, Joanna pulled out of his arms and headed for the bedroom on shaky legs. "I won't be but a minute," she tossed over her shoulder.

Smiling, Sean watched her until she disappeared into the bedroom. He took a step toward the sofa, noticed the crumpled sheet of paper on the floor and stooped to pick it up. He glanced at it, saw immediately from the standard form that it was a radiogram and started to toss it onto the coffee table, when suddenly his own name seemed to leap off the page at him.

He stopped, and very carefully smoothed out the sheet. By the time he finished reading the brief message his jaw was tight, his eyes flint hard. Except for the hand that slowly crumpled the paper into a tight ball, he stood rigidly still in the middle of the floor.

He was still there when Joanna returned a few minutes later.

"Will this do?" Arms wide, she twirled around to give him a complete view, causing the bronze chiffon to flutter and float around her calves. He didn't reply. When she saw his face her smile faded, and she grew still. "Darling, what's wrong?"

"I think this dropped out of your pocket," he said in a hard, flat voice.

Joanna's puzzled gaze dropped to his outstretched hand, and when she saw what it held she paled. She raised stricken eyes to his face. "Sean, let me explain. I—"

"Oh, I think this is fairly self-explanatory. You're working for Senator Hartwell, aren't you?"

"Yes, I—"

"I seem to recall Matt telling me that he'd gotten you a job on some senator's staff, but I really didn't pay much attention. I figured you'd grow bored with it in a few months and quit." Sean gave her a hard, cold look, his hands bunching into tight fists at his sides. "It seems I was wrong. You must like your job one helluva lot to accept this kind of assignment."

"Sean, no! You don't understand. Yes, I came on this trip to try to talk you into running for office, but I didn't do it for Senator Hartwell. Actually, this whole thing was my idea. You see, I was hoping that you would give me a job on your staff if you won the nomination."

"Is that supposed to make me feel better?" Sean threw his head back and laughed mirthlessly at the ceiling. "Hell! I thought you had changed, but you haven't. You're still a scheming, manipulative spoiled brat. If there's something you want you just grab for it, with no thought for anyone else." He gave her a look of pure disgust and snarled bitterly, "You'll do anything to have your own way, won't you, Joanna? Including prostitute yourself." He threw the wadded up radiogram down on the coffee table so hard it bounced off and hit the wall, and Joanna jumped. "What was your plan? Seduce me? Soften me up with sex, then make your pitch? Well I saved you the trouble, didn't I?"

"No, Sean, please. It wasn't like that, I swear it."

She might as well not have spoken. Sean raked both hands through his hair and snorted. "Lord, and I thought you'd come on this cruise because you had a crush on me."

"I did!" Joanna cried. "All the other was just rationalization. Deep down, I just wanted to be with you. I love you."

"Oh, come off it, Joanna! I may be a fool, but I'm not that big a fool."

"Where are you going?" she cried when he stomped toward the door.

He paused with his hand on the knob and looked back at her with such fury that Joanna almost cringed. "Away from you," he spat. "Just as far as I can get on the confines of this ship. If we were back in the States I'd put miles between us."

Desolate, Joanna stared at the closed door for several seconds after it slammed behind him. Tears streamed down her face and sharp, wracking sobs began to shake her. She pressed her lips together and struggled to contain them, but it was no use. Bent from the waist, her arms wrapped tightly around her middle as though she were in mortal pain, Joanna staggered into the bedroom, flung herself across the bed and gave in to the emotional storm.

With her face buried against her crossed arms, she cried as though her heart would break. *Sean. Oh, Sean.* Harsh sobs shook her and hurt her throat, but she didn't try to fight them. The piteous, anguished sounds tore from her endlessly and reverberated in the quiet room. Tears flowed from her eyes in torrents, wetting her forearms until they were slick and forming a dark, spreading circle on the green silk bedspread. Her misery was soul deep. Fathomless.

The convulsive sobs went on and on until her chest ached and her throat was raw. At last, wrung dry, the wrenching cries gradually subsided to sniffles, then choppy sighs. Joanna rolled to her side and curled into the fetal position. She lay perfectly still and stared out the window through wet, spiky lashes, seeing nothing. Her eyes burned and her heart felt like a dead weight in her chest.

I've lost him. She closed her eyes and let the thought soak in, fighting back a renewed freshet of tears. She was going to have to get used to it. Accept it. *But, oh, God, it hurts so.*

It was her own fault, she knew, and the knowing merely made the pain worse. Sean had been right. She was an immature, spoiled child, always trying to manipulate things to suit herself. Joanna knew she wasn't guilty of the charges he'd thrown at her, but she *had* set out on this trip intent on influencing Sean's decision, on having her own way. That it hadn't been her real reason for coming didn't matter. Even on a subconscious level she had been behaving true to form: she loved Sean and wanted him, so she grabbed at the first convenient excuse and chased after him. When was she ever going to learn?

Joanna sat up slowly and wiped her wet cheeks with the heel of her hand. Her gaze dropped to the bronze chiffon twisted about her thighs, a silent reminder of the boundless joy she had felt only an hour ago. Joanna drew in a shuddering breath and swallowed hard to ease the painful constriction in her throat.

The sound of voices in the companionway told her that it was getting late. Passengers were returning from their day ashore to get dressed for the evening meal. They would be sailing soon.

Listlessly, Joanna's gaze wandered around the luxurious suite. I can't stay cooped up on this ship with Sean, she thought in sudden panic. After what they had shared, the thought of being so close to him, and yet so very far, was more than she could bear.

Shedding her robe on the way, Joanna hurried to the closet and pulled out the warm suit she had worn on the trip from D.C. to Florida. Despite the seducing sunshine outside, it was still late November in Washington.

When dressed, Joanna called the purser's office and asked for assistance. She dragged out her cases and spread them open on the bed. Working as fast as she could, with no regard whatever for neatness, she snatched the designer clothes from their hangers, scooped frilly lingerie from the drawers and stuffed them and the rest of her belongings into the bags.

Twenty minutes later, leaving the ship behind the burdened steward, Joanna paused once on the gangway and looked back. The past four days had been intensely beautiful, the most wonderful in her life. And for a brief, sweet time it had seemed as though all her dreams were about to come true. Biting the inside of her lip to force back the threatening tears, Joanna tilted her chin and continued down the steps to the dock. *Grow up, Joanna. Only a child or a fool believes that dreams come true.*

Was I too hard on her? The answer came a split second after Sean's mind posed the question. *No, dammit! I was not!* Yet, once again he slanted a glance at the empty chair beside him.

With grim determination, Sean cut another bite of steak, forked it into his mouth and chewed. Around him the table conversation flowed freely. Tony, Gloria and the Adamsons had spent the day at the beach while the Wrights had browsed the shops, and they were all in good spirits. Sean was barely aware of their presence. On arriving, they had asked him where Joanna was, and after his clipped, "I have no idea" they had taken the hint and left him alone.

God, he hurt. He hadn't known it was possible to hurt so much...and live. He hacked off another chunk of choice steak and rammed it into his mouth. It could have been sawdust for all he was aware of its succulent flavor. He loved her, dammit! And she'd just been using him.

The thought tore at his gut like a rusty grappling hook. Sean didn't want to believe Joanna was capable of that type of deceit. For hours he had been trying to convince himself that he was wrong, that he had overreacted, but he couldn't quite manage it. The evidence was just too strong. Hell, she'd even admitted why she came on this trip. He took a long swallow of the scalding coffee the waiter had just poured and hissed as it seared his throat.

Joanna was used to getting her way, but did she really want that damned job bad enough to sleep with him for it?

She did accept your proposal, remember, a niggling voice coaxed.

Yeah, but I had just told her that I was going to run for the Senate. She sure as hell wasn't going to turn me down at that point. As my fiancée, what would be more natural than for her to pitch in on my campaign?

But it's also possible that she really does love you.

Maybe. Against his will, Sean thought of the anguished expression on Joanna's face when he'd made those cutting remarks. *Maybe.*

A concern he didn't want to feel crept up on him when he shot another glance at her empty chair. Maybe he ought to check on her, just to be sure she was all right.

Oh, hell, Fleming, you've gone soft in the head over the woman. Sean tossed his napkin on the table, muttered a terse, "Excuse me" and strode from the dining room. *Joanna Andrews is a self-centered, grasping spoiled brat who will stop at nothing to get what she wants. She's probably just sulking.*

The thought brought his anger back full force. Jaw set, Sean loped down the stairs and headed for Joanna's suite. He'd be damned if he'd let her hide out in her room again. She'd created this mess, and she was going to face it.

Five minutes of banging on her door produced no results. Neither did a thorough search of the ship. For the next hour Sean checked out every shadowed corner on every deck, and poked his head into the theater, the casino and each of the nightclubs, but there was no sign of Joanna anywhere. By the time he had covered all the public areas twice he was growing concerned.

In desperation, he returned to her suite and banged on the door again. Just as he was about to give up, her room steward appeared.

"Are you looking for Miss Andrews, sir?" he inquired tentatively, looking a bit uneasy when he spied Sean's fierce expression.

"Yes. Have you seen her?"

"Miss Andrews is gone, sir. She got off the ship in Cozumel, just before we sailed."

"What! Are you sure?"

"Yessir. I carried her bags off myself. She said she had to fly home because of an urgent family matter."

In a blinding flash, Sean's concern turned to impotent fury. As civilly as he could, he thanked the man and stalked to his cabin. Cursing fluently, he paced the narrow confines. He checked his watch and made a quick, mental calculation. She'd gotten off the ship three hours ago. Even if she'd managed to get a flight out, she wouldn't have arrived in D.C. yet. But maybe, just maybe...

Sean yanked up the phone, dialed the operator, and told him he wanted to make a ship to shore call. In a matter of minutes he was listening to the ringing tones at the other end of the line and cursing impatiently when Matt answered.

"Hello."

"Matt, this is Sean. Is Claire all right?"

"Sean? What the... I thought you were at sea. And why the devil wouldn't Claire be all right?"

"Then she hasn't had the baby?"

"No. It's not due for another six weeks."

"I see." Sean paused to grit his teeth, then asked, "Have you heard from Joanna today?"

"Joanna? No. Why do you ask?"

"Because she jumped ship in Cozumel three hours ago. I'm assuming she's on her way home. I thought maybe she'd called to let you and Claire know."

"Why would she leave the cruise?" Matt barked. "What the devil is going on between you two?"

"It's a long story, Matt. One I think you'd better ask Joanna. Look, I need her phone number in D.C."

"What do you—"

"Dammit, Matt. This isn't the time to go into it. Just give me the number, okay."

Grumbling, Matt complied, and a few minutes later when Sean hung up he stalked to the porthole and stared out at the night-dark ocean. "Urgent family matter, my ass."

Joanna entered her Georgetown home on a blast of frigid air. The wind had whipped color into her pale cheeks but there were dark circles beneath her eyes and a look of fragility about her that no amount of long solitary walks could cure. She pulled the knit cap from her head and shook out the snowflakes. She took off her coat and hung it and the cap on the brass coatrack to dry, before making her way to the kitchen at the back of the house.

Mechanically, Joanna turned the fire on under the kettle, got out a thick mug and emptied a packet of cocoa into it. Waiting for the water to boil, she leaned her hip against the counter and glanced around the room. It was not as immaculate as it had been when Mrs. Hall had worked there as housekeeper. There were a few dishes in the sink, a wadded towel on the counter, an apron slung carelessly over the back of a chair. But Joanna was fiercely glad that she had let the woman go. The last thing she needed to contend with at this point was Nora Hall's stiff formality. On her own, Joanna was free to weep or rage as she wanted.

Joanna had inherited the housekeeper along with the house. It had been her parents' home. Claire had signed it over to her when she married Matt, claiming she no longer had a use for it, but Joanna suspected that the place held unhappy memories for her mother.

Joanna understood. She was learning just how painful memories could be.

She poured the boiling water into the mug, and the scent of chocolate rose with the curling wisps of steam. Cradling the mug in her hands, Joanna turned and was heading for the door when her gaze fell on the wall phone. She stopped and stared at it uncertainly. On arriving home two days ago she had unplugged it. She had needed the time and the solitude—craved it still—but Joanna knew she couldn't go on hiding forever. Her mother and Matt were expecting her back from the cruise today.

With a resigned sigh, Joanna walked to the phone and plugged it in. Before she could take a step away it rang, and she jumped, causing her cocoa to slosh over the side of the mug and splatter onto the tile floor.

Aggravated, Joanna snatched the receiver and snapped, "Hello."

"Joanna? Oh, thank God, you're home," Claire said with heartfelt relief. "Where in the world have you been? I've been calling for three days."

"You have? But why? I wasn't due back until today."

"Sean called us the night you left the ship," Claire said, and Joanna's heart jerked. "He's called every day since, and he's absolutely furious, Joanna."

Joanna was too stunned to reply. She hadn't expected that. She had thought, if he even noticed that she was gone, that he would be relieved.

"We assume that you two have had an argument," Claire said in a concerned voice, breaking into the taut silence.

"Yes, I guess you could say that." With a calm she was far from feeling, Joanna gave her mother an extremely watered-down version of what had happened.

When she had finished Claire murmured, "Oh, darling, I'm so sorry. But I can't say I'm surprised that Sean is angry. I was afraid something like this would happen. He's easygoing, but he's not a man who can be pushed or manipulated. And, though he doesn't lose his temper often, when he does it's explosive. What does surprise me, though, is that you let yourself get involved with him. I mean, darling, I like Sean very much. You know that. But...well...where women are concerned, he's not known for his constancy."

Joanna blinked back tears and forced out a blasé laugh. "Oh, well, you know how it is, Mother. You tend to get carried away with all that sun and surf and romantic, moonlit nights at sea. It was just a shipboard fling. No harm done." Joanna's heart felt as though it had split in two at the words, but they were necessary. The last thing she wanted was to cause Claire worry. Especially not now, with the baby due in just a few weeks.

"Well, maybe so. But as angry as he is, I doubt that Sean is going to pass it off that easily. If I were you I'd brace myself. I'm fairly certain he intends to pay you a visit."

Joanna fervently hoped that her mother was wrong, but a short while later, just scant seconds after she had hung up the phone, her doorbell sounded. With a sinking feeling in the pit of her stomach, she went to answer it. Before she reached the entryway the bell sounded twice more, and then a hammering fist took up the summons. Drawing a deep breath, Joanna squared her shoulders and opened the door.

"It's about time."

Sean stormed past her like an enraged bull and stalked into the living room. Shakily, Joanna closed the door and followed him. He was standing in the middle of the room, radiating anger, his back to her, but when Joanna entered he whirled around.

"I should have expected an irresponsible stunt like this from you," he snarled through clenched teeth. "You connive and finagle to get what you want without a thought for anyone else, and then when things turn unpleasant, you turn tail and run like the spoiled, selfish brat you are."

"I'm sorry."

"Sorry! Sorry doesn't cut it, Joanna. What you did was inconsiderate at best. If I hadn't run into your room steward I would have thought the worst."

"Wh-what do you mean?"

"I *mean*, you just disappeared without a word after we'd had a serious argument. For all I knew you could have fallen overboard or been kidnapped or been seriously ill. And didn't it occur to you that your mother would be worried."

"If you hadn't called—"

"Was I just supposed to ignore the fact that you had disappeared in a foreign country without a word? The steward said you'd rushed off the ship because of an urgent family crisis. The first thing that came to my mind was that Claire had run into trouble with her pregnancy. So I called."

"I see," Joanna said weakly.

Sean gave her a disgusted look and turned away, then just as quickly turned right back, his eyes narrowed. "And while we're on the subject, just where the hell have you been since you walked off that ship in Cozumel? Claire has called a hundred times. She's been going out of her mind with worry."

"I . . . I've been here. I unplugged my phone."

The stream of expletives that shot from him were sharp and searing. Joanna flinched with each one.

He was angrier than she had ever seen him, and as she watched him pace back and forth across the oriental rug, Joanna felt wretched. She couldn't even work up any anger, because she knew that Sean was right. Once again she had thought only of herself and acted impulsively. Despite all her good intentions and the earnest attempt she'd made to change, the habits and conditioning of a lifetime were difficult to shake.

Joanna listened to Sean's scorching comments with the calm of utter hopelessness, and when he was through, said quietly, "You're right, Sean. And I'm sorry. I didn't mean to worry or upset anyone. I know that's inadequate, but it's the best I can offer."

Her calm agreement stopped Sean in his tracks, and he looked at her with a mixture of confusion and caution. Where was her anger? He'd come spoiling for a fight and had expected her to rage right back at him. After the frustration of the past three days he had relished the prospect of clearing the air. And now this.

He frowned as he watched her edge toward the door, leaving him with no option but to follow.

"I . . . I'm sorry things didn't work out between us, Sean, but I do thank you for your concern. I hope, despite everything, that you will run for the Senate." With her head held high, Joanna gave him a wobbly smile and opened the door, keeping one hand on the knob. "Goodbye, Sean."

Sean hesitated and looked at her closely, then nodded. "Goodbye, Joanna."

It was over. He told himself it was for the best. That he'd had a narrow escape. Joanna Andrews was all that he'd accused her of being: shallow, selfish, thoughtless. She was incapable of loving anyone.

Yet, as Sean walked past her and stepped out into the frigid afternoon all he felt was a terrible, consuming sense of loss.

Chapter Thirteen

Snow lay over the Virginia hillsides like a heavy layer of whipped cream, blown by a capricious wind into smooth, swirling patterns in some places, mounded into high drifts in others. Skeletal trees stood in sharp relief against the leaden sky, their branches piled high with snow and drooping forlornly beneath its weight. It was utterly quiet, except for the occasional loud crack of a limb breaking and the mournful soughing of the wind around the eaves of the farmhouse.

Over and over, Joanna's eyes strayed to the wintry scene while her fingers automatically carried out the task of breaking pecan halves into small pieces and dropping them into the measuring cup. It could be a painting, she thought as she gazed out the frosted panes of the kitchen window. The still, stark, haunting loveliness of it appealed to her somehow. In her present mood, blue skies and bright sunshine would be offensive.

"It looks like we're in for another snow before morning," Claire commented as she deftly fluted the edge on a fresh made pie crust.

"Mmm."

"On a day like this I'm always glad to stay inside where it's cozy and warm." Letting her gaze roam over the homey kitchen, Claire's soft gray eyes glowed with contentment as they took in brick patterned floors, pecan cabinets, massive beams and hanging copper pots, their polished surfaces reflecting the cheery fire crackling in the massive hearth. The large room was redolent with the tantalizing aromas of burning wood, spices, fresh-baked pies and warm, yeasty bread. "And it's a great time for baking."

Joanna gave her mother a faint smile. "Is that why we're having this marathon bake off? Because the weather is gloomy?"

"Well . . . kind of. Besides, with the Drummond clan coming for Christmas it's best to stock up on goodies."

But the real reason is you're trying to keep my mind occupied, and off Sean, Joanna thought fondly, her gaze sliding once more to the dismal beauty beyond the windows.

It wasn't working. She'd been home over three weeks, and during that time she'd thought of little else. And after last night, she was hurting worse than ever.

Oh, God, if only she hadn't let herself be talked into going to that embassy party. She hadn't wanted to, but her mother and Matt had been insistent, and because she had known they were worried about her, she had given in.

Bitter, silent amusement rippled through Joanna when she recalled the pep talk she'd given herself as they had entered the embassy. *It's time to pick up your life again,* she'd lectured. You can't pine away forever. And anyway, Washington is a big town. Just because you're going to a party doesn't mean you'll run into Sean.

Brave words. And totally inaccurate. She had practically bumped into him the moment they entered the ballroom.

He had been standing just a few feet inside the door, and at the sight of him she had come to an abrupt halt, her heart crashing against her ribs. Even now, Joanna could remember, with painful clarity, every tension fraught moment of that disastrous encounter.

"Sean."

She hadn't even known she had spoken, but as his name whispered past her lips he had looked up, straight into her eyes. For a small eternity they simply stared at each other. Then, at last, he said quietly, "Hello, Joanna."

"Hello," she managed to choke out. Her heart was booming in her chest like a kettledrum, and for a panicked second she feared she would pass out.

Sean's gaze switched to Claire and Matt, who were standing on either side of Joanna, alert and wary as they watched the tense tabloid unfold. He nodded, and his mouth moved in a semblance of a smile. "Claire. Matt. Good to see you."

They returned the greeting, but Sean's gaze had already slid back to Joanna.

"How are you?"

"Fine. And you?"

"I'm doing okay."

"I...uh...want to wish you luck with your campaign. I read in the newspaper that you're making a bid for the nomination."

"Thanks."

"I . . . I was afraid you'd change your mind."

"I thought about it," Sean admitted, his eyes hardening a fraction. "But I decided it would be stupid not to, since it's what I want."

All through the banal conversation Joanna drank in the sight of him like someone dying of thirst who has just discovered a clear bubbling spring. She was so enthralled, it was several minutes before she even saw the blonde by his side, and still another before she realized that the woman's arm was linked with Sean's.

Seeming to become aware of the woman at the same time, Sean glanced down at her and looked back at Joanna sharply. "I'm sorry. I don't believe you've met Natalie Stone. Natalie, this is Joanna Andrews, and Claire and Matt Drummond."

"It's so nice to meet you. When Sean invited me to this party he said I'd probably meet some famous people but I certainly never expected to meet Claire Andrews," the woman gushed, eyeing Claire's protruding abdomen with avid interest.

"My name is Drummond now," Claire corrected with gentle firmness before glancing worriedly at Joanna's white face.

Helplessly, Joanna's stricken gaze went back and forth between Sean's face and the slender white arm resting on the dark sleeve of his tuxedo. In that moment, she thought she would surely die from the crushing pain that pressed in on her.

Joanna picked up another pecan and snapped it in two. During the past three weeks she had wondered if he was seeing other women. The uncertainty had been horrible, but knowing, she discovered, was worse. So much worse.

She wasn't sure how she had gotten through the rest of the evening. Now it was all a hazy blur of pain. She had thought that she'd concealed her feelings well though, until her mother had shown up on her doorstep bright and early that morning.

Joanna's gaze warmed when it lit on her mother. Over the past few years she had come to realize how lucky she was to have a mother like Claire, but never more than this morning. She hadn't pried or rendered judgment or offered advice, but had simply taken Joanna's hands in hers, and said, "You love him, don't you, darling?" And when Joanna had nodded and burst into tears, she had held her close until the storm had passed.

Then she had asked Joanna to move to the farm until after the baby arrived. "It will be good for you, and you can keep me company. And now that you've quit your job, there's no reason why you can't."

Joanna had tried to refuse, but where her loved ones were concerned, Claire wasn't above using a little emotional blackmail. "Please, darling. You'll be doing me a tremendous favor. With my due date so near Matt is absolutely terrified to leave me alone at the farm during the day. If you don't come I'm sure he'll end up hiring a nurse to stay with me."

Put that way, Joanna had really had little choice, but she didn't mind. There was some comfort in being with people who loved you.

A smile curved Joanna's mouth as she followed her mother's waddling progress around the kitchen. She wore plum-colored maternity slacks and a plum-and-lilac top that looked wonderful with her gray eyes. Short curls framed her face beguilingly and gleamed like spun gold in the warm light of the kitchen. Flour covered her hands and arms up to her elbows, and there was a smudge of it on her cheek, yet Joanna had never seen her look more appealing. Claire had always been beautiful, but now there was a Madonna-like quality to her loveliness that took your breath away. It was no wonder that Sean had almost lost his heart to her four years ago, Joanna mused with love and pride, and just a touch of envy.

As she watched her mother, Joanna wondered wistfully if she would ever attain that kind of serenity, the kind that comes with loving and being loved in return.

Sean's fingers drummed an impatient tattoo on the table. He darted another look across the dimly lit bar to the entrance and shifted restlessly. *Where the devil is Matt?* A glance at his watch told him that Matt wasn't even due for another ten minutes, but knowing that did nothing to curb his restiveness.

Cupping his hand around the back of his neck, Sean squeezed the knotted muscles and rolled his head from side to side. God, he was tired. Between strategy sessions, hiring a staff, setting up a headquarters and scaring up backers, he'd been run ragged these past few weeks. It had been years since he'd actively worked on a campaign; he had forgotten just how hectic it could be.

But not so hectic that you don't think of Joanna a hundred times a day, he thought with both resentment and longing. Sean glanced at the door again and took a sip of bourbon. *Hell, face it, man. Nothing is going to wipe her out of your mind . . . or your heart. Even if she is too young, even though she's reckless and willful and spoiled—you love her. Which is why you're here, and why you asked Matt to meet you for a drink.*

Had he been mistaken? No. No, he was almost certain that had been pain he'd seen in Joanna's eyes last night when she'd realized he was there with Natalie.

The memory of that wounded look brought a grimace to Sean's face. The last thing he wanted to do was hurt Joanna. Why the devil had he even asked Natalie to go with him to that party? He hadn't wanted to. But like a pigheaded idiot, he'd been determined to prove to himself that he didn't need Joanna, that he could still enjoy the company of other women. What a laugh.

Still, his date with Natalie may not have been a total washout. If that was pain he'd seen in Joanna's eyes, then that meant she did care. Didn't it? And if she cared, that changed everything.

What Joanna had done was pushy and presumptuous, but he could overlook that, as long as he could know for sure that she had gone to bed with him out of love, and not for what she could get from him.

While Sean was lost in his anxious thoughts Matt sat down in the chair opposite him.

"How's it going, buddy?"

"Matt! Hey, glad you could make it," Sean responded just a shade too jovially. "What'll you have, your usual?"

"No, nothing for me, thanks," Matt said when Sean started to signal for the waiter. "I can't stay long. I want to get home to Claire. And anyway, it looks like we're in for more snow. I need to head out before the roads get too bad." Leaning back in his chair, Matt eyed Sean speculatively. "So, how's the campaign coming along?"

"So far, great. Jerry Calder's managing it for me. Of course, he was my second choice." A lopsided grin crooked one side of Sean's mouth as his eyes met Matt's. "But I knew better than to ask you. I figured once that baby gets here you're going to want to stay close to home."

"You figured right."

Sean's expression grew serious, and he looked down at the squat glass he was absently rotating. "And then there's this..."

"This thing between you and Joanna," Matt finished for him when he hesitated.

Sean's head jerked up, and he found himself pinned by his friend's keen blue gaze. "Yeah, there's that," he admitted grimly. Sean tossed back the last of his bourbon and set the glass down. Black eyes met blue ones in a long, searching look. "How is Joanna?"

Matt's impassive expression did not so much as flicker, and at that moment Sean recalled why he never played poker with the man. He stared back at Sean for what seemed like minutes. "Do you really want to know, or is that a polite question?"

"I want to know."

"All right then...she's miserable."

The quick flare of hope Sean could not hide brought a hint of a smile to Matt's mouth. "Look, I don't know what happened between you two on that cruise. I don't think I even want to know, but it's about time you patched this thing up. Because to tell you the truth, old friend, you don't look too hot, either."

"Do you think it's possible?"

"You won't know until you try, will you?" When Sean didn't answer, Matt gave an impatient sigh. "Look, Joanna is staying with us until after the baby is born. Why don't you come home with me for dinner and talk to her?"

It was tempting. Very tempting. Sean looked at his friend searchingly, torn between doubt and longing.

What if I'm just kidding myself? Seeing something because it's what I want to see?

Finally, a look of determination tightened his face. Pushing back his chair, Sean stood up and tossed some bills on the table. "Let's go."

"Matt's home," Claire announced as they saw the car headlights flash by and continue on to the barn.

Standing by the sink preparing a salad, Joanna looked up and had to suppress a grin when she saw the way her mother's face had lit up. Her amusement grew as she watched Claire quickly dry her hands, then fluff her curls and smooth imaginary wrinkles from her maternity smock before going to the back door to greet him. Shaking her head, Joanna returned her attention to the celery she was dicing. She'd never known two people that much in love.

Joanna heard the door open and felt the blast of frigid air against her back, but, discreetly, she didn't turn around.

Matt's "Hello, darling" was followed by a few seconds of heady silence that signaled a lingering kiss.

"Mmm. How's my favorite pregnant lady?" he asked finally in a caressing voice.

"Still pregnant."

"Good. Uh…as you can see, I brought company for dinner. You don't mind, do you?"

"I…why no. No, of course not." Claire rushed to assure him. "Uh…Joanna, darling, look who's here."

The note of uncertainty in her mother's voice, as much as the request, brought Joanna around to face them, but her smile of greeting froze and faded away when she spotted Sean.

He was standing beside Matt, watching her in that intent way of his, still and silent, waiting for her to say something. Joanna felt as though an iron fist had knocked all the wind from her body. Her eyes skittered to Matt. How could you? How *could* you, they asked silently. She had thought he cared about her. Didn't he know how much this would hurt?

Joanna felt panic welling up inside her like a geyser. She couldn't endure an evening of polite conversation with Sean, act like he was no more than an old family friend. She couldn't.

With a silent plea, her gaze went to Claire. In her eyes Joanna saw compassion, in the regal lift of her head an unspoken call for courage. Joanna's jaw clenched and her hands curled into tight fists. Every muscle in her body quivered with the urge to flee, but from somewhere she found the strength to battle it down. Tilting her own chin in a way that unconsciously mirrored Claire's elegant dignity, she stepped forward and said calmly, "Hello, Sean."

"Joanna," he replied with a nod, still watching her with that disconcerting intensity.

Even in the midst of shock and panic, Joanna's mind registered a myriad of irrelevant details about him: his upturned overcoat collar, the tiny pieces of sleet peppered across his shoulders and in his blue-black hair, the look of fatigue around his eyes and the deeper lines that bracketed his mouth, the faint shadow of beard, the scent of cold winter night that clung to him. He looked tired, worried and unhappy. Even so, to Joanna's aching, lovelorn heart he looked wonderful.

More than anything, she wanted to throw herself into his arms, but she couldn't. Sean was lost to her. She had to accept that, and she would. Someday she would be able to look at him without feeling as though her heart had just been ripped from her chest. But not now. Not yet. It was too soon.

"Here, let me take your coats," Claire said, breaking into the tense silence. "While Joanna sets another place at the table you two go wash up. Dinner will be ready by the time you're finished."

For Joanna, sitting across the table from Sean was exquisite, excruciating torture. While the others talked she kept her eyes on her plate and moved the food around with her fork. Her stomach felt as though it were tied in a hard knot, and throughout the meal she only managed to choke down a half-dozen bites.

Sean regaled Matt and Claire with stories about the cruise, telling them about the people they'd met, the places and things they'd seen. With his teasing, devilish charm, he managed to make incidents that had been only mildly amusing sound hilariously funny. The others laughed uproariously, but every word tore at Joanna's heart and scraped her nerves raw.

Several times Sean tried to draw her into the conversation, but she spoke only when he asked her a direct question, and then she kept her replies as brief as possible. She could feel his gaze burning into her, but she refused to look at him. All she wanted was for the interminable evening to end, for a chance to escape to her room and cry.

To Joanna's vast relief, after the meal the men retired to the den, leaving her and Claire to deal with the dishes. Knowing that they would join them as soon as they were through, Joanna worked with meticulous care, drawing out the task as long as possible. When at last everything was put away and the dishwasher was chugging monotonously, she started to sweep the kitchen, but after only two swipes Claire took the broom from her.

"I know what you're trying to do," she said, giving her a mildly reproving look. "But, sweetheart, it's pointless. You can't hide in the kitchen forever."

Panicked defiance flared in Joanna's eyes for an instant, then faded as her shoulders dropped. "I don't want to go in there, Mother. I can't."

"Yes, you can, Joanna. I know it's hard, but it's something you must face and accept, because the problem isn't going to go away. Sean is a dear friend of ours. He has always been welcome in this house, and he always will be. Unless there's something you're not telling me." Claire cocked her head to one side and gave Joanna a long, thoughtful look. "Should we be angry with Sean? Has he done something unforgivable?"

"No, of course not." Pressing her lips together in a grim line, Joanna sighed her defeat. "And you're right. It's time to stop running away."

"That's my girl." Claire gave Joanna a quick hug, and with a hand at her back urged her toward the door. "Now, come on, we'll— Oh, my God!"

With the startled exclamation, Claire stopped in her tracks, and Joanna turned to find her staring straight ahead, her eyes wide with shock. As one, they both looked down at Claire's drenched slacks and the spreading puddle at her feet. When their eyes met again both women had paled. "My water," Claire said, in a faint, amazed tone. "Joanna, my water has broken."

At the words, Joanna's heart jerked. She looked around wildly for a second. Then she leaped forward to put a supporting arm around her mother and at the same time screamed for Matt at the top of her lungs.

Five seconds later he came barreling through the door with Sean at his heels. "What is it? What's the ma—"

He stopped abruptly, his eyes going wide with horror when they lit on Claire.

"My God! It's the baby!"

"Now, Matt, calm down," Claire cautioned as he rushed forward, but before she could get all the words out he was scooping her up in his arms.

He swung around and barked, "Sean, call Dr. Harris. His number is by every phone in the house. Joanna, you run upstairs and get her bag. It's right beside our bed. Move! Both of you!"

Sean's face was even whiter than Joanna's, but when she rushed out the door he swallowed hard and followed right behind her. He grabbed the phone in the hall, and as she sprinted up the stairs on legs that felt like rubber sticks she heard him demanding to be put through to Dr. Harris. When she raced back down with the overnight bag a few seconds later, he was just hanging up the phone, and Matt was striding toward the front door with Claire in his arms.

"Sean, go get my car and bring it around to the front. Joanna! Hurry with that bag!" he yelled without even looking around.

"Matt, I can't go out in this weather without a coat," Claire reminded him.

Swearing, Matt swung back toward the closet. Before he got there Joanna had already pulled Claire's coat from its hanger, but when she held it out to Matt he just stood there with his wife in his arms and scowled.

"Darling, you have to put me down so I can put it on."

Matt looked at Claire in sheer horror. "Do you think you can stand?"

"Of course. I'm fine, darling. Really."

With a great deal of reluctance, Matt very gingerly lowered her to her feet. Joanna helped her mother into her coat, but she had barely gotten the first button fastened when Claire gasped and bent over, clutching her distended abdomen.

"What is it?" Matt cried in alarm.

"It's...okay, it's...just...a labor pain," Claire gasped.

Matt's face turned ashen. His curse turned the air blue.

He started to snatch her up in his arms again, but Joanna stopped him. "Give it time to pass first. And in the meantime, here, put your coat on."

Cursing fluently under his breath, his eyes never leaving his wife, Matt snatched the coat from her outstretched hand as Joanna pulled her own from the closet. By the time they had scrambled into them the pain had eased and Claire had started to straighten. Before she could finish, Matt swept her up in his arms again.

"Dammit! What the hell is keeping Sean?" he roared as he headed for the door.

As if on cue, a car horn blasted outside. Carrying the overnight bag, Joanna rushed out the door after Matt, and gasped when she was hit full in the face by blowing snow.

"When did this happen?" Matt grumbled as he bundled Claire into the back seat, and Joanna scrambled in beside Sean. "The weatherman said we were in for a light snow, for Pete's sake!"

Sean sent the car shooting down the gravel drive toward the highway, a mile away. "He miscalculated," he said tersely, leaning forward to peer through the swirling flakes. "This has all the earmarks of a blizzard."

Matt muttered a curse and Claire murmured soothingly to him. Staring straight ahead Joanna held the overnight bag in her lap and gripped the handle with both hands.

Visibility grew worse by the minute. By the time they reached the highway it didn't extend the length of the headlight beams. Grimly, his jaw clenched, Sean eased the car onto the paved road, but they had barely gone ten feet when it began to fishtail. By the time he brought it to a stop they were almost in the ditch.

"It's no use, Matt. That sleet has formed a solid layer of ice over the road. We've got to go back."

"We can't!"

"Matt, we have to. If we don't we'll end up freezing to death in a ditch."

Matt opened his mouth to argue, but at that moment another pain hit Claire, and he clutched her to him, his panic-stricken eyes seeking out the other two over the top of her head.

Joanna checked her watch and swallowed around the knot of fear in her throat. Striving to keep her voice calm, she said, "It's only been six minutes since the last pain. Matt, we have no choice but to go back."

Without waiting for his reply, Sean put the car in reverse.

When Matt rushed back into the house with Claire in his arms she was in the grips of another wrenching contraction. With Joanna and Sean right behind him, he took the stairs two at a time and hurried to the master bedroom. Joanna darted around him and flipped back the covers, and Matt eased Claire onto the bed, then sat beside her and gripped her hands tightly.

"Hang on, sweetheart," he said with gruff tenderness when the pain had passed. He snatched up the phone on the bedside table and began punching out numbers. "We'll get you to the hospital, don't worry."

Two minutes later, Matt had Dr. Harris on the phone. Quickly, in a voice bordering on panic, he told him what had happened. "I want a helicopter out here, Bob, and I want it now," he ordered. "The damned pains are already less than six minutes apart."

There was a moment of silence, then, his face livid, Matt shouted, "What the hell do you mean, they can't fly in this weather? They have to!"

Chapter Fourteen

Dammit, man! Don't you understand? Claire is in pain! She's going to have the baby! She needs help!''

Sitting on the opposite side of the bed, Joanna held her mother's hand and cast anxious glances at her stepfather. The knuckles on Matt's left hand were white where they gripped the phone. His face was a rigid mask of fear and rage, his eyes wild. He looked ready to commit mayhem. Joanna didn't have to be told that the news was not good. She had seen Matt angry before, but never this close to losing control.

"*What!* Are you crazy?" he roared into the receiver. "We can't deliver this baby! You've got to do something, dammit!''

As Matt listened to the doctor's reply Joanna watched his expression grow more desperate, and fear crawled up her spine. "Now listen to me, you sonofa—''

Claire cried out and clutched her abdomen, and the vitriolic curse cut off in mid-spate. The phone slid from Matt's grasp and dropped to the floor unnoticed as he sank back down on the edge of the bed and grasped both her shoulders. "Easy, sweetheart. Easy," he crooned desperately as Claire writhed in the grip of a clawing pain.

Joanna looked at Sean, but he was standing at the foot of the bed, an expression of sheer horror on his face. Gathering her courage, she rose, circled around to the other side of the bed and picked up the receiver from the carpet. "Dr. Harris? This is Joanna Andrews, Mrs. Drummond's daughter."

"Ah, good," Dr. Harris said in a relieved tone. "I'm glad you're there, Miss Andrews. From the sound of Matt, he's not going to be of much use. I'm afraid it's going to be up to you to deliver that baby."

Terror washed over Joanna in an icy wave, sending a shudder rippling through her. She wanted to run and hide. Dear, Lord! She couldn't deliver a baby! But when her panicked glance fell on Claire's pale face Joanna drew in a deep breath and clamped down on the fear. "Tell me what we have to do."

Joanna listened intently to the doctor's instructions, and scribbled on the notepad by the phone the list of supplies she would need. "You will stay on the phone and guide me?" she asked shakily when he had finished.

"Yes, of course. Now you just stay calm and do what I say, and everything will be fine."

"All right, doctor. Hold on just a moment." Joanna put the phone down on the bedside table and started issuing orders as she headed for the master bathroom. "Sean, you man the phone and relay Dr. Harris's instructions. Matt, you stay right where you are and do what you can to help Mother.''

Matt came up off the bed with a roared, *"No!"*

Joanna spun around and found him glaring at her, his rugged features distorted with anguish and stark fear.

Putting a bracing hand on his shoulder, Sean said, ''Matt, take it easy. Can't you see we don't have a choice?''

''He's right, Matt.'' Joanna walked back to him and gripped his upper arms, feeling the tense muscles ripple beneath her hands. ''There is no way on earth we can get to the hospital, and like it or not, that baby is going to be born tonight. Probably within the hour, Dr. Harris says. We just have to do what we can to help Mother.''

A shudder shook Matt's big frame, and he squeezed his eyes shut as though in agony.

''Darling, please don't worry,'' Claire called softly, and Matt spun around and dropped down on his knees beside the bed. He grasped one of her hands between both of his and brought it to his mouth, his blue eyes darting frantically over her face, wide with fear and concern. She looked at him tenderly and touched the silvered hair at his temple with her other hand. ''It will be all right, my love. Women have been having babies since the beginning of time.''

''Oh, God, Claire!''

Joanna left them and went to look for the things she needed. She returned a few minutes later carrying clean sheets and towels, scissors, a ball of string, a bottle of alcohol, newspaper, and a plastic dry cleaner's bag.

With Matt's help, she stripped Claire of her soiled clothes and dressed her in a warm gown. Joanna then spread several layers of newspaper over the plastic, covered both with a sheet and slid the makeshift pad under her mother's hips. As she covered Claire with a sheet another pain bore down on her.

Joanna checked her watch and looked at Sean. "Tell Dr. Harris the pains are now four and a half minutes apart."

Matt muttered a frantic "Oh, God" and gripped Claire's hand tighter as he dabbed the beads of perspiration from her forehead with a tissue.

Stepping to the side of the bed, Joanna touched her mother's shoulder and studied her with concerned eyes. "Are you okay?"

"I . . . I'm fine," Claire panted.

Swallowing down another rush of fear, Joanna hurried away to finish her preparations. When Matt came storming into the bathroom a few minutes later she had just finished removing her nail polish and was hurriedly clipping her nails.

"For God's sake, Joanna!" he yelled. "What the hell are you doing? This is no time for a manicure!"

At any other time Joanna would have taken offense at his tone, but she knew that Matt was distraught. "Matt, I'm trying to make my hands as germfree as possible," she explained patiently. "As soon as I scrub I'll be there. Now go back to your wife."

"Well hurry it up," he snapped, only partially mollified. "Claire needs you."

As if on cue, they heard a stifled scream from the bedroom. Matt paled, cursed, and shot back through the door. When Joanna followed him a couple of minutes later another hard contraction was building. Anxiously, her eyes sought Sean, and he muttered, "Two minutes apart."

Fear clawed at Joanna. Claire was drenched in sweat, her golden curls darkened and plastered to her head. Her hands gripped two of the oak spindles in the headboard above her head, and she was pulling and straining, writhing from side to side. Her lovely face was ravaged with pain, her eyes and jaws clamped tightly shut, but little sounds of distress came out with every breath.

Joanna climbed onto the foot of the bed and knelt between Claire's knees. She placed her hand on her stomach, and her eyes widened as she felt the rippling movement against her palm. Claire's moans built to a hoarse scream that seemed to tear from her throat, and her back arched off the bed as her abdomen tightened into a tortuous hard ball.

"Dr. Harris says not to fight it, Claire," Sean advised in a strained voice a moment later as the agonized sound faded away. "Pant with the pains and relax in between."

When the next pain hit a minute later Claire tried, but toward the end her breathless pants dissolved into a high, keening wail. Two more spasms came before Joanna cried out, "I can see the head!"

Sean related the news to Dr. Harris and announced, "He says it won't be long now."

The undulating contractions were so close together now there were only scant seconds of respite in between.

"You're doing fine, Mother. Just fine. Okay, here comes another one. You're going to have to push now."

Claire gulped in air and strained with all her might as the wrenching pain twisted her insides. Her face turned an alarming purple-red with the effort. She dug her heels into the mattress and pushed, and her hands pulled at the oak spindles until her knuckles were bone-white and the tendons in her neck, shoulders and arms stood out like taut wires.

"That's it. That's it. You're doing great. Just a little harder," Joanna coaxed.

As Claire strove to comply the sharp crack of splintering wood sounded above the guttural moans that rasped from her throat.

Three pairs of eyes went to the split and bowed oak spindles still held in Claire's iron grasp.

"Oh, God. Oh, God. Oh, God," Matt chanted weakly.

Sean stared and swallowed hard. "Christ."

Gritting her teeth, Joanna forced her gaze back to the birth area, and her eyes widened in delight. "Oh, here it comes! The baby's coming! Oh, this is so beautiful!" she cried, laughing and sobbing as the head emerged. "You're doing terrific, Mother. Just a little more. There, that's it. That's it. Oh, my," she murmured in breathless awe as she caught the slippery newborn in her hands.

Joanna looked up, her eyes swimming with emotion. "Oh, Mother, you have a son. A beautiful little son."

The baby choked, then squalled lustily.

"One with a healthy set of lungs," Sean quipped, and everyone chuckled in relief. But a few seconds later, when Joanna had dealt with the cord and laid the infant on her mother's stomach they were all blinking back tears.

"Oh, Matt, look," Claire exclaimed. "Isn't he perfect."

Before he could answer, her features contorted as another pain hit her. Matt jerked in alarm. "What? What is it?"

"It's okay," Joanna assured him. "This is the last of it. There. That's it." She looked up at her mother and smiled. "Feel better now?"

"Yes, darling. Thank you." A look of deep understanding and love passed silently between mother and daughter, and Claire added softly, "For everything."

Sean talked quietly to the doctor while Joanna made her mother comfortable and removed the soiled linen. Claire, her face glowing, counted tiny fingers and toes, touched the rosebud mouth and quivering chin, the delicate soft spot in the top of the baby's head. Matt watched her with open adoration, tears running unashamedly down his face.

"Oh, Matt, we have a son," Claire said in wonder. She looked at him with eyes brimming with inexpressible happiness and love. "Isn't it wonderful?"

"Yes, love, it's wonderful. You're wonderful."

"Wouldn't it be perfect if next time we had a girl?"

"No!" Matt almost shouted the word. He shook his head, his expression growing bleak. "No, darling, I'll *never* put you through that again," he declared vehemently, in a voice gone rough with emotion.

"Matt—"

"No, I mean it." He bent and pressed his face against her breast. "Oh, God, Claire, it was awful. I was so scared. So scared..."

"It's over now, darling. Don't think about it." Claire stroked her fingers lovingly through his hair, and over the top of his head her eyes sought the other two with a silent plea.

Understanding, Joanna lifted the crying infant and carried him into the bathroom as Sean slipped quietly out the door.

As Joanna cleaned and dressed her protesting baby brother, her heart was filled with emotions so intense they formed an aching knot in her chest. The experience they had all just shared had been the most profoundly beautiful, exciting and frightening of her life. That she had had a part, no matter how small, in bringing this perfect little human into the world both touched and thrilled her beyond words.

When the baby was tucked into a warm knit gown and swaddled in a receiving blanket, he quieted. For a moment, Joanna cuddled him close, rubbing her cheek against his downy head and breathing in the delicious scent of baby.

Matt and Claire were holding hands and talking quietly when she returned to the bedroom. Joanna laid the baby in her mother's arms, murmured a few appropriate words, which she doubted either of them heard, gathered up the soiled linen and slipped out the door, leaving them engrossed in each other and their child.

In the hall, Joanna leaned weakly against the wall and closed her eyes as the enormity of it all hit her.

"Come on," Sean said beside her, and her eyes popped open in surprise as he slipped a supporting arm around her waist. "What you need is a good stiff drink. At the very least a cup of very sweet tea." Taking the bundle of linen from her, he led her down the hall toward the stairs.

Joanna leaned on him heavily, grateful for his assistance. "I feel so weak and shaky," she complained in a bewildered voice.

"I think it's called delayed shock. And after the evening you've had, I'm not at all surprised."

He guided her into the den and sat her down in a chair. "Take it easy for a minute. I'll be right back," he said, and disappeared through the door. When he returned he went to the bar and poured a glass of brandy. Squatting down on his haunches, Sean pressed the glass into her hand. "Drink this, sweetheart. It'll make you feel better."

The endearment brought Joanna's head up, and she looked at him sharply. At his urging, she took a tentative sip of the brandy and felt it burn its way down her throat. When she would have put the glass down Sean shook his head. She took several more sips, watching him cautiously over the top of the glass.

When at last she had finished he took the glass and placed it on the table beside her chair, but he didn't move. His dark eyes bore into her. "Joanna, we have to talk."

"About what?" she asked warily.

"About us."

"Sean, please. Not now. Not tonight."

"Yes, now. I came here with Matt to talk to you, and I'm not leaving until I do."

Joanna slumped back against the chair. "All right. Since I seem to have no choice, go ahead."

"First of all, I want to apologize." He smiled crookedly when her eyes widened with surprise. "I called you a lot of uncomplimentary things, and said that you were spoiled and immature, but I was wrong. Anyone who can do what you did tonight is certainly not a child."

"Just because I did what had to be done?" She gave him a sad smile and shook her head dejectedly. "No, you were right before."

Sean frowned. "By that, do you mean I was right about you looking for a father substitute?"

Fatigue and emotional turmoil had taken its toll and Joanna's laugh bordered on hysteria. "Hardly. If that was what I wanted, why on earth would I pick you? You're nothing at all like my father. Nor do you even remotely resemble the type of man I've always envisioned myself loving, but that doesn't seem to be something we can control."

A look of hope flickered across Sean's face. "You do love me then? Even now? After all that's happened?"

Tears she could not control welled in Joanna's eyes, and she looked at him reproachfully. Why was he doing this to her?

When she didn't reply, Sean took hold of her hands and stood up, pulling her to her feet. He looked at her intently and smiled. "Do you, Joanna?"

"Yes. Yes I do. Does that make you happy?" she said peevishly as the tears spilled over her lower lashes.

"Yes, it makes me very happy. Because I love you too." Sean's expression was filled with tenderness, but when he went to pull her into his arms Joanna pushed his hands away.

"That doesn't change anything, Sean," she insisted tearfully. "I'm still headstrong and impulsive. I've been indulged and petted all of my life, and to some degree I will probably always be spoiled. Maybe...maybe someday—" She stopped and drew a shuddering breath, fighting against the urge to fling herself in his arms and bawl. "I'm trying very hard to be the kind of woman you want, the kind of woman my mother is—mature and giving and...and unselfish. But I'm not there yet," she admitted in a shaky, dispirited voice, her eyes swimming with sadness and longing.

Sean grinned and folded her into his embrace. His dark gaze skimmed over her woebegone face like a loving touch. Then his lids dropped partway and his head began a slow, inexorable descent. "Maybe not. But you do have promise, my love," he whispered tenderly against her lips. "Pure, sweet promise."

The kiss was shattering. Warm, tender, blatantly possessive, it set off explosions that shook Joanna to her very soul. The strain of the past three weeks and an evening fraught with emotional trauma had her drawn taut and fine, and at the first touch of his mouth her precarious control snapped.

She clung to him helplessly, quivering within his embrace. The sweet, searing kiss went on and on, throbbing with the aching need of three lonely weeks apart, of love too long denied. Lips rocked together hungrily. Tongues teased, tasted, entwined. Passion built quickly and the kiss became hotter, deeper, recklessly greedy, until their hearts raced and their pulses pounded.

When at last the kiss ended Sean's eyes burned hotly over Joanna's dazed face. "We've both made mistakes, Joanna, but the biggest one would be if we parted. I love you, darling, and I want you for my wife. I want to spend the rest of my life loving you."

"Oh, Sean, are you sure? I—"

"Hush. Hush." A finger over her lips stopped the anguished flow. "None of us is perfect, Joanna. I'm certainly not. But that doesn't matter." He touched the mole at the corner of her mouth and gave her a lopsided grin. "Because, I love you just as you are, faults and all."

"I love you, too," Joanna whispered shakily, gazing at him with dewy, emotion-filled eyes.

"So, will you marry me?"

Joanna blinked and strove for a stern expression. "On one condition."

"And that is?"

"That you give me that little black book of yours so that I can rip it to shreds."

Sean threw back his head and laughed, then kissed her hard. "You've got a deal. In fact, we'll make a ceremony of it, first thing tomorrow. But tonight—" the laughter in his eyes was replaced by a hot, hungry look, and his smile changed to sensuous anticipation "—tonight I have something else in mind."

He bent and scooped her up in his arms and started for the door.

"Sean! Where are you taking me?"

"To bed." He took the stairs with ease, grinning into her startled eyes. "You'll have to show me which bedroom is yours."

"Here! But Mother and Matt—"

"Are so wrapped up in each other and their son at the moment, I doubt they even remember we're here." He stopped at the top of the stairs and looked at her, his expression tender but unyielding. "In the morning I'll tell them that we're going to be married. I think they'll understand. But if there's any flack, I'll deal with it. Now which way is your room?"

Wordlessly, her heart pounding in her chest, Joanna showed him.

He set her gently on her feet beside the bed and, cupping her face between his hands, he kissed her. Then he stepped back and gripped the bottom edge of her sweater in both hands. Holding her gaze, he slowly pulled the coral sweater up over her head and tossed it aside. Her bra came next, baring the smooth fragrant skin that he had dreamed about for weeks.

Joanna quivered beneath his hungry look, and when he reached out, almost reverently, and cupped her breasts she caught her breath. His hands were warm and calloused and exquisitely tender. Their gazes met and held for a long heady moment.

"What are you thinking?" His voice was soft and velvety, his eyes caressing.

"That I love you," she whispered. "More than life."

"And when I do this?" His thumbs skimmed the silken peaks and they beaded with desire.

Joanna's head tipped back and her breathing became labored. "That I want you...so much." His thumbs swept again. "I...I...oh, Sean, I can't think when you do that."

"Good. Don't think. Just feel. Feel how much I love you. How much I want you." He lifted her breasts, pushed them together and buried his face in the tender mounds. With lips and tongue he worshiped her, dipping evocatively into the tight cleavage, stroking the pearly swells, suckling the rose velvet tips.

"Oh, Sean." Joanna bent over him and clutched his head, her silky brown hair spilling over his shoulders as she held him near.

His hands slid down her ribcage to the button on her slacks, and Sean dropped to his knees before her. When he had divested her of slacks, panties, stockings and shoes he worked his way back up, pausing to kiss her knee, her thigh, the silky nest of feminine curls, her belly, her breasts, the soft hollow at the base of her throat. Sliding his arms around her waist, he brought her close and kissed her trembling lips last.

His mouth was hot and demanding, the abrasive rub of his clothes against her bare skin oddly erotic. Joanna pressed close and clung, losing herself in sensation.

With his mouth still fastened to hers, Sean lifted her in his arms and placed her on the bed. His own clothes were dealt with swiftly, and then he was there beside her, pulling her into his arms again, his sigh echoing hers as warm flesh met warm flesh.

They held each other for a long, appreciative moment, savoring the closeness, the warmth, letting anticipation build. Joanna's breasts pressed achingly against his muscled chest, the nipples turgid buttons of desire. His masculine shaft throbbed against her soft belly, yearning, seeking.

Joanna's hands roamed over his back, then down his spine to cup his buttocks. Sean's knee lifted to separate her silken thighs, then pressed hard against her moist, pulsing flesh.

"I want you so much, Joanna. So very much," Sean rasped as her body arched in response to his touch.

"Oh, yes, Sean. Please!"

After the three lonely weeks apart their desire for each other had reached a fever pitch, and neither could wait any longer. Rolling her to her back, Sean rose above her. Gazing into her lambent eyes, he whispered tenderly, "I love you" as he made them one.

Epilogue

Soft strains of organ music filled the small chapel. The pleasing scents of flowers and burning candles wafted in the air. The pews were filled with close friends and family, waiting with hushed anticipation. It all reminded Claire poignantly of her own wedding, almost four years ago. It was the same chapel, the same minister, the same witnesses. The only difference was that then it had been spring, and now it was winter, and snow covered the ground.

"Are you ready, Mrs. Drummond?"

Smiling up at the young man beside her, Claire nodded and placed her hand on his sleeve, and with four-week-old Daniel Ethan Drummond tucked securely in the crook of her other arm, she allowed him to lead her up the aisle.

When Claire was seated in the first pew she looked across the aisle at Maggie Fleming and smiled. As Sean and his father entered the chapel through the side door, Claire's eyes were drawn to him, and her heart filled with thankfulness that this man, whom she and Matt loved so dearly, had chosen her daughter.

As though sensing her gaze on him, Sean's eyes met Claire's, and held, and after a moment of silent communication, he smiled and lowered one eyelid in a lazy wink. Then the stirring strains of the "Wedding March" rose from the organ, and his gaze sought the ivory clad figure at the back of the church. As Matt led Joanna toward the altar Sean had eyes only for her.

Tears pooled in Claire's eyes as she saw the look of love that passed between Sean and her lovely, radiant daughter. With a heart overflowing with happiness and a throat so tight it ached, she watched Matt place Joanna's hand in Sean's.

A short while later the minister asked who gave the bride in marriage, and at Matt's strong, "Her mother and I," Claire's tears spilled over.

She was crying unashamedly when Matt joined her on the bench. As Joanna and Sean repeated the solemn vows Matt picked up Claire's hand and squeezed it, and their eyes met in a long, poignant look, each remembering that day four years ago when they had spoken the same words.

The minister pronounced them man and wife, and Sean lifted Joanna's veil and drew her into his arms. The kiss was so loving and tender that Claire's tears began to flow again. One plopped on the baby's cheek and he awoke with a start and immediately began to wail his displeasure. Everyone laughed, including Joanna and Sean when they broke apart.

The recessional began and the swell of the organ music covered the baby's crying as the newlyweds started their walk down the aisle. When they drew even with the first pew, Joanna stopped and kissed her squalling, red-faced baby brother on the forehead, before doing the same to her mother and Matt.

Then, her eyes shining with love, she turned to Sean and held out her hand.

The Silhouette Cameo Tote Bag Now available for just $6.99

Handsomely designed in blue and bright pink, its stylish good looks make the Cameo Tote Bag an attractive accessory. The Cameo Tote Bag is big and roomy (13″ square), with reinforced handles and a snap-shut top. You can buy the Cameo Tote Bag for $6.99, plus $1.50 for postage and handling.

Send your name and address with check or money order for $6.99 (plus $1.50 postage and handling), a total of $8.49 to:

**Silhouette Books
120 Brighton Road
P.O. Box 5084
Clifton, NJ 07015-5084
ATTN: Tote Bag**

SIL–T–1R

The Silhouette Cameo Tote Bag can be purchased pre-paid only. No charges will be accepted. Please allow 4 to 6 weeks for delivery.

N.Y. State Residents Please Add Sales Tax

Offer not available in Canada.

Silhouette Special Edition

COMING NEXT MONTH

SOMETHING ABOUT SUMMER—Linda Shaw
State Prosecutor Summer MacLean didn't know what to do when she
found herself handcuffed to a suspect determined to prove he was
innocent . . . and who happened to look like her late husband.

EQUAL SHARES—Sondra Stanford
When Shannon Edwards inherited fifty-one percent of a troubled
business, she went to check it out. She expected a problem, but not the
sexiest man alive . . . her partner.

ALMOST FOREVER—Linda Howard
Max Conroy was buying out the company where Claire worked, and used
her to get the vital information. What he didn't figure on was falling in
love.

MATCHED PAIR—Carole Halston
The handsome gambler and the glamorous sophisticate met across the
blackjack table, and it was passion at first sight. Neither realized they were
living a fantasy that could keep them apart.

SILVER THAW—Natalie Bishop
Mallory owned prize Christmas trees, but had no one to market them. The
only man willing to help her was the man who had once sworn he
loved her.

EMERALD LOVE, SAPPHIRE DREAMS—Monica Barrie
Pres Wyman had been the school nerd. But when Megan Teal hired him to
help her salvage a sunken galleon, she found the erstwhile nerd had
become a living Adonis.

AVAILABLE THIS MONTH:

FOUR UNIQUE SERIES FOR EVERY WOMAN YOU ARE...

Silhouette Romance

Heartwarming romances that will make you laugh and cry as they bring you all the wonder and magic of falling in love.

6 titles per month

Silhouette Special Edition

Expanded romances written with emotion and heightened romantic tension to ensure powerful stories. A rare blend of passion and dramatic realism.

6 titles per month

Silhouette Desire

Believable, sensuous, compelling—and above all, romantic—these stories deliver the promise of love, the guarantee of satisfaction.

6 titles per month

Silhouette Intimate Moments

Love stories that entice; longer, more sensuous romances filled with adventure, suspense, glamour and melodrama.

4 titles per month